Mayhem at Nepenthe Manor

Ψ

A Pandora Belfry Adventure
(Book One)

Kristina Schram, Ph.D.

*Mischief*Maker*Media*

Published by Mischief Maker Media (USA)

First printing: September, 2013

Cover Design, Interior, and Technical Expertise: GorKee

ISBN: 978-1-939397-05-8

Visit Kristina Schram on the World Wide Web at:
www.KristinaSchram.com

Acknowledgements

I'd like to thank my readers, Elizabeth Schram, Heather Duane, Kendra DeCota, and Gordon Unzen. I know that entering the worlds I create can be hazardous, but you do it with uncommon grace and courage. Thanks for all your input - you make me a better writer!

A big shout out goes to my husband, Dan, for all his technical help and support. He keeps me sane. Mostly.

To all the staff, teachers, and professors I've worked with over the years who have taught me everything they know about the vast and difficult field of mental health. They have always emphasized the importance of being open-minded, accepting, and kind towards those who march to a different drummer. I thank you for that.

~~~~~~~~~~

Dedicated to all victims of mental illness...

~~~~~~~~~~

Sometimes the job of a writer is to reveal the truth, and sometimes it's to create a more palatable truth. In writing about the residents of Nepenthe Manor, I have attempted to do both. While I hope to turn a light on the very real issues with which the mentally ill struggle every day, I also want to give these unique individuals a chance at a life I imagine few get to experience in the real world—one full of adventure, mystery, healing, and plain old fun.

1

𝒜 Live One

PANDORA BELFRY HEARD the muffled, but undeniably furious, howls in the middle of eating the horrid offal that was being passed off as her dinner. Immediately she perked up. A new inmate had arrived.

And he, or she, was fighting incarceration all the way.

Pandora leaned over the slatted railing of her painted black bunk bed and released her dinner tray. It smacked against the gray and matted carpet, bucked back up, then settled into a perfect landing. She took in the results with a satisfied, slightly devious smile. Another success.

Still grinning, she pushed herself off the bunk, landing beside the tray like a ninja. Quick as a flash, she picked up the remains of her dinner and tossed the puke-colored tray onto her desk, no longer caring what happened to its contents. Grabbing a long-handled, silver flashlight and stuffing a ring of old keys she wasn't supposed to have into her Scottish sporran, she let herself out of her room via a hidden door in her closet, a door that led to a secret passageway.

Feeling particularly giddy—it had been a while since a new inmate had been admitted (two months and three days, to be exact)—she raced down the musty passage, which connected to an endless number of other passages, which threaded their way through the walls of the massive stone building like a mutant spider web.

And I'm the mutant spider, she thought as her black, rubber-soled shoes thumped along the wood floor and her equally black braids swung back and forth like a hangman's rope.

The passage was narrow and darker than the Grim Reaper's eye sockets, but Pandora knew her way as though spotlights lit the area. Even so, she always brought along her handy-dandy flashlight, 'borrowed' years ago from Joey, a security guard who had long since left for a job with better pay and less aggravation. The flashlight also served as an effective weapon for walloping vermin if one happened to cross her path. She'd had to use it against a non-vermin only once, but that was another story.

Pandora reached the central wing—the part of Nepenthe Manor where all new inmates were processed—in exactly one minute and twenty-four seconds. Noting the time, she cursed vigorously despite her panting breath. She was either getting out of shape—all those awful meals eaten alone in her room, along with little exercise—or in her excitement she'd let her focus slip. Probably a bit of both.

She tiptoed toward Door Number Eight, affectionately known as the Gate to Hell and lectured herself to get it together. "Keep your eyes on the prize, Belfry! Become one with the shadows. Move like a snake."

She paused a moment to visualize herself looking like Jabba the Hutt oozing down the hallway and only just managed to bite down on a snigger. Luckily, because Frank Steen, the security guard, was passing by on the other side of the door that, like all the secret doors, was indistinguishable from the magnificent walnut paneling that composed the manor's walls. She could hear his size-fourteens clomping down the dimly lit hall as he swayed back and forth like an overgrown duck. She didn't see any of this, of course—she couldn't see through walls—but she knew full well what he looked like. She also knew why she shouldn't mess with him. Frank was obsessed with routine and he followed his own carefully planned route religiously. And woe be to anyone who got in his way. He did *not* like interruptions. All the inmates knew that and made their plans accordingly.

The new arrival obviously didn't know Frank.

Once he'd passed by, Pandora pushed open the door a slight crack just in time to see his rubber billy club, which he kept hidden from prying eyes in a little pouch hung from his leather belt, bang on the specially installed metal door of Room Thirty-Four, Better Lock Your Door, or BLYD for short. Upon arrival, the violent inmates were sent straight here, trussed up in a frayed straightjacket—a.k.a. the Crazy Cocoon—until they calmed down. Sometimes a tranq was used to help that process along. More often than not, though, time was the drug of choice.

At that moment the new inmate screeched like a banshee. Clearly he or she hadn't been drugged.

Hurray! Pandora cheered. *A live one!*

She watched Frank closely now, his full, pockmarked cheeks and heavy jowls almost gaunt in the sterile light shining through the small, chicken-wired window in BLYD's door. Slightly stooped, he peered into the room, his low brow menacing as a villain's and his beady eyes squinting and disgruntled. Though his sandy-brown hair was slicked back with gel, Frank could never quite eliminate the twin cowlicks riding the crown of his head. His dark brown uniform—heavily creased and straining at the crotch—was growing tighter, too. He was the only one in this place who ever gained any weight. Well, him and the cook, Mrs. Corker. The old fraud considered leftovers her bonus for putting up with 'this lot,' which were, of course, the inmates of Nepenthe Manor.

To sum up, Frank was big, not too bright, strangely fussy about his hair, and perpetually cranky. Pandora rather liked the old git.

"Quiet now in there! You'll upset the whole place with your screechin' and that'll make Frank mad. We don't want Frank getting mad."

"I'm not supposed to be here!" the stranger behind the door cried. "You've got to let me out!" Although the voice was loud, it was muffled just enough to make it difficult to determine gender. Pandora leaned forward, taking care not to widen the crack too much. Frank's hooded eyes, like those vultures you see in cartoons, were sharp, and if he caught her, she'd be in for it good.

"Like it or not, for the next forty-eight hours your new home is Nepenthe Manor." Frank said Nuh-pen-*thee*, instead of its proper pronunciation, with the accent on 'pen' and the 'th' like think.

"But I didn't do anything wrong!" the prisoner protested.

"Yeah, yeah, yeah," Frank grumbled, glancing down at the massive, cheap silver watch encircling his equally massive, hairy wrist. "Neither did Jack the Ripper." It was his favorite retort.

"But they took my shoelaces and my belt!"

"That's so you don't use 'em to off yourself. Now shut it so Frank won't get mad cause you made him get behind schedule." Whoever was behind the door at least had enough sense to 'shut it.' When there was no response, Frank gave a satisfied nod and headed off to complete his rounds.

Once his impressively large hind end disappeared around the corner of the long hallway, Pandora straightened up and pushed on the door. She was just about to step into the hall when a sound at the end of the corridor caught her attention.

Crap.

She shrank back. The nurse was doing her rounds. Whenever an inmate was tied up in the Cocoon, someone needed to check on the victim every thirty minutes. Pandora supposed it was necessary, but the rule made her life more difficult. The nurse on duty tonight was Miss Joanna Burns, twenty-two years old, and as perky as a puppy. Her sun-streaked blond ponytail swung from side to side as she practically bounced down the dimly lit hall. A part of Pandora worshipped and envied her—she really was perfection. Clear, tan skin. A smile that stretched from ear to ear, with ruby lips framing blinding white teeth. Yet another, darker part of Pandora wanted to do something to blemish that perfection. Like give it a bad haircut, or better yet, a round of electro-shock therapy.

Five minutes later, Joanna emerged from BLYD, still smiling. Even the new arrival's pathetic pleas of "for the love of God, get me out of here!" didn't affect her perpetually good mood. Not for the first time Pandora wondered just how natural that mood was. Everyone got grumpy sometimes. But not Joanna.

When Miss Sunshine was gone, Pandora slowly pushed open the Gate to Hell, which on its spring-loaded hinges, shut quietly as a whisper behind her. Stealthy as a burglar, she tiptoed up to BLYD. Not particularly tall, nor particularly short at five foot four and three-quarters, she couldn't see through the window, which was set at a height for giants like Frank, not normal humans like herself.

Bending at the knees, one of which popped like an air gun, she pushed off with her clenched toes and leaped into the air. Through her reflection, which showed a pale, oval face truncated by a fringe of black bangs, she caught a brief glimpse of spiky, blond hair and wide eyes before coming back down. Hmmm. She jumped again. The white lump was struggling to sit up. Cool.

She fished the key ring out of her sporran, looked to the left, then to the right, then slid the correct key into the lock. It turned, clicked, and entrance was gained. Twisting the cool steel knob in her hand, Pandora slowly opened the door. It creaked. She pulled the door shut and opened it again. It gave another satisfying creak. One more time for good measure, and only then did Pandora step inside the room. Just as she hoped, by that point her victim was well and truly nervous. Normal people don't open and close a door three times.

Unfortunately, when the new arrival saw her, an expression of relief crossed his face. Yes, *his*. The white lump was a boy, about her age, which was fourteen. His long, thin face appeared tan under smears of dirt; his coffee-colored eyes were big as 50-cent pieces. The straight-jacket, along with cream-colored chinos, made him look like a giant, white caterpillar.

He was scared, she noted, but not of her. *Bugger.* She wanted him to fear her, she wanted him to squeal and cower before her like a sissy baby. She took a step toward him and widened her eyes psychotically. He smiled tentatively.

Bugger-squared.

"Did you come to get me out?" he asked hopefully. She took in his pointy chin, his pale lips, his shock of blond hair that looked like it had been cut with a weed whacker, and the gold hoop earring piercing his right earlobe, which someone on the staff had neglected to remove. He actually wasn't all that bad looking, she conceded, which could work for him or against. She hadn't yet decided.

Pandora squinted at him. "What makes you think that?"

He ignored the question. "Listen, I'm not like..." His eyes darted back and forth and the nostrils of his snub nose, its bridge spattered with pale freckles, flared excitedly. "I'm not like *these* people."

"These people?" she questioned, deciding to go along with the ruse. He thought she'd come to help him. *Not terribly smart, then*, she mused. Good.

"The other people here."

"You mean, people like me?"

"What? No!" He shook his head desperately. "You look normal enough." He lowered his voice to confide, "I mean the *loonies*!"

She gave him her best Mad Hatter stare. "You do understand that I'm one of these loonies to which you refer?"

His whole body jerked backward. "What? You're... Oh, crap."

This time she couldn't stop the air traveling up her nasal passages and out her nose. She snorted. The flabbergasted look on his face was priceless. If only she had a camera, or her sketchpad. If only she could draw. Still, she filed away the mental image to pass onto the inmates later. She might not be an artist, but she could tell a story that could compete with the likes of a drunken Irishman.

"Yup," she nodded, letting her head bobble. She'd practiced doing that the other day in the mirror and liked what she saw. "Mind you, I don't agree with their assessment. They put me in here simply because I like to have people for dinner."

"But that's not a crime!" He was amusingly indignant.

"It is when they're the main course, my friend!" *Ah, an oldie but a goodie.*

His mouth screwed up, his brain finally catching on. "I don't know who you are or why you're here, but I'm telling you this. I. Don't. Belong. Here."

Pandora smirked. "I may not know much..." *Lie.* "But I do know you don't get the mummy treatment for good deeds." Her eyes swept over the straightjacket.

He frowned. "Yes, well, I suppose. But it wasn't... I didn't..." He gave up and slumped back on the narrow cot. "I just want out of here."

"Yeah, well, you and everyone else in this place." Another lie. But a necessary one. They had a reputation to maintain.

She turned to go, but his next words stopped her. "You didn't really eat people…"

She gave him a ghastly grin. "I made them into stew. Added a few carrots and potatoes, some garlic and onion for flavor." She stuck the feathery end of a black braid in her mouth and chomped on it. "It was delicious, if I do say so myself." Smacking her lips and making yummy noises, she slipped out the door, making sure to lock it. Behind her the Newbie howled.

Per-fection, she congratulated herself, already plotting her next visit to the new arrival as she ran off to tell the inmates everything.

Evils of the World

2

HALF AN HOUR later, Pandora and four of the five members of her posse sat in what was known as *their* corner of the Leisure Room, a.k.a. the TV room/lounge. A bay window reflected their shadowy figures, all of which were sitting in various positions ranging from long legs dangling over the arm of a chair, to upright and rigid as a soldier. The chairs were as overstuffed as scarecrows and surrounded a dinged-up coffee table with burn marks leftover from the days when inmates were allowed to smoke indoors. It was nearly dark outside. Only one lamp lit the area, which made the large room feel like a cavern.

Pandora was nearly finished telling the inmates all about her incredible and daring adventure meeting the new arrival when a short, roundish girl, with a surprisingly husky voice for her size, interrupted. "So *he's* the caterwauling I've been trying not to hear for the past million and a half hours." She clapped child-like hands to her head, missing her ears by a couple inches because two frizzy pigtails, which looked like giant pom-poms, were in the way. "I hate caterwauling. It makes my eardrums mad."

Pandora nodded importantly, her finger working in conjunction with her thumb to twist her braid around and around like an auger. "That's him all right, Lucy. What's more…" She paused for dramatic effect— the inmates *adored* dramatic effect—"…he says he shouldn't be here because *he's* not a loony!"

"Me, neither!" Lucy asserted, her thick tongue slurring her words a bit. She dropped her hands and peered at her blunt cut fingernails with an avid expression, the tip of her raspberry tongue sticking out. She looked as though she expected something to grow out of them at any moment. Something with heads.

"No, you just like to start fires," a lanky, dark-haired boy drawled as he affectionately tugged on Lucy's pigtail. Acne scars pitted his chin and cheeks like miniature craters. He wore round glasses with arms that curved like a shepherd's staff around his prominent ears, which he kept hidden with shoulder-length hair and a hat. He never went anywhere without a hat, and in fact, looked naked without one. Today it was a black bowler.

"Stop pulling, Skippy, or I'll burn all your dumb hats!" Lucy threatened, her honey brown skin darkening with fury. He let go with a grin. Once her pigtail was free of Skippy's grasp, her hand slid up like a hypnotized snake and began to tug at the big, puffy ball. It was a temptation too hard even for their owner to resist. Lucy didn't mind when Pandora pulled on her pigtails, because she admired Pandora, but everyone else who tried it she threatened to torch. It was a valid threat, considering her history of arson.

"Do you want me to take care of him?" a small-for-thirteen, painfully thin boy asked, his blue eyes wide with excitement. This was Charles and his skin was so pale you could see his veins running beneath the surface. His whole body, especially his lips and fingertips, had a purplish hue. His health records cited that he had a dicky heart that didn't always do what it was supposed to, skipping beats and sometimes not beating hard enough to keep up. The way Charles talked, though, you wouldn't know it. He flexed his miniscule muscles and straightened his red Superman cape. "Cause I can do it if you want me to, Pandora. *Kerpow!*" he shouted and punched the air, his head, covered with angelic gold curls, dodging back and forth as he fought his invisible enemy. "*Bop! Bam!*" He stopped swiping at the air and peered at Pandora expectantly.

She laughed. "It wouldn't be a fair fight, I'm afraid. You'd slaughter him, Charles."

He gave her a look of disappointment, but was soon nodding in agreement. "I probably would. To have such awesome powers is a great responsibility. I must use them wisely." With that he put his thin, purple hands together, prayer-like, and bowed.

"That you must," she replied, returning the bow.

"So you really talked to him?" Skippy asked. No longer allowed to pull Lucy's pigtails, he had moved on to rubbing at his eyes beneath his glasses, then straightening his hat, then tapping on the cushioned arm of his chair. The arrival of a new inmate had kicked him into a manic phase, making staying still nearly impossible.

"Talked to who?" A breeze blew into Pandora's face as a voluptuous teenage girl with platinum blond hair trotted past her and plopped dramatically onto a nearby chair. After lots of grunts and exclamations, she finally settled in, her plump chin resting on her equally plump, gorgeously manicured hand. "What have I missed? Fill me in!" She snapped a wad of grape Bubble Yum several times. "I have just had a terribly difficult session with the Snake—he thinks I might have a hysterical womb, of all things—and I need to be cheered up!" She fluttered her fake eyelashes, which framed dragon-green eyes (courtesy of her new contact lenses). Usually they were plain brown, kind of like river mud. Birdy Peacock thought brown was totally boring, like her real name, Beth, which few used, especially after she threatened to kill them if they made the attempt. The name Birdy wasn't much better, she admitted, but her father, whom she adored, had come up with it. So she kept the nickname, saying, "at least it's unique." Today Birdy's blond hair was styled to look like Marilyn Monroe—her latest fashion idol. She wore a blue and white polka dot, fifties-style dress, white heels, and lots of make-up. Birdy always dressed as though she were in a play. She definitely stood out, and that's just the way she liked it.

"We're discussing the Newbie, and how Pandora got to meet him," Lucy told her. "He called us loonies, Birdy!"

"He did *not!*" Birdy gasped, looking thrilled. "How could he?" Dramatic as a silent-screen movie star, she laid the back of her hand across her forehead. "Oh, the shame of it!" She paused and leaned forward. "I know. Let's kill him!"

"Now, now. Let's leave the killing to the authorities," Pandora jumped in, taking back control of the conversation. Birdy was a scene-stealer and Pandora didn't like having her scene stolen, especially one as juicy as this. "Besides, if we killed him, we wouldn't have the fun of torturing him."

Lucy giggled and Birdy clapped her hands excitedly. Charles looked pale, as usual, and a little worried after the mention of torture. Skippy was tapping his foot and staring out the window, distracted by the mirrored reflections of other inmates wandering in and out of the room. Only Sinclair, the sixth of the Secret Six, as they called themselves, remained his stoic self, upright and still, gazing directly at Pandora without moving. At least, he *appeared* stoic, with his red hair combed perfectly into place and his spotless attire. But on the inside, he was a mess of anxieties and rules and endless rituals. Nonetheless, he kept his mouth shut a good deal of the time and Pandora liked that about him. She got enough interruptions from the others.

"I'm going to see him tomorrow morning, during staff change. He should be processed by then. Can you guys create a diversion for me?"

Birdy looked affronted, the palm of her hand smacking against her chest indignantly. "I cannot believe you even asked us that question!"

"I apologize. What I meant to say was, *Will* you guys create a diversion?"

"Oh, yes. Most definitely yes," Lucy answered. "Should I pretend to choke on a cracker? Or...or do you want me to start a fire?" Her small, round face glowed at the thought.

"I get to be the casualty this time!" Birdy wailed. She threw herself back against the chair and kicked her heels into the air. The chair's curved front legs briefly lifted off the ground before returning with a thump. "You got to do it last time, Lucy!"

Lucy scowled. "No, I didn't. You're an attention hog, Turdy Birdy!" Pandora stifled a laugh, quickly glancing out the window. Lucy was fifteen, but she had the mental age of a five-year-old so her insults weren't exactly brilliant, but they *were* stupidly funny. The trick was to not let Lucy see that Pandora found them amusing, otherwise she'd abuse her ability every chance she could and the posse would start acting out in accordance with their mental illness and generally make life hell. Pandora liked to run a tight ship, but it wasn't easy.

"I am not an attention hog!" Birdy declared vigorously. "You're just jealous, Lucy. I can't help it that I naturally attract attention. That I have a certain flair, or glamour, if you will, that draws people to me. And don't you call me Turdy, you retard!" Charles gaped at Birdy, then glanced over at Lucy, his blue lips pressed tightly together. He had a terrible crush on Lucy, and what's more, calling her the 'R' word was strictly forbidden. Besides, Birdy should know that it wasn't smart to upset Lucy. She would happily burn them all in their beds, feeling only the slightest twitch of remorse at seeing her friends perish in such a horrible manner. The girl loved her fire.

Charles sighed and Pandora guessed exactly what he was thinking. While he didn't want to take out Birdy, he may well be forced to do so to save Lucy's honor. Pandora quickly held up her hands, saving him from abusing his powers. "I don't see why you both can't play victims. You know my theory..."

"The more chaos, the better!" they all shouted with gusto, fists raised in the air, argument forgotten.

Even Sinclair joined in. No emotion accompanied his spoken words, nor did he raise his fist, but his response showed he was listening. Of course, now he had to keep saying the words over and over. *The more chaos, the better.* Once spoken aloud, they had to be repeated eleven more times (to make a nice even twelve), with no mistakes, or a great world catastrophe would occur. Pandora often thought Sinclair carried a heavy burden on his shoulders. Luckily for the rest of the world, she'd trained him to make his repetitions softly. He used to shout them, but yelling, she'd convinced him, caused too many negative airwaves, rendering his chants useless. A whisper would be much more effective.

As he mumbled to himself, his finger tracing a yellow diamond on one of the twenty or so Argyle sweaters he always wore over a crisp white, button-down dress shirt (in the summer he changed over to Argyle vests and short sleeve button-downs), Pandora drew in a deep breath. "All right, Secret Six. We have a job to do." *Finally!* she added under her breath. Lately, life had been pretty boring around Nepenthe Manor. You'd think for a loony bin, the day would be filled with excitement. Not so. Sometimes Pandora was forced to create pandemonium, if only to relieve the tedium of daily ritual necessary to keep a massive place like this from running into the ground. Or at the very least, burned to the ground. She glanced at Lucy, who was banging her head against the back of the chair.

"Your mom's not going to like this," Charles said softly, looking worried.

"My mom's not going to find out, is she?" He shook his head, his blue eyes trusting. "Besides, what's a girl supposed to do? Languish away in this frigid, dusty old place and die a wizened heap of a loser? No way!" She pounded the coffee table and the polyhedral dice from Charles's Dungeons and Dragons game jumped into the air. He quickly gathered up the pieces. "Vicki's always telling me..." here, she lowered her voice to sound terribly serious, "...'Life is what you make of it, Pandy.'"

Her mother, despite giving her the name most associated with all the evils of the world, refused to call her Pandora. She thought she was making up for the momentary lack of reasoning she'd experienced after a prolonged and difficult childbirth to a child she hadn't wanted in the first place. Pandora got that. But to go with Pandy instead? The nickname sounded awfully close to Pansy, and more like something you'd call a panda bear. Anyway, Pandora preferred going by her whole name. All the inmates called her Pandora. They understood the importance of a name. Nobody bowed down to a Pandy, but they did to a *Pandora*.

Names being important, Pandora decided when she was eight years old to start calling her mother by her first name. Vicki had fought it at first, yelling and practically frothing at the mouth, but she was a busy woman, and soon gave up the battle. She had better things to do than fight with a sullen kid.

"I, for one, would like to see the new inmate myself," Birdy said as she straightened her dress. "I don't see why Pandora gets to have all the fun."

"Pandora gets to have all the fun," Skippy sniped, "because she can come and go as she pleases." He yanked a pair of drumsticks—a gift from Professor Robertson, a fellow inmate—out of his back pocket and started to play *Smoke on the Water* on the coffee table.

"It isn't fair!" Birdy pouted. "Why can't I come and go? I mean, I know why the rest of you losers are in here. But me? Sure, I have terrible luck. Sure, I get blamed for more than my fair share. But I'm sixteen! I'm plenty old enough to look after myself. I quit the Six." She crossed her arms and blew a big, purple bubble.

Everyone stayed silent. On some level, they all knew why they were here. It was just that no one liked to dwell on the fact...or what it meant beyond simply not fitting into "normal" society. Pandora frowned. This was getting out of hand.

"Oh, Birdy," she scolded. "You know the Secret Six wouldn't be the same without you."

"Yeah, because then it would only be the Secret Five," Skippy muttered. "Not quite the same ring." Pandora gave him a sharp look, meant to put him in his place, and his bony shoulders drooped. His head dropped forward and his hat nearly toppled off, but his long fingers caught it at the last moment.

"You've got to be kidding me!" She looked around at the rest of the pathetic bunch, already mimicking Skippy's posture of despair. Whenever he started to sink into an abyss of depression, he had a tendency to pull everyone in with him. He was like his own black hole. "This is the first adventure we've had in ages and you want to let it slip through our fingers?"

Skippy sighed, but Lucy, bless her heart, perked up. "Can I start a fire?"

Pandora shook her head. "No, but you can pretend you did. They might even call in the fire trucks!"

Lucy laughed gleefully, the sound rich and deep. "Oh, I love those fire fighters! They're even hotter than fire!"

"Lucy!" Birdy screeched, tossing a bedraggled throw pillow at her. "You old dog, you!" She threw back her head and laughed, delighting in the wickedness of it. Lucy giggled, Charles brightened, and Sinclair finished his recitations. Skippy jumped to his feet, leaving his depression behind, and jammed his drumsticks into his back pocket. His roller coaster mood was heading back uphill.

"Let's get plotting, people!" Rubbing his hands together and grinning like a lunatic, he added, "And I know exactly what we need to do."

Pandora smiled to herself. *Life is what you make of it, you say, Mother dear? Well, let's see what you make of this!*

3

Best-Laid Plans

IN THE END, ninety-nine percent of Skippy's numerous and completely impractical ideas were rejected. Where he thought the posse was going to get a hold of napalm was beyond Pandora. But she had to let him vent or he'd sink into a depression again. So she half listened to his rambling and afterwards, proceeded to make him feel like his ideas were tantamount to the cure for cancer.

Then, and only then, did she begin to whittle away at his grand, and fatuously dangerous, schemes until they had a much more simplified version to follow for early the next morning. The simpler, the better. Pandora wasn't exactly dealing with Ph.D. candidates here. On the other hand, she'd met a few doctors in her day that really ought to be taken out and shot, they were so moronic. They made the posse look like Harvard graduates. A few such doctors worked at Nepenthe Manor and each time she saw one of them her trigger finger would itch. Lucky for them, Pandora wasn't big on going to jail for murdering idiots. Still, a girl could dream, couldn't she?

It was late now and she lay in her bunk, pondering the mottled ceiling, which was so old it cracked like desert sand in some places and bulged like blisters in others. She thought about Newbie and what he'd said about not being like the inmates here. Could he really be that delusional? Anyone arriving at Nepenthe Manor via the Madmobile, a mode of transportation typically used only for the tough cases, had to have done something to piss off the powers that be. The inmates all had that in common. They had drawn attention to themselves in a manner unbefitting good citizens. And they were still paying the price for it.

But what if he was telling the truth? What if he really didn't belong here? It was a thought Pandora had never considered in her fourteen years living in this messed-up Gothic manor. She'd always assumed if a person was sent here, they were meant to be here, even if only temporarily. But now that she considered the idea, she realized the new guy didn't exactly fit the profile. She'd met enough crazy people (including many who should be incarcerated, but weren't) to get a feel for what lunacy looked like, especially upon first arrival at Nepenthe Manor. And typically, that look wasn't scared. Newbie had been with it enough to be afraid of his situation. Most people in the throes of a breakdown acted everything but scared. Angry, lost, sad, spaced out, even giddy, but scared? Not the truly sick ones.

If Newbie wasn't a legitimate Nepenthe Manor candidate, then what had he done to end up in an insane asylum? It was the 1980s, after all. Loads of progress had been made in the mental health field since the days when all it took to lock someone up was somebody else's word that the victim in question was crazy, along with a few coins to sweeten the deal. These days people couldn't be locked up without due diligence. There was a process for admitting inmates—important papers had to be looked over and signed by important people Who Know Best before anyone could be held against their will. So what was his story?

It was a mystery, all right, and one she was aching to solve. Her fevered brain kicked into overdrive. Was he experiencing a drug-induced psychosis? He certainly hadn't seemed psychotic—no ravings, no attacks, no begging her to get the bugs off him. Schizophrenic paranoia maybe? Probably not. He'd thought she'd come to help him and no paranoid schizo worth his salt would trust *any*one. Perhaps he'd simply been walking around town buck-naked singing *Joy to the World*. That was certainly possible.

Finally, after a rousing internal debate that lasted for hours, but solved nothing, Pandora fell asleep with a satisfied smile on her lips. Whatever came out of this, it would be interesting.

After dreaming all night about running from a pack of vigilante therapists toting notepads and determined to make her tell them about her childhood, Pandora woke with a start at precisely 6:30 a.m. Lately she'd been sleeping in until ten or eleven. But today, like the late April spring air, the comings of fresh blood offered new hope that life here might be worth living after all. She slid out of her bunk and padded in bare feet over to one of two eight-foot tall, multi-paned windows lighting her room. She climbed up onto the padded velvet window seat and peered out. A pink-orange glow from the rising sun behind the manor gave rare color to her long, pale face, though she'd have rather done without it. Blushing cheeks rather spoiled her carefully cultivated gothic look.

Her bedroom faced the lawn that encircled the house like a bold, green crown, then stretched westward for half an acre. A wrought-iron fence, rising fifteen feet into the air and ending with spear tips that could skewer your gut with one slip of the foot, ran around the entire thirty acres of the manor's demesne, even closing off the cliffs that overlooked the Atlantic Ocean...to discourage the jumpers.

From her window Pandora had an excellent view of the gravel drive that cut through the lawn like a pale river, putting her in the prime position of being able to see anyone coming or going. After about fifty yards, the driveway skirted around a copse of massive trees—mainly oak and maple interspersed with white pine—then disappeared from sight.

After traveling forty yards through a tree-lined tunnel, you would come upon the main gate and a two-story house that resembled a turret. Ronny and Lonny were identical twin brothers who, with their skinny, slouched figures, humped noses, and black, pony-tailed hair, greatly resembled Ichabod Crane. They lived in the turret. Social misfits, they discouraged visitors and rarely spoke more than one or two words at a time, preferring to nod or grunt. Pandora was pretty sure their odd manners and appearance did nothing to dispel the rumors about Nepenthe Manor. Their job was to unlock and open the massive gate, then close and lock it once more. They also drove the Madmobile, the asylum's version of an ambulance, which they parked in a two-car garage next to the gatehouse. A plain brown van was used for carting inmates into town for visits to the dentist or eye doctor or whatever else could not be taken care of at the manor. The twins took turns doing each job, but they looked so much alike that nobody, except Pandora, ever noticed the difference.

Her roving eyes returned to the main grounds where benches and picnic tables could be found lounging beneath the protective canopy of the trees. Close by, a giant labyrinth took up most of the southern corner of the lawn. Behind its tantalizing fifteen-foot wall, covered in a thick blanket of English ivy, a locked-up tight maze of gargantuan proportions languished unused, much to Pandora's disgust. If she had a key, she'd use it to get inside. But she'd yet to even find the door. And she couldn't go over the walls—the tops were covered with sharp spikes, all different sizes, and all lethal. She called the maze the Labyrinth of Lunacy—it seemed a very appropriate title under the circumstances.

To the south, just beyond the fence, sat a series of white cottages that, with their squat chimneys and profusion of wild flowers, would look right at home in the midst of an English village. Most of the therapists who worked at Nepenthe Manor lived in the cottages. They had to put up with a lot of crap at the institute, or so an annoying few kept reminding anyone within twenty feet whilst on a rant, but in return, they got to live in paradise. A cottage on the ocean, a bit of earth to call their own, and a short commute—what else could anyone ask for?

Even so, having a lovely cottage wasn't enough for some of the staff. Pandora referred to such individuals as Fragile Flowers (FF) or Spineless Simpletons (SS), depending on the person. Just two weeks ago, Fragile Flower, Ms. Thomson, who held a Master's degree in Social Work, had scuttled out the front door of the manor, down its grand staircase, past the decorative twin griffins, wings spread like hawks swooping in for the kill, and into her boyfriend's waiting car—all in heels, no less. She was crying. Pandora had been sorry to see her go. Ms. Thomson had been great fun, and an easy target, being the unfortunately naïve type of individual who believed anything a person told her.

So now the search was on for yet another new therapist. Pandora sighed and jumped down from the window seat. Why did things have to change? She shook her head despondently as she headed for her dresser. Maybe she shouldn't have encouraged the posse to call her Ms. Bombson. She also might have avoided suggesting they spin tall tales of woe during therapy with the FF.

Ah, well. If they ended up with someone worse, it was Pandora's own fault. She should have just let the poor girl be. Better the devil you know, and all that. Poor Ms. Bombson wasn't really a devil, though, only a victim. Pandora had been trying to toughen her up, mold her into a warrior. And this is the thanks she got from the ingrate? Leaving without a word? Well, poo on her.

Thoroughly indignant now, Pandora yanked on black tights and matching Doc Martens, a black mini-skirt and a black turtleneck. Her contraband mirror, hidden behind the door, revealed a Wednesday Addams look (with the exception of her repulsively vivid blue eyes, and fringe-cut bangs) that was quite pleasing. Her appearance—black Goth and innocent braids—represented a sort of yin and yang. Pandora thought she looked sweet, yet sinister. By the time people figured out which one she was, it was too late.

Whistling the tune to *The Andy Griffith Show*, she grabbed her sporran, which she always wore wherever she went, and which stored an assortment of items necessary for survival in an insane asylum, and pulled it over her head, settling it to fall at her hip. Then she picked up her flashlight and headed for the opening to the secret passage.

Years ago she'd found the passages while hiding in her bedroom closet. A closet was an unusual feature in such an old house, but then, it obviously wasn't this house's only unusual feature. When she was four, she'd broken an ornately carved newel post on the curved central staircase leading up to the second floor. At the time, bored and looking for a way to pass the lonely hours, she'd been hanging from it. Who knew the dang thing would be so delicate? At this young age, she'd still been afraid of getting into trouble and so she'd hidden in her closet.

Sobbing with fear, her little fingers picking at any knob or protrusion they could find, she pressed hard on one particularly wobbly piece of wood and a click sounded. Her red eyes gaped at the black crack that appeared before her and she immediately stopped crying. After wiping her tears and her runny nose on her sleeve, she stood and pushed open the panel. Trembling slightly, she entered a dusty and cobwebby passage that looked like it hadn't been used since the Nepenthe family had built the manor back in 1885. Seeing how dark it was, she scuttled back out, quickly found a tiny flashlight, and returned, her fears of being punished forgotten.

After that initial foray, Pandora spent countless hours exploring the many passages snaking throughout Nepenthe Manor. Whoever had drawn up the plans for the house had possessed a fascinating mind, installing on every level, several spring-loaded, hinged doors, some of which were mere paneling, but others that were set behind built-in bookcases or attached to massive paintings. Special buttons at toe level unlatched the door to allow for re-entry. For the most part, Pandora avoided using the paintings simply because the openings were about three feet off the floor and hard to return through in case of an emergency. Countless little stairways, with only three or four steps, led from one passage to another for no apparent reason. There were longer staircases, too, which allowed one to travel from one floor to the next. About fifteen of the passages dead-ended. Peepholes had been bored into the walls of all the public rooms, like the old ballroom, which was now the dining room, and kept Pandora from feeling too left out of things. In the heart of Nepenthe Manor there was a secret room, as well. It was one of her favorite places to visit when life got too hard to handle.

Pandora firmly believed that this vast, hidden world had saved her life countless times over the years and she did her best to keep everything clean and in good working order, oiling hinges on a weekly basis and, once a month, sweeping the floors, a chore which she hated because it made her wheezy for the next two days. But she did it anyway. The suffering was worth it.

Pandora hurried along the dark corridor, sporran thumping against her hip, and thought about their plan for Newbie. He would've been processed by now, then moved to another room on the second floor. The straightjacket would be gone—likely removed shortly after Pandora's visit. The Director didn't like them (though some of the staff swore by them, and Pandora had to admit she wouldn't mind getting hold of one herself) and personally made sure the restraint was removed from new inmates sooner rather than later. Pandora preferred later—the later the better, in fact. She liked having plenty of time to size up new arrivals while they were still physically restrained. The helpless were so much easier to control. So far, though, Newbie hadn't turned out to be all that easy to manipulate. Pandora's pulse quickened. She'd soon change that.

The second floor was where the inmates slept. If Newbie was going to stay, he would start out in a special room designed to ease the inmate into his new life as a ward of the state. After proving he was going to play nice, he'd move in with a roommate.

Nepenthe Manor was a sort of catchall institute for difficult 'cases' and one of the last of its kind in the area. Locals called it "The Dump" because people nobody wanted were dumped here. Inmates ranged in age from ten to ninety-five (that was Mr. Harley), had all sorts of problems that nobody could quite figure out or didn't know how to handle, and were split about equally between males and females.

Most people who checked in to Nepenthe Manor never checked out. The frequent fliers were few, staying for a few weeks to stabilize, then leaving again, only to return after their next breakdown. Some of those who stayed indefinitely were unable to function independently; others couldn't make it on their own without destroying something (like Lucy and her fire setting) or someone (like Birdy and her threats of bodily harm, which were sometimes followed through on). But most who came simply didn't want to leave. For many, this was the only home they'd ever known. That's why Pandora worked so hard to make it a fun place to be. Her motto, "It's all about others..." made life worth living for the inmates. She didn't make trouble simply for her own pleasure; she did it to bring joy to their otherwise miserable, little lives.

Access to Floor Two, South Wing, was through door number 13, Pandora's most favorite and luckiest number. She called it the Ratched Route, after scary Nurse Ratched in *One Flew Over the Cuckoo's Nest,* and in honor of Head Nurse Rackett, who bore an eerie resemblance in both appearance and name to the anal-retentive, rule following Ratched. Pandora's favorite part of *Cuckoo's Nest,* the videotape of

which she kept hidden away in her closet, was when the inmates re-
belled against Nurse Ratched. Her least favorite, but most intensely
watched bit, was when Jack Nicholson got a lobotomy and ended up
drooling all over the place. That kind of stuff didn't happen at the
manor anymore, though the rooms where such grisly operations had
taken place still existed, and all the operating tables, machines, and
various implements of torture had not been touched or removed. Although off-limits (along with the labyrinth, the manor's small stage
theater, and the catacomb-like cellar), Pandora liked to visit the operating rooms whenever she was in a restless mood. Sometimes she'd lie
on the table and pretend she was about to get zapped in the brain, or
actually did get zapped, and was now convulsing with seizures.

After listening closely to ensure the coast was clear, she slowly
pushed open the door and peeked out into the main hallway of the
South Wing. The South Wing was where the gentlemen lived—the
North Wing was where the ladies stayed. The night and day nurses
shuttled back and forth between the wings, but typically spent more
time on the male side because boys were supposed to be so much
more trouble than girls. *Ha!* Strictly speaking, the male wing was off-
limits to females (and vice versa), a rule that the posse planned to use
to their advantage while instituting their latest scheme.

After much debate, it was decided that Lucy would chase Birdy into
forbidden territory, threatening to light her hair on fire. When the head
night nurse, Nurse Hunter, came out to shoo them off, Pandora would
make her move. Charles and Skippy would come out of their rooms at
the same time, adding to the pandemonium. Sinclair's job was to get in
the way of the nurses, if need be.

Pandora glanced at her watch. 7:05. Birdy and Lucy were due to commit mayhem at any moment. At the end of the hall, where the glassed-
in office/station was located, the staff (three from the night shift, and
three for the upcoming day shift) was drinking bitter coffee and
chatting as they waited for Nurse Hunter to brief them on any issues
that had arisen during the previous 12-hour shift. If Pandora thought
she could walk undetected to the Newbie's door, she would. But the
room for new admissions stood only two doors down from the
office—they'd spot her for sure. Being that word was out that any time
Pandora was somewhere she wasn't supposed to be was a dangerous
time for them all, she decided not to take any unnecessary chances.

Pandora glanced at her watch again. 7:10. Where were Birdy and
Lucy? The door to the hallway wasn't kept locked—the Director didn't

believe in such draconian measures, at least not in this respect—so access wasn't a problem. They should be here by now. Had something happened? Was someone ratting her out at this very moment? It wouldn't be the first time. Pandora twisted and untwisted her braid again and again as she waited impatiently. Finally, she stepped out into the passage and ducked low. She couldn't be caught peeping through a door no one knew about. She'd rather be caught in the hallway and face Nurse Rackett's wrath than have someone find out about the secret passages.

At 7:12, the heavy metal door to the second floor slowly opened and Lucy popped her head around the corner. Her eyes darted about, then zeroed in on Pandora. When she saw her, she lifted her pudgy hands and shoulders in a "What do I do?" gesture. Damn. Birdy was late. As usual. That girl would be late to her own funeral, which would be occurring soon if she didn't shape up. Lucy would have to go it alone. Luckily, she was more than capable of creating a scene all by herself.

Pandora waved her on. Lucy grinned and stepped into the hall. Within moments, she was outside Skippy and Charles's room, which was four doors down from the station, and on the opposite side from the Newbie Room. Pandora retreated, unseen, behind the hidden door and waited to see what Lucy would come up with. Whatever it was ought to be good.

Lucy pounded on the door. "Skippy, you get out here this instance! I know you took it, you booger brain! Give it back *now!*"

Two of the staff perked up. Trouble was brewing. Still, they didn't move, just waited to see what was up. The staff that worked at Nepenthe Manor weren't always the brightest bulbs, but they'd learned how to survive, and that meant avoiding confrontation if at all possible, hoping against all hopes that any potential crises died out on their own. "I'll light you on fire if you don't open this door. I'm warning you!"

That got their attention. The same two workers—a psych assistant and a male nurse—hustled out the door. "Now, now, Miss Lucy," the p.a. soothed. "What's this?" The male nurse tried to grab Lucy's arms and she shrieked like a demon. His hands jerked back as though she'd spewed fire at him. He was pretty new, Pandora realized, and her resulting smile was decidedly devilish.

"Who're you?" Lucy demanded, her dark eyes blazing. "Don't make me torch you!"

The nurse smiled a patronizing smile. It was, perhaps, the last time in his short career at Nepenthe Manor he would make that dumb mistake. "I think we should go back to our rooms, don't you?"

Lucy whipped out the pink lighter Pandora had given her. "I think we should just back off!" She waved it at the two staff. As ordered, the p.a. and the nurse backed off, hands in the air. Pandora groaned. She had hoped to use the lighter only as a last resort. She didn't have very many left. Ah, well. All for a good cause.

"Nurse Rackett!" the p.a. turned and shouted. While Nurse Hunter was an adequate nurse, it was the end of her 12-hour shift and she was just about done in, and anyways, everyone knew who was really in charge—The Rackett. "We need you!"

Pandora gave a mental cheer as the entire staff—all of whom were watching the events unfold—poured out of the office, with Nurse Rackett taking the lead like a modern day Attila the Hun. At that same moment, Skippy's door opened, a long-fingered hand reached out, grabbed Lucy's plump arm, and pulled her inside. The door slammed shut. Seconds later the staff swarmed the area, all talking at once. Nurse Rackett rapped on the door and demanded to be let in.

In the ensuing chaos, Pandora slipped through the crack and began to sneak down the hall like a thief. She kept her back pressed against the wall and her eyes focused on the crowd at Skippy's door. The door behind her suddenly swung open and she fell backward. Turning her head, she spotted Sinclair's smooth, round face, blank as the moon. He put his hand on her back, pushed her out of his room, and calmly closed the door. Sinclair was no dummy.

By now the staff was really getting worked up, banging and hollering for Skippy to open up. No doubt he was holding the knob. In his manic phase that boy possessed inhuman strength.

"Open this door now!" Nurse Rackett shouted, her cold voice penetrating to the bone. Suddenly the door flew open and the staff, all sort of leaning on each other, fell into the room like water through a broken dam.

Here was Pandora's chance! She scampered down the hall, twisted the knob to the Newbie's door, leaped inside, and quickly shut it behind her. Panting, she turned to face him.

"What are *you* doing here?" The boy, now free of the straightjacket, was lying on his bed, head propped up by a pillow, arms crossed. His scowling face was clean and he wore the Nepenthe Manor uniform for incoming inmates—ill-fitting blue PJs, a beltless robe, and fuzzy slippers.

Pandora took a step forward and a lemony smell wafted toward her. "I'm a member of the Nepenthe Manor Welcoming Committee." She smiled sweetly and spread her arms wide as she approached him. "Welcome!"

"No, you're not. You're evil."

Pandora did her best to look affronted, her blue eyes wide, her mouth forming a small o. "Excuse me? I can't believe you just said that. I came here to find out more about you. Give you someone to talk to, give you a chance to tell your side of the story." She stopped two feet from his bed and looked down on him.

His scowl deepened. "You're the last person I'd confide in." He ran a hand over his spiky blond hair, then down the back of his neck where the hair was longer and curly. "Now leave me alone before I start yelling." His brown eyes narrowed. "I'll bet you're not even supposed to be in here." He leaned to his left to look around her. "What's going on out there, anyway?"

Pandora ignored all that. "Listen, Newbie. You're going to be here a while, so you might as well spill it. What did you do?" She took another step closer.

He shook his head, his lips pressed firmly together. Seeing him like this, Pandora had to admit that he didn't really look like the typical Nepenthe Manor resident, especially now that he was clean and the straightjacket was gone. She'd been right. There *was* something different about him. He seemed calmer, more rational than the other inmates. Intrigued, she found she truly was curious about what had brought him here, and not just because she wanted to use the information against him at a later date.

"Come on. You can talk to me. I won't tell…" *the police, Nurse Rackett, or the Nazis. Everyone else is fair game.*

He sat up. "You think I'm going to trust you after you purposely misled me? I don't think so."

So he'd figured her out. "Listen Newbie. This might be a loony bin, but that doesn't mean a girl doesn't get bored. I do what I have to do to keep from letting the ennui suffocate me."

"It's pronounced, on-wee, Wednesday. Not en-u-i." He gave her a smug look. Possibly his last.

"You know what happens to Newbies who get on my bad side?"

He shook his head, looking infuriatingly calm.

"I give my good friend Crazy Chuck the go-ahead to perform a lobotomy on your little brain." She made a motion indicating an ice pick getting shoved up her nose.

He had the good sense to blanch. "For the last time…if you don't get out of here I'm going to start yelling."

His mouth launched into yelling mode, but before he could make good on his threat, the door flew open and Birdy burst in, leaving the door wide open. Pandora rushed to close it. "Sorry I'm late! My stockings got a run in—" She screeched to a halt, as best one can in heels, and took in the Newbie, eyes wide with appreciation. "Well, well, well. No wonder Pandora wanted to keep you all to herself."

Newbie's eyes widened. "Who are *you*?"

Doing her best Marilyn Monroe impression, she sashayed up to his bed in her red heels and red halter-top dress, which had to be freezing. Near the ocean and incredibly huge, Nepenthe Manor was *never* warm. "I'm lonely…and you're cute. Ask me out on a date, Cute," she said in a breathy voice.

Newbie gave a harsh bark of a laugh, most likely elicited by shock. Birdy was a lot to take in all at once. "Um, we're in an asylum. I don't think dating is allowed."

"Sure, it is. Just as long as nobody knows about it. Right, Pandora?"

"You're late, Birdy," Pandora replied, feeling quite put out as she inched closer to Newbie's bed, hoping to regain the advantage she'd had. Once again Birdy had stolen the show, and just when Newbie had been about to crack.

Birdy ignored her, plopping down next to Newbie on the bed. He tried to scoot away as her red fingernails prowled up his thigh. "What's your name, other than Handsome?"

"Um, er…"

She gave a throaty laugh. "Let me guess. Gorgeous?"

"Xavier," he sputtered. His eyes darted to Pandora. *Save me*, they said. She crossed her arms and shot him a *you're on your own, bucko* look back. That's what he got for not confiding in her and then threatening to turn her in.

"Xavier. I like that," Birdy purred.

"*Burn, heathen scum!*" Lucy's hearty cry sounded from the hallway like an alarm. Dang! They'd gotten her out of Skippy and Charles's bedroom. Pandora suddenly realized their own precarious position. If someone came in right now and found them sitting with the Newbie— well, it would not be good.

"We have to get out of here, Birdy," Pandora warned.

"I never had a lighter!" Lucy protested loudly, her voice carrying loud and clear through the door. "It was candy and I ate it!" She laughed. "Fooled you, fooled you!"

"I knew you weren't supposed to be in here!" Newbie exclaimed, sitting upright and pointing at Pandora.

"Yeah, well, c'est la vie! Gotta go." She grabbed Birdy's arm and ran for the door.

But before they could reach it, it swung open, revealing a frightful figure dressed all in white. "Are you all right, Mr.— Pandora? Birdy? What are you girls doing in here?" Nurse Rackett advanced toward them like an iceberg and they, mere dinghies in her path.

"We were just checking to be sure the new arrival was okay," Pandora rushed to say.

"She was spying on me," Xavier said loudly. "I want her out of here."

Pandora spun about and glared at him. "You'll regret that, Newbie," she mouthed, drawing a finger across her throat. He shrugged.

Nurse Rackett grabbed Pandora and Birdy's arms just above the elbows and spun them around. With an iron grip that would make grown men cry, she dragged them into the hallway. It was completely empty. Skippy and Charles's door was closed and not a peep came from behind it. The p.a. must have taken Lucy back to her room and Charles and Skippy were apparently hiding out. Upon spotting Nurse Rackett, several cracked-open doors in the hallway clicked shut.

"Ms. Hessian!" Nurse Rackett called, her voice cold and calm, yet carrying. Ms. Hessian, a heavyset p.a. with a sloping brow and short, chopped bangs that made her look more like a throwback to ancient man than a nurse, plodded out of the station. "Take Ms. Peacock to her room. I'll deal with this one."

"Stay alive, Pandora!" Birdy cried, fist lifted high in the air as the Hessian dragged her away. Pandora raised her fist in acknowledgment as she watched her friend stumble off in her high heels.

"I'm taking you to the Director," Nurse Rackett announced, her blue eyes icy. Pandora nearly gagged. *Not the Director*, she groaned inwardly. *Anyone but the Director!*

She lowered her fist in defeat. The thing about best-laid plans around this place? They *always* went awry.

Lessons to be Learned

4

PANDORA WISHED NURSE Rackett would say *some*thing. But the wretched woman knew just how to twist the knife of shame, her pale lips thin with disapproval, her straight back rigid with condemnation. She was a tall woman, possibly six feet, and solidly built. She wore her graying blond hair in an elaborate up-do—her only *visible* (who knew what she wore under that white uniform?) nod to vanity. It must have taken ages to perfect each morning. With her long Scandinavian face, plain as a rutabaga farmer's and nearly wrinkle-free except for some scowl lines around her perpetually downturned mouth, she looked like she could be a nanny for the Munsters. The only jewelry she wore was a small silver watch pinned just above where her heart would be, if she had one. If only she'd wear a little eyeliner, Pandora mused, maybe some lip-gloss, she'd look less like the Grim Reaper's mother. Maybe. Pandora was all for the living dead look, but this was taking things too far.

The march down to the first floor where the Director's office was located seemed interminable, like the sacrificial virgin trudging up the side of a volcano to her death. Each inmate they passed on the stairway watched them go by with wide, worried eyes. Nurse Rackett had a freakish reputation for getting her way, and this time, she was determined to see that Pandora pay for her little shenanigans. As they crossed the foyer, Pandora's footsteps seemed to chant, "You're in for it, you're in for it, you're in for it."

They finally reached the office and Nurse Rackett rapped sharply on the solid oak door. Pandora tried to pull away. She couldn't face it. Not again. She knew what was going to happen—it always happened—and the thought of it made her woozy. She wasn't up to this. She said as much to Nurse Rackett.

"I'm just not up to this today, Nurse Rackett. I'm sure you understand."

Nurse Rackett peered down at her. Her pale blue orbs looked like what a drowned person's eyes would look like, glassy and unforgiving as death. Pandora should know. When she was eight she found the body of a bag lady on the beach. She never forgot that day, or the sight of the bloated body and its staring eyes. She sometimes dreamed about it and often sketched poorly drawn pictures for study at a later date. She wondered if the victim—no one she knew—had suffered terribly. She couldn't help dwelling on what the old woman must have gone through: limbs thrashing, water splashing, the first pricks of panic, then at last giving in to the inevitable—sinking in slow motion, hands grasping at the sky, lungs filling with saltwater, the brain's blood vessels popping like fireworks, then one last, mighty explosion before oblivion.

Pandora kind of felt like that now. Only there'd be no welcome oblivion.

Nurse Rackett knocked again. Three more sharp raps, like a judge's gavel.

"What? Who is it? Oh, come in, come in!" The voice behind the door sounded distracted. The reason for the distraction was apparent when Nurse Rackett pushed open the door. The Director, seated behind her mahogany desk—an ornate Victorian monstrosity that Pandora coveted for its many nooks and crannies and secret drawers—was talking on the phone.

When they entered, she held up a finger without looking at them. "I see. Yes, well, I'll be sure to take care of that as soon as I get the check from the state. Yesterday was Sunday, so no mail. But I'm expecting it to come today." Irritated pause. "Yes, I know it's late. But surely—" The Director impatiently tapped a ball-point pen on the desktop. "Do you seriously want that to happen?" More tapping, the pen growing increasingly irate. "I didn't think so. Just give me two more days and I'll deliver the check myself. Better yet, I'll have Bennington do it. She remembers that sort of thing better than I do." She leaned forward and peered through a doorway between two built-in bookshelves and waved at a wren-like Asian woman sitting in a smaller office, hunched over her computer keyboard. Bennington, the Director's personal assistant, barely paused in her typing to flip an acknowledging wave back. "Fine. You tell him that. You can also remind him about the ramifications of— Oh, does he?" She glanced up and grimaced.

One of Nurse Rackett's pale eyebrows rose haughtily and her fishy lips curled in disdain. "We can wait outside—"

The Director held up a finger again. "Yes, well, next time tell him to fight his own battles instead of getting his trained monkeys to do it for him!" She slammed down the phone and stared off into space, her eyes narrowed. "Stupid man!" she grumbled. "Who does he think he is?"

Nurse Rackett cleared her throat. "Do you have a moment?"

"Hm? Oh, yes." The Director ran her hands, square and competent, yet still feminine, through her curly brown hair, and blew out a big breath of air. "What can I do for you, Nurse Rackett?" She glanced at Pandora and one dark eyebrow lifted dubiously. "I hope you're here to tell me something good, though I have a feeling you aren't."

Nurse Rackett's back went even more rigid, something Pandora didn't think was possible being that her spine was undoubtedly made of steel. "No, I'm not. You see—"

But the Director didn't let her finish. She turned to Pandora. "What were you up to this time?"

Pandora shrugged. "Nothing much. I just wanted to greet the new arrival."

Nurse Rackett gasped indignantly. "You plotted to sneak in to see him and judging by his reaction, it wasn't your first time. She manipulated several of the patients to create a diversion so she wouldn't be seen. Really, Director—"

The Director held up her hand. She wore an oversized leather wristwatch that slid up and down on a wrist that wouldn't be so thin if she ate when she was supposed to. She meant to, or so she always said, but interruptions in her position were inevitable and the manor's food wasn't nearly tempting enough to return to once left. "I'm sure she was just trying to be helpful." The Director started sifting through a pile of paperwork on her desk, her brow furrowed. "Now where did I put those forms? He'll be arriving at any moment—"

Pandora watched the Director's movements, hoping against hope that this time she'd surprise her and do something different. That she wouldn't let Pandora off the hook like she always did. But the Director's mind was already on something else and Nurse Rackett was looking more furious by the second.

"You're not going to do anything?" she demanded.

The Director looked up, confused. "About what?"

"About Pandora! She is constantly stirring up trouble. I have enough on my plate with too many patients and not enough staff without having to deal with her, too. There are Lessons to be Learned. They *must* be learned!" If Nurse Rackett had a ruler she would've slapped the palm of her hand, and very likely Pandora's behind, too.

The Director sighed and rubbed her forehead. "I'm sure she'll be good from now on, won't you?" She stared pointedly at Pandora.

Pandora shook her head, her finger tracing the decorative Celtic knots and thistles embossed on her sporran. "It's not really in my nature to be good."

The Director frowned. "Oh, sure it is. You just have to try harder." She leaned back in her chair. "But you are only thirteen—"

Pandora bit her lip. "I'm fourteen now, remember?"

"Oh, yes, that's right." She looked at Nurse Rackett. "See? She's a teenager. She's bound to want to test the limits, find her boundaries. You know all about that psychological stuff, right? And she didn't hurt anyone, did she?"

Nurse Rackett sniffed. "I'm a psychiatric nurse, not a *counselor*." Nurse Rackett thought all counselors were quacks. Her methods consisted of strict control, ample medication, and swift punishment, whenever deemed appropriate. If the use of whips were allowed, she'd own a whole arsenal of them. Counselors, in her mind, were namby-pamby, touchy-feely wusses, and therefore, useless not only in Nepenthe Manor, but to the world in general.

"Right. Of course." The Director smiled, her stressed and tired face suddenly lighting up. "Speaking of which, our new counselor starts today!"

Nurse Rackett looked as though she'd swallowed something half-alive, and which was fighting its way back out. "I was hoping to add another nurse to the staff. At least another full-time psychiatric assistant. You know how unreliable those college students from the university can be. They think they're doing us a favor, working here."

The Director snorted. "With what we pay them, they *are* doing us a favor." She waved her hand to dismiss the topic. "You'll like this one, Rackett. Trust me."

"I highly doubt that." Nurse Rackett sniffed again. Pandora was tempted to offer her an antihistamine, washed down with an arsenic chaser. The combination would surely stop all sniffing...*permanently*.

There was a knock at the door, which echoed in the high-ceilinged room that had once been a charming Victorian parlor, but was now painted a professional and ghastly dull eggshell with gray undertones. The Director popped up out of her chair and swiftly straightened her navy blue skirt, dotted with tiny, pink flowers, then pulled down the hem of a matching shaker knit sweater, which she wore over a pink blouse. She was looking quite feminine for once—she typically wore brown corduroys or khakis accompanied by blouses and blazers in practical colors (navy blue, black, brown—*never* pink). Her shoes were always comfortable flats, as opposed to the navy blue heels she wore today. Her hazel green eyes were bright, her cheeks flushed. Whoever was knocking, the Director was anxious to see him. "Come in!"

Pandora and Nurse Rackett turned around just as the door swung open and the newcomer entered the room, bringing with him a whiff of cologne that reminded Pandora of pine trees and hot sun. Bennington dashed out of her office and stood behind the Director, hands clasped together, dark eyes behind large, black-rimmed glasses, unusually excited. If a photographer took their photo right at that moment, he would have captured identical expressions on all four females' faces, even Nurse Rackett's, who was rumored to be asexual, and therefore, without longings.

The look was *stunned.*

The new counselor was well and truly a god. He stood over six feet tall—lean, yet muscular, and his black, curly hair was a little long, its raven color bringing out the blue in his sparkling eyes. His wide, crooked grin made the lucky person receiving its effects feel as though he saw only them. His tan skin spoke of good health and the great outdoors. The man could be a model.

What the heck is he doing in this *place?* Pandora wondered, then promptly followed that thought with, *Who cares?* He was the most perfect human specimen she'd ever seen, and for the first time in fourteen years, her sleeping hormones stirred like bees after a long winter.

I won't rest until he's mine. She stifled a startled giggle.

"Hello?" he called, looking at them all. "Is this my welcoming committee?"

Nurse Rackett gave a strangled titter. Bennington snorted unbecomingly. The Director smiled brightly and Pandora, to her dismay, roared with laughter. She even slapped her knee. "Welcoming committee. That's a good one!" Egad, what had come over her? Feeling hot and cold at the same time, she struggled to stop doing what she was doing. The near-dead did not *guffaw,* nor did they slap knees!

"We were just having a little meeting. Come in," the Director motioned. "Sit." She indicated a high-backed chair for him to take. Nurse Rackett stepped out of the way, but Pandora, frozen like a deer caught in headlights, was unable to budge an inch. He ended up weaving around her with an "excuse me" before sitting down.

Introduce me, Pandora begged, giving the Director a bug-eyed plea.

But the blastedly oblivious woman, seated once more, was devouring the newcomer with her eyes. "I'm so glad to have you on our staff," she stated warmly. "To think you've just finished your doctoral internship at the prestigious Mentis Institute—you could have gone anywhere, really. We're honored to have you."

"I wanted to make a difference," he said. His voice carried a hint of an accent, one that summoned up echoes from another time—when duels were fought to defend the honor of a lady. "I thought I could do that here."

At that moment, Nurse Rackett cleared her throat, though it sounded more like a growl than a cough. The Director glanced up at her, temporarily nonplussed. "Oh, yes! Sorry. Andrew…I mean, Dr. Steele, this is our Head Psychiatric Nurse—Nurse Rackett. She keeps us on track. I'd be lost without her." She beamed at Nurse Rackett, who only had eyes for Dr. Steele.

He stood and reached for her manly hand, taking it in his and squeezing lightly. She stared at him like a catfish out of water. "It's an honor, Nurse Rackett. I've read some of your work on psychotropic medications and the need for routine. Very well done."

Nurse Rackett giggled, then smothered her traitorous mouth with her free hand. "Oh, those papers were just something I threw together," she said around it. "I have so much more to say on the subject."

He gave her a charming smile. "I'd love to hear it. But probably another time? I imagine you're a very busy woman and I believe I have a mountain of paperwork to complete." He nodded at the Director without taking his eyes off Nurse Rackett.

Her pale lashes fluttered rapidly. "Oh, yes. Another time. We'll schedule it in. Paperwork must always come first."

"I'd like that." He bowed over her hand, squeezed it one last time, then let it go. "Until then…"

She nodded dumbly and Pandora realized she was witnessing a miracle. Nurse Rackett, seemingly immune to all things human or otherwise, was twitterpated. "Come along, Pandora," she motioned without taking her eyes off Dr. Steele. "We must leave them to their work."

The nurse herded Pandora out the Director's door and then turned her toward the main entrance to the building. "Make yourself useful, girl," she said distantly. "I have work to do."

Then, in another miracle, she walked away without a single reference to a punishment of any form. Pandora had completely gotten away with her escapade!

As she veered away from the door to go track down the inmates, Pandora realized two things. One, Dr. Steele had rescued her, albeit unknowingly, from Nurse Rackett's wrath. And two, her mother had not introduced her own daughter to the most amazing man ever.

It seemed the Director had better things to do.

5

To Break Another Rule

WHEN PANDORA FOUND the other members of the Secret Six, they were sitting in their usual places in the TV room, watching *Hogan's Heroes*, one of Charles's favorite shows. There were definite rules about seating arrangements, not to be trifled with, and each member would fight to the death for 'their' chair. Pandora was fine with that. She'd claimed the best chair for herself—an emerald green velvet, King Louis XVI knock-off, which resembled a throne, and had been donated by the Ladies of Bedlam Auxiliary Club. Typically Pandora thought of LoBAC as a group of interfering old biddies with nothing better to do than stick their noses where they didn't belong, but this time they'd actually done something useful.

"Oooh, Hooogan!" Colonel Klink declared unhappily, shaking his black-gloved fist in consternation as he glared at the dashing American colonel through the monocle clenched in his eye socket.

"I know nuthink!" Pandora cried in a flawless German accent. The group turned in unison, their faces excited, almost avid, as if expecting to find some body parts missing—or at least a little gore somewhere on her person. They knew how her mother could be, but they also knew how determined Nurse Rackett was to bring Pandora down a few pegs, preferably with a sledgehammer.

"You're still alive!" Lucy announced in the midst of twirling her springy hair around a tiny finger. Pandora was pleased to note she looked rather happy about the fact. Give the girl a lollipop.

"And unscathed…" Pandora added, making a grand bow.

"That's not fair!" Birdy howled. "Just because you're not an inmate doesn't mean you should get special attention. That Horrible Hessian made me take an Ativan, which I spit out when she wasn't looking— she never checks to see that I swallowed it. She also made me do thirty sit-ups. She says I'm getting fat! Like she should talk. I'm thinking of calling her Buffalo Butt from now on. But first I'm going to kill her!" In her red dress and matching heels, Birdy actually looked dressed to kill. "And I know just how I'll do it!" Her white teeth, surrounded by Raunchy Red lipsticked lips, glistened like a wolf's. "I'll rip off her arm and beat her Buffalo Butt with it!"

Although Pandora was not happy with Birdy for muffing their plans, she decided to talk her out of bludgeoning the Hessian to death with her own arm. "You know we need the Hessian, Birdy. Her cerebral cortex resembles that of a mushroom's, which makes her astoundingly easy to trick. We have to keep her around."

Birdy's lower lip stuck out and she crossed her arms over her ever-expanding bosom—Pandora would swear the girl had to be stuffing her bra. Nobody doubled in size in a week. "I suppose so. But still...isn't there *something* we can do?"

"Why don't you just talk to her for a couple hours?" Skippy offered. "I'm sure that will kill whatever brain cells she might have left." He was wearing his typical outfit of torn jeans two inches too short, a Beatles t-shirt, red suspenders, and worn black, high-top sneakers, with a hole in one toe, plus a hat—a black beret this time.

She rounded on him. "You shut up! I did my best to save our plan from complete disaster and this is the thanks I get!" She blew a pink bubble, then popped it with her fingernail.

"Save?" Skippy snorted. "You nearly got us all in trouble! Lucky for you I can think on my feet."

"I done good, didn't I, Pandora?" Lucy asked, looking deceptively sweet as she clasped her tiny hands together and fluttered her curled lashes. Times like this Pandora remembered why the girl was their greatest weapon. Even those victims she'd burned (pun intended) for-got her past record whenever she widened those big brown eyes. She looked like a koala bear, making a person just want to hug her tight. And while they were doing that, she'd be trying to light their hair on fire. She was one special gal.

"You did wicked good," Pandora said. "And you, too, Skippy and Charles. Sinclair, you made the right decision to turn back around. No sense us all getting in trouble."

Birdy's unnaturally green eyes narrowed. "I haven't heard you men-tion my name yet, Pandora."

Pandora felt an urge to poke out those eyes, but restrained herself. She needed Birdy, she reminded herself, and Birdy couldn't help being the way she was—annoying and self-centered. Now was the time for understanding and maturity. "Your boobs have gotten bigger," she said instead.

Birdy giggled wickedly, reminding Pandora why she kept her around. The girl had no shame. "I'm so glad you noticed. Because if you're noticing, then surely the boys must be."

Skippy shook his head. "I didn't."

"That's because you're a queer," Birdy shot at him.

Skippy leaped out of his chair as though he'd just been given a shock with a cattle prod. "I am not!" A blush mottled his cheeks. "I like girls. A lot!"

She laughed. "Methinks thou doth protest too much."

"Skippy really does like girls," Charles offered, his thin, purple-hued face innocent. "Every night before bed he looks at a girlie magazine that he got from Beetle for two dollars."

Skippy's face turned red as a Bloody Mary. "I-I…"

"Do you?" Birdy looked suddenly thoughtful, which was strange, because Birdy was not exactly what a person would call a thinker. Pandora watched her carefully. "How very interesting."

The color drained from Skippy's face as he plopped back down on his chair. "I don't care if other people are gay, but *I'm* not," he mumbled. With one hand, he pulled off his glasses, blew a breath on a lens, then began to clean it on his shirt.

"Mr. Lord is gay," Lucy offered. They stared at her. "I've never seen anyone as happy as him."

Birdy's eyes widened and she clapped a hand over her mouth. Everyone else blinked really hard, trying not to laugh. Lucy didn't like being laughed at. She said it made her heart mad.

"Yes, well, he is quite gay, isn't he, Lucy?" Pandora offered, then bit her lip.

"Yes," Lucy nodded, looking very serious. "I think he's the gayest man I've ever seen."

That was too much. The others totally lost it (even Sinclair, who actually smiled), and their subsequent howling could be heard ten doors down, disturbing Mrs. Johnson in the arts and crafts room, who hollered at them to shut up. Lucy glared at the group until Pandora explained, through heaves and tears, that sometimes Lucy didn't know how funny she was and how much joy she brought to others. It was a line that worked every time she had to use it, though Pandora dreaded the day it didn't. Lucy liked being entertaining, but not at her own expense.

Wiping away a tear, Skippy put his glasses back on and turned to Pandora. "So what did happen with your mom?"

"Oh, Vicki was her usual empathic self," Pandora drawled, trying to look as though she didn't give a fig. "She wondered what was going on with me to make me get into trouble all the time. She persisted until she dragged the truth out of me. She really cares about me, about what I'm up to." She sniffed twice. "Yes, a paragon of motherly devotion, that woman." She rolled her eyes. "Yeah, right. She still thinks I'm thir-teen! Then she said teens will be teens and they have to test bounda-ries, or some crap like that. And then…" Pandora paused momentarily before deciding to keep Dr. Steele to herself for the time being. "Well, Rackett tried her best to see that I was suitably punished, but Vicki let me go. I guess she had other things on her mind."

"I still don't know why you want her to get mad at you," Charles asked as he tied the ends of his red cape into knots. "I don't like it when people get mad at me." He blinked worriedly. "What if I can't control my powers? What if I start hitting them and can't stop?"

Pandora patted him on the shoulder. "Charles, I've known you for ten years and not once have you hit a single human being who didn't deserve it. You are a paragon of self-control."

He straightened up, looking a little more hero-like. "I suppose you're right. But I still don't understand why you want your mom to punish you."

Pandora shook her head. "It's complicated. A Freudian thing, I think."

Charles nodded wisely. "You have a mother complex."

She shrugged. "Like I care, anyway. She can do whatever she wants." She paused and grinned. "And so can I. Which brings me to the next phase of my plan." The others, with the exception of Sinclair, uncon-sciously leaned forward. No doubt he was counting the dents in the wall. Still, he was listening. He always listened.

"We all agree that Newbie's a total jerk, so I say we—"

"I thought he was cute," Birdy interrupted, licking her lips like the tart that she was.

"—teach him a lesson," Pandora continued, ignoring her. "He was rude and he ratted me out."

"What?" Lucy gasped. "He told on you?" Lucy hated narcs. Too bad she never remembered that when she told on the other inmates. To give her credit, she never meant to. Things just slipped out. Some-times, though, Pandora had the feeling that Lucy knew exactly what she was doing when she spilled the beans. She was a survivalist. One had to be at Nepenthe Manor.

"He didn't mean to—" Birdy began.

"Oh, yes, he did!" Pandora roared. "He said, and I quote, 'She was spying on me and I want her out of here before I start screaming.'"

"He didn't say, 'before I start screaming,'" Birdy sniped. "And you notice he was only talking about Pandora?" She looked around at the group. Charles was wide-eyed. Lucy was staring at her fingernails again.

Sinclair mumbled under his breath as his reddish-brown eyes darted up and down the wall. Only Skippy seemed to be taking anything in.

"You're saying he likes you and not me?"

Birdy gave a throaty laugh. "Who wouldn't?" She put her hands under her strangely expanding bosom and heaved upward a couple times. "Not with these babies."

"Was he looking at her chest?" Skippy demanded of Pandora and she stared at him.

"I don't know. Like I'd notice that!" She groaned with annoyance. "We are in a crisis here, people. He's a subversive. He's going to bring us all down if we're not careful."

"Maybe I *want* him to bring me down." Birdy giggled as she grabbed the wad of bubble gum clamped between her teeth and pulled half of it out of her mouth, stretching it like a rubber band.

"Gag me with a spoon!" Pandora exclaimed, feeling an overwhelming desire to gag Birdy with a spoon…better yet, a shovel.

"Hear, hear." Skippy clapped.

"What did Birdy mean, Pandora?" Lucy wondered, her fingernails temporarily forgotten.

"I don't know!" Pandora cried, feeling hot under the collar. Though she had a sneaking suspicion she really did know and the thought made her want to stick a fork in her eye. "You're grossing me out, Birdy, so knock it off. We have business to discuss."

"What's the plan, Pandora?" Charles wanted to know. "Should I fly up to his window and look into his room? Maybe I can use my super hearing to listen in on his conversations."

"No flying!" Lucy shouted at him. "You promised, Charles."

He looked chagrined. "You're right, Lucy, I did. I'll try hard to remember that."

"You better remember, butthead," she threatened. "I don't want you to go splat."

"All right, all right," Pandora moaned. "Enough with that. Now, what I think we need to do is find out why he's here. Skippy, can you break into the records room again?" It was the one key Pandora did not possess and the one place she could never hope to enter. Being the daughter of the Director had its limitations.

He clapped his hands together and rubbed them furiously. "I could do better than that. I could get all our papers signed…get us out of this dump. We'd be free! Then I could wire some money to my Swiss bank account. We'll head to the Bahamas. Jamaica. Wherever we want! And then—"

Everyone sighed. Skippy was zipping toward full-blown mania like a bullet train. "Calm down, boy!" Birdy snapped. "We just need the goods on our new friend."

"He's not my friend," Pandora spat. "Traitor!"

"Jealous much?"

"Oh, yes. I wish *I* had fake boobs."

"You could use something." Birdy eyed Pandora's chest. "I have a box of tissues in my room I haven't opened yet. Dr. Hannah thought I wanted them to dry my tears. She's always so happy when she makes me cry."

"She is, isn't she?" Skippy agreed. "I think she's a sadist beneath that calm, sweet exterior."

"Can we focus here?" All eyes turned on Pandora. Instantly she felt better. "All right. Skippy, your job is to break into the records room tonight. You know the best time to do it. Right before shift change."

He nodded. "Though I wouldn't mind a bit of a challenge. Can I try it now? I could do it, you know. And get all our release papers signed!"

"Thanks, big guy, but not today. Today we break that little toad."

"What do we do in the meantime?" Birdy stretched and yawned.

"Stay out of trouble."

"All right, you scoundrels," came a raspy voice from the far side of the room. "Vamoose, scat, get lost!" It was Mrs. Johnson. Everyone jumped to their feet as she entered the room. Her pink, fuzzy slippers made shushing noises as she shuffled across the floor. Her dress, a shapeless flower print that bulged over her flour bag figure, was old, but clean. Half glasses perched at the end of her bulbous nose. Mrs. Johnson had moved into Nepenthe Manor twenty years ago when her schizophrenic husband was sent here to recuperate. He never did recover from his illness and ten years ago he died from a heart attack. Mrs. Johnson stayed, though Pandora had yet to figure out how she managed it. Mrs. Johnson might be mean as the devil's own, but she wasn't crazy.

The ornery old woman made her slow way to the television and changed the channel to NBC, where her favorite show was about to begin. Sally Jesse Raphael, in red glasses and a polka-dot dress with a red belt and monstrous shoulder pads, popped up. Today she was talking about sisters who steal each other's boyfriends.

"Oh, I thought I'd tell you that *Days of Our Lives* isn't on today," Birdy spoke up.

Mrs. Johnson didn't even turn around. "I don't recall askin' for your opinion, you Jezebel."

Birdy tilted her head. She might just as well have lowered it, like a bull readying to charge. "I'm only repeating what J.T. said." J.T. was in charge of recreation. The inmates idolized their rec director, not for his looks, but for his peppy personality. Plus, he kept them from losing what was left of their minds. *Ha.*

"J.T. is a fool." Obviously, Mrs. Johnson did not hold the same opinion of J.T. as everyone else.

Birdy was undeterred. "I think there's going to be a presidential address on instead."

Pandora groaned inwardly. They had better things to do than torture a mean old woman who chose to waste her life in this depressing place. "Well, I'm outta here," she announced to the group. "I need your *orders.*"

That was the magic word. Not another peep was uttered as the group followed Pandora out of the room, into the privacy of the empty hallway. Well, not completely empty. Professor Robertson was using his magnifying glass to search for bug specimens, but he was typically too out of it to hear, or understand, anything anyone said, so Pandora didn't worry about him.

"Boston crème," Birdy declared, licking her lips.

"Glazed blueberry." Skippy's dark eyelashes fluttered with anticipation. "I had the sugar donut last time, but it was a little plain. I want something more in my donut. Something with life—"

"A jelly donut with rainbow sprinkles," interrupted Lucy.

"Me, too," Charles added, his blue lips quivering a little.

"What about you, Sinclair?"

Sinclair took two steps forward, faced Pandora squarely, and said, "One cranberry walnut muffin, please." Then he took two steps back and the recitation began. "One cranberry walnut muffin, please…"

Pandora didn't bother taking notes. Except for Skippy, they all pretty much ordered the same thing every week.

"All right, guys. I'm off to see the wizard. Be good!" And with a wink, Pandora left the posse, whistling the theme song to *Hogan's Heroes*, a skip in her step.

She was about to break another rule.

To Bedlam

6

PANDORA STEPPED OUTSIDE into the fresh April air and clattered down the mansion's broad staircase. At the bottom, she took a right and headed toward the stable. A large part of Nepenthe Manor's thirty acres was considered a working farm. There was a massive white barn that needed a paint job, a stable to house the manor's six horses and four milk cows, and a fenced-in chicken coop full of chickens and one vile rooster. Carl Perkins, a prematurely gray, confirmed bachelor who rarely wore anything fancier than overalls, was the groundskeeper and lived in one of the rooms over the stable. A field behind the barn provided the grain and hay necessary to feed the animals.

On her way, Pandora passed by the vegetable garden, which at the moment was only black dirt. Cracker Jack, a victim of Vietnam and posttraumatic stress disorder (shell shock for the uninitiated), waved to her and she gave him a crisp salute. He grinned and returned to preparing the rich earth for planting. Every year the garden produced a bumper crop of vegetables that, along with the fruit from the apple and peach trees, and the raspberry and blueberry bushes in the various orchards running parallel to the field, was used to feed the inmates. Extras of milk, fruit, and eggs were sold to Bea Taylor, the eighty-year-old owner of Bea's Country Store, an old-fashioned store that catered to tourists, and to the kooky Natalia (no one knew her last name) of Natalia's Natural Nook, which sold everything from natural foods, like organic coffee and granola crunchies, to beeswax lip balm and healing crystals. The dreadlocked, Birkenstocked, and heavily beaded Natalia also told fortunes on the side.

The Director, a.k.a. mother, a.k.a. Vicki, thought it was important to make Nepenthe Manor pay for itself whenever possible. Judging by the phone call she'd been in the middle of when Nurse Rackett so rudely interrupted her, and from many comments thrown out here and there over the years, paying for itself wasn't exactly the manor's forte. Still, it did meet another one of Vicki's goals and that was to give the inmates—she, of course, called them residents—something worthy to do, which, as she was fond of saying, was better than any therapy.

For some strange reason, Vicki was determined to keep Nepenthe Manor running despite everything working against it. A few people, like Pandora herself, might say Victoria Belfry was obsessed with the idea. She was an ambitious woman and she didn't like to lose. Why she had chosen such a strange forum upon which to ply her skills, nobody really knew. It was a mystery Pandora one day hoped to solve.

The stable, when she entered it, smelled of dusty hay, fresh manure, and leather—a combination that was nectar to Pandora's nose. The scent alone was enough to stir her blood and ignite images of her galloping across the Irish moors astride a wild, black horse, dark hair streaming loose behind her.

Speaking of which... "How's Shadow?" she asked Carl, who was mucking out the cow stalls. His only answer was to toss his John Deere capped head toward the last stall. He did this without missing a beat, his pitchfork swinging back and forth in a soothing rhythm. "Thanks, Cap'n." Pandora tipped an invisible hat to him. He ignored her, as he often did. He was a busy man and had no time for tomfoolery. He had one weakness, though. He and Pandora shared a passion for horses, and most especially a love of Shadow, a horse who'd nearly died from starvation after her previous owners had dumped her outside Nepenthe.

Together the two of them spoiled her, though they really shouldn't have. More often than not, Shadow acted up worse than the devil himself (which was probably why she was dumped). You had to brush her velvety black coat a certain way—first the left side, then the right—or she'd bite you. When saddling her, the rider had better check to see that the little bugger wasn't pushing air out so that her girth fitted too loosely, causing the saddle, and rider, to fall off. And she was scared of, among many things, mushrooms, mainly the white ones. Pandora dreaded riding during humid weather or after it rained.

Right from the start Pandora had taken it upon herself to break the ornery beast. Three years later, she was still working on it. Luckily, Shadow knew Pandora meant freedom and fresh grass, perhaps a carrot or two in town. And for that reason, she didn't give Pandora too much guff—just enough to make life interesting. She was like the inmates that way.

A contemptuous snort followed by a scolding whinny greeted Pandora as she approached the back of the stable. Shadow had a gate on her stall, unlike the others—all old farm horses that were gentle and steady. They had no wish to go far. In exchange for food, they served as therapy horses. The horses more than earned their keep, and the inmates loved them unconditionally in return. Except for a few. Birdy, for one, thought horses were stinky beasts not all that far removed from goats.

"Are you ready to go, you she-devil?"

Shadow stamped her hoof. Knowing Pandora's Monday schedule, which almost never varied, Carl had already saddled up the mare, and she was waiting impatiently, snorting and tossing her shiny, black head. Pandora climbed up on the gate and grabbed the reins, pulling Shadow toward her. Making sure she had a secure grip, she jumped to the ground, opened the gate, and led Shadow out. Whispering of sweet grass and the open plains, she finally calmed the jittery horse enough to mount her. Shadow was ready to run. Pandora wanted to be sure she was firmly in the saddle before the horse took off. A broken arm, several bruises, scratches, and stitches, and countless hours spent tracking down the runaway horse, who'd slipped out the main gate after breaking free, had taught her a valuable lesson.

Never let your guard down.

Pandora slid her left foot into the stirrup and with one easy movement pulled herself up onto the horse, who at seventeen hands, was quite tall. Pandora felt certain the mare was a hot-blooded thoroughbred. Like Pandora, she was smart, spirited, and headstrong. Maybe that's why they clicked. Unfortunately, in addition to her mushroom phobia, Shadow was also a bit of a wimp when it came to bad weather of any kind. Today—hallelujah—looked to be perfect. Not a cloud in the sky. Maybe for once Shadow would behave herself.

"I'm off!" she called to Carl. The cheeky old bugger didn't even look up.

The story Pandora told everyone about her daily rides differed a bit from what she was actually going to do today. Vicki, Carl, and anyone else who might care (except for the Secret Six and they had good reason to keep their mouths shut), thought she was simply exercising Shadow. They did ride several times a week at varying times, following the paths that laced through the ten acres of woods, then along the cliffs overlooking the ocean, and finally past the ancient Nepenthe family cemetery. Except on Mondays. Mondays she and Shadow took a detour. Mondays they headed to Bedlam.

"Yah!" she cried, tapping Shadow with her heels, but not before she gripped the reins firmly and bent forward so low she could smell the horse's distinct musky smell. Shadow bolted forward and the burst of speed sent waves of exhilaration through both of them. The wind rushing past made Pandora's heart beat faster and the two became one as they raced along the edge of the field toward the woods. Off in the distance, the old tennis court with its cracked pavement and two basketball hoops, sans net, came into view, then disappeared just as quickly behind them as they galloped along.

Too soon they entered the dark stand of trees and had to slow down, but instead of taking their usual right along the path, they took a left, ending up, after ten minutes of trotting, at a hidden gate. Pulling Shadow to a stop, Pandora slid off the saddle and unlocked the heavily rusted gate, which she'd discovered seven or eight years ago while wandering the woods in search of hidden treasure. The entire fence was ancient and in need of a good paint job, but the gate's hinges were kept well-greased with infusions of olive oil borrowed from a crate in the kitchen. Mrs. Corker never noticed any oil missing as she never used the 'foreign' stuff, even though Vicki kept urging her to try it for its health benefits. Old Corker preferred good old-fashioned spray oil—the kind that made everything taste like plastic.

Pandora led Shadow through to the other side, relocked the gate, and mounted the skittish mare once more. Fortunately, they were able to ride unseen most of the way on a trail through the trees that ran parallel to the road. After a mile and a half, the woods ended abruptly at a large meadow, which Shadow loved for its plethora of tasty grass and clover. After passing through a curtain of bittersweet, Pandora turned, as she always did, to check on the state of the path's entryway. As she hoped, nothing had changed. The bittersweet vines, which hung from the tree branches like ropes, still hid the entrance. Only someone who knew that the path was there would see it. And then, only if they were really looking.

After assuring herself that no one was coming, Pandora urged Shadow away from the woods, giving the horse her head. Shadow's gait was smooth and pure and within minutes they were at the outskirts of the small seaside town of Bedlam. Here the vista opened up and the sight of endless ocean greeted Pandora. She inhaled deeply as she rode, savoring her brief freedom. She loved it out in the big world. What a crime that it was forbidden to her, and through no fault of her own.

When she was four she had accompanied her mother to the town library to participate in story hour for the summer reading program. While waiting in the children's room for the librarian to come read, a group of older kids, around seven or eight years old, demanded to know her name. After learning what it was, a snotty-nosed boy cried out, "She's the girl that lives at the funny farm!" He started calling her Loony Tunes and Batty Belfry, and the rest, after laughing uproariously, joined in on the name calling. Vicki had been looking for books at the time, but overheard the ruckus and found Pandora ready to tackle the whole lot of them, arms flailing, mouth wide and screeching, "I'm *not* a loony, you pus-filled bedsores!"

After that incident, Vicki left Pandora at Nepenthe Manor when she went into town. For her part, Pandora couldn't believe she was being punished for something she didn't do. She wasn't afraid of those kids. "I'll show 'em not to pick on me!" she'd told her mother with an up-raised fist on the car ride home. But Vicki said that fighting would only make things worse; that it was better to stay home and be safe.

Pandora didn't believe her mother was right about that, so a few weeks after the library debacle she successfully sneaked out through the gate that Lonny had briefly opened to let Ronny drive the Madmo-bile through. After a lovely day of wandering around town, looking at store window displays and begging bits of donut from the nice bakery lady, she returned home to find she couldn't get back inside. Hours later, her mother found her at the gate, angry fists gripping the black iron bars, lower lip protruding defiantly. Without a word, she signaled Ronny to open the gate. Once inside, she told her daughter not to leave the grounds of Nepenthe Manor on her own ever again, or she'd have to hire another nanny to look after her. The threat was enough to scare Pandora into staying within the bounds of Nepenthe Manor, un-til she found the hidden gate, that is.

The funny thing was, while Pandora snuck into town all the time af-ter that, none of the townsfolk had ever spilled the beans about her being there, accidentally or otherwise. Or maybe they *had* said some-thing and Vicki decided long ago she didn't really care anymore what happened to Pandora. Even so, Pandora wasn't taking any chances. She didn't want another nanny any more than she wanted a lobotomy and was careful to keep her outings as incident free as she could.

Feeling a burning urge to forget everything about her life at Nepen-the Manor, Pandora pushed Shadow to a faster gallop, heading across the field and toward downtown Bedlam. When she grew close to where the old buildings crushed against one another like people in a crowd, she pulled on the reins, forcing Shadow to a trot. While she didn't exactly hide herself while visiting town, she also didn't set her-self up as a moving target for the townspeople. Luckily most of the town kids were in school right now. When they were bored, they made a special point of reminding Pandora that she was a freak.

Pandora herself was home schooled, if one could call it that. She could read whatever she wanted—from Plato to Freud to Garfield, study anything she found interesting—she especially loved any kind of history involving loss of life and/or body part (preferably the head via Madame Guillotine), and learn life lessons from the inmates that just couldn't be taught in school (like how to hide meds in your cheek or how to convince your therapist you aren't crazy). Pandora knew stuff. Important stuff. Seriously, how many fourteen-year-olds could perform a frontal lobotomy after reading about the procedure in a book? Pandora would bet her white, grandma undies the answer would be just one...Pandora Belfry.

Without being told, Shadow headed down a narrow, back street, which led to the Chowder Shack and Bakery, and her hooves clip-clopped proudly on the damp cobblestone. At one time the business had been called simply, the Chowder Shack, but when Mrs. Hathaway bought it twenty years ago, she added the bakery part.

"I love a good chowdah, followed by an éclair chasah!" she'd chortle whenever anyone asked with a furrowed brow, "Why soup *and* pastry?" Pandora knew what a chasah, or chaser, was. Professor Robertson referred to it as his favorite kind of medicine. Whenever she could, she'd "borrow" a bottle of whiskey from Mrs. Corker's stash and pass it along to him. Luckily the woman occasionally went on benders and lost track of what she'd imbibed. In return, Professor Robertson would show Pandora his specimens—a rare honor that few got, or even wanted, to enjoy.

Outside the back of the building, Pandora slid off Shadow and tied the cracked, but well-oiled, leather reins to the wood hitching post, one of many in the ancient town. While in Bedlam, she made it a rule never to enter through the front entrance of a building if she could help it—one, because she liked to know what she was heading into, and two, because she wouldn't dare leave her horse out in the open like that.

Pulling out the small copper bell she carried with her on such trips, she clipped it to Shadow's halter then hid it in her thick black mane. Last month a group of ten-year-olds had thought it would be funny to steal her. Shadow nearly killed them. She did not like strangers touching her. Thankfully Mrs. Hathaway bribed the three boys and two girls with a bag of donuts each to keep their smarmy little mouths shut. For good measure, Pandora threatened them with the Madmobile if they so much as thought about telling anyone, or, for that matter, ever crossed her again. Most likely they told their friends about the adventure, but since none of their parents ever called the manor complaining, she figured she and Shadow weren't going to be accused of murderous intentions.

After scouting out the area and assuring herself the coast was clear, Pandora slipped through the screened back door, which banged shut behind her. The combination of briny chowder and sweet pastry made her mouth water. She was hungry today. Because of their morning plans to interrogate Newbie, she'd had to skip breakfast. Ah, well. More room for Mrs. Hathaway's delights!

In seconds, Pandora had seated herself in her favorite, slick red vinyl booth in the corner of the café, hidden from the rest of the world by the seat's high back. While the building was painted a plain pink on the outside, inside was a virtual rainbow of colors, from royal purple curtains to cherry red seats to lime green tiles and an orange counter. The table tops were baby blue.

"Pandora, dear!" Mrs. Hathaway cooed, bustling over. She wiped her hands on a worn yellow and green-striped apron as she slid into the seat opposite. "How lovely to see you."

Pandora smiled. Round, little Mrs. Hathaway, with her vibrant dresses and apple cheeks and silvery beehive hair-do, was always good for a boost to the self-esteem. Pandora's mother might not want her around, but Mrs. Hathaway sure did.

"How's business, Mrs. H.?"

"Oh, fair to middlin'," she replied as she straightened the sheep-shaped salt and pepper shakers. Like Skippy, she could never sit still, her hands constantly fidgeting with one thing or another. "It should be picking up soon with the tourist season starting." She leaned forward, the tip of her pink tongue showing between her moist, plump lips. "And how are things…out your way?"

"Mayhem, Mrs. H. Pure mayhem."

The little woman clapped her hands delightedly, then quickly rearranged her expression to that more suited to hearing bad news. "Oh, dear me. More trouble?"

Pandora threw up her hands. "Is there ever anything else?"

"Oh, you poor thing. You must tell me all about it. But first, let me get you a bite to eat. If you ask me, you're way too thin. A female ought to be pleasingly plump. That's what Mr. Hathaway always says. Girls these days are too damn—er, I mean, darn, skinny. Would a bowl of chowder do it for you?"

Pandora nodded solemnly, letting her eyes well up a bit. "You're so kind, Mrs. H. Mrs. Corker means well, but she just—" She let her head drop forward, as though she didn't have the energy to hold it up.

Mrs. Hathaway patted her hand—her own was as soft as the dough she used to make her famous breads. "Say no more. Agnes Corker couldn't cook her way out of a paper bag." Pandora laughed to herself. It was true. "I'll be right back. You like Coke, right?"

Pandora's head swung up. "The most refreshing taste around!" she sang, like she was Annie on Broadway.

Mrs. Hathaway laughed heartily. "Oh, you are a card, Pandora Belfry." With a wink, she hustled to the kitchen to gather Pandora's meal. Pandora would feel worse about taking advantage of Mrs. Hathaway's hospitality, but six years ago she'd saved Woofy, Mrs. Hathaway's beefy, dyspeptic bulldog, from a delivery truck that was about to flatten him. Mrs. Hathaway didn't have any children of her own, so her animals—eight cats at last count, two goats, and a dog—were near and dear to her heart.

Woofy actually accompanied Mrs. Hathaway to work and slept behind the counter in a bright green wicker basket with daisies painted on it. Last year Ms. Arnery, the town tax collector, had put up quite a stink, telling everyone who came into the town hall that, "keeping an animal in a place where food is served is unhygienic and repulsive!" She nearly got run out of town for her troubles. Bedlamites loved their dogs. Anyway, Mrs. Hathaway was so grateful that she insisted on giving Pandora free food after that. Pandora didn't exactly feel this was fair so she had come up with the idea of passing along gossip from Nepenthe Manor to even things out. Mrs. Hathaway fed Pandora food, and Pandora fed the kind woman, who lived for a good gossip, stories in return.

Mrs. Hathaway soon returned with a warm bread bowl filled with fish chowder, a bottle of Coke, its glass hazy with cold, and a fresh garden salad. Pandora gratefully tucked in while the bubbly Mrs. Hathaway served several customers. It was still early enough for Pandora to miss the lunch crowd, which was fine by her. The fewer people who saw her in town, the better. She didn't want to push her luck with Vicki.

There was a brief lull in the morning flow of customers and Mrs. Hathaway hurried over to the booth, slipping her pen behind her ear. She plopped down and fanned her flushed cheeks. "What a rush! I should close up shop on Mondays and have it just you and me for our little tête-à-têtes."

"Good thinkin', Mrs. Lincoln."

Pandora said this phrase every visit, and Mrs. Hathaway would respond the same way, every visit. "Oh, you! How do you come up with such crazy sayings?"

Pandora raised an eyebrow, feigning surprise. "Well, Mrs. H., considering where I was raised…"

Mrs. Hathaway's eyes, the color of a donut just out of the fryer, and which were set almost ridiculously close together, widened on cue. "Oh…Oh, dear! I didn't mean it that way."

"I know you didn't, Mrs. H." Pandora sighed gustily. "I wish everyone could be as understanding as you are about, well, you know…"

Mrs. Hathaway nodded sympathetically, her eyes blinking mistily. "I tell everyone I know that you're as normal as can be, Pandora Belfry. Especially being raised in that *place*."

Coming from a woman who believed aliens and ghosts were as "real as you and me" and who didn't make a decision without first consulting her horoscope or Natalia next door, Pandora was pretty sure how well that went down with the local folk. "You don't know what that means to me, Mrs. H." She demurely lowered her head.

Mrs. Hathaway rapped on the table, her soft knuckles sounding uncannily like little woodpeckers. "Now you just turn that frown upside down, Missy!"

Pandora looked up and smiled a wavering smile. "I'll try. It's just so hard, though, with all that stuff going on at that place I have to call home." She took a deep breath and focused all her energy on giving her weekly soap opera presentation of *Nepenthe Manor Mayhem*.

"Go on," Mrs. Hathaway leaned forward, her very ears trembling with a gossip's longing to hear more. "Let it out."

Pandora proceeded to make up a long tale about how one patient, whom she called Mr. X—to protect his identity, of course—went after another patient, Mrs. J, in a most frightfully amorous way, and then had to get shock treatment because he wouldn't stop singing bawdy love songs to her. But after thinking it over, Mrs. J decided she loved Mr. X after all and he didn't have to get electrified.

When Pandora finished telling her story, she took a long swig of Coke, then burped into the crook of her arm. By now Mrs. Hathaway was nearly a puddle of delight. "You poor, poor thing," she mumbled dreamily, staring off into space. No doubt she was calculating the hours until she could rush home and tell Mr. Hathaway all about Nepenthe Manor's latest escapades. "Such strange things you go through."

Pandora shrugged, happy to see she'd once again managed to please the little woman, even though this week's installment wasn't her best work. "Oh, it's all right. It helps that I get to see you every week. You're my guiding light, Mrs. H., my one solace."

Mrs. Hathaway blushed, looking thrilled. "I'm so glad I can be of help. If only your mother—"

"Oh, Vicki is terribly busy," Pandora hastily interrupted. She wouldn't put it past the woman to confront her mother about the sinful neglect of her daughter. Mrs. H. wasn't one to hold her tongue. "I can't be bothering her with all my little troubles. Without her, Nepenthe Manor would go under. Just imagine, Mrs. H., what would happen if it closed?"

Mrs. Hathaway gasped and went pale. "A tragedy, that's what it would be. Over my dead body, I say!" Thoroughly flustered at the very idea, Mrs. Hathaway popped to her feet, her eyes wide with worry. "That won't happen, will it?" She absently began clearing away Pandora's dishes, her eyes troubled.

"Not if Vicki stays in charge," Pandora assured her.

Mrs. Hathaway breathed a sigh of relief. "Then I won't bother her, dear. Though I really wish things were better for you at that…that place." She tsked, tsked several times.

"I'll be okay, Mrs. H. Just knowing you're on my side helps." She stood up, too, desperate to change the topic. "You've really outdone yourself this time. The chowder was creamy without being overly rich, the bread bowl baked to perfection, firm yet soft as a cloud. How do you do it?"

Mrs. Hathaway tapped the side of her flour-dusted nose. "I'm never satisfied, dear. Always tinkering with ingredients, testing things out. I guess that's why I've put on a bit of weight since my girlhood days."

"You've got to be kidding me!" Pandora made a show of peering closely at Mrs. Hathaway's face and figure. "I bet you look exactly like you did twenty years ago."

Mrs. Hathaway tittered. "Twenty years ago? Oh, you silly girl. You flatter me!"

"Not in the least." Pandora grabbed her Coke bottle and brought it up to the counter. Okay, maybe she was exaggerating a little bit, but not much. Mrs. H., though plump and silver-haired, really did look quite youthful for her advanced age, which was forty-five. All that gossiping must keep her young. "Shadow's outside so I'd better get going. Thanks a lot for the meal. Be sure to remember me to the mister, all right?"

"I will, dear— Wait!" Mrs. Hathaway scurried around to the back of the counter. "You almost forgot your order."

"Oh, Mrs. H. You shouldn't…"

"Nonsense. We need to fatten you up." She handed two bags over the counter to Pandora.

"At least let me pay you." Pandora grabbed the white paper bags, warm from their fresh contents, and peeked inside. "You didn't happen to make any glazed blueberry donuts today?" she asked, remembering Skippy's request.

"Oh, good choice! The last to be baked and fresh as can be." She reached under the counter with a square of tissue paper. "And no need for that." She waved away Pandora's attempts to dig in her pockets for money, though it was only a pathetic ploy—she rarely had extra money to spend.

"Wow, thanks!" She held out the bag and Mrs. Hathaway plopped a glazed blueberry donut inside. "But if you won't let me pay you for the donuts, at least let me clean out the grease traps next week, okay?" She helped Mrs. Hathaway with this nasty and messy project once a month. Free lunches were one thing, free donuts was pushing it. Cleaning the grease traps helped keep Pandora's conscience, and her pride, appeased.

"Oh, dear me. I always forget about those…and I do hate doing them. Mr. Hathaway would help but you know he has troubles with his sciatica. All right," she gave in, as she did every time. "Sunday?"

"Sunday, it is. See you then." Pandora started to walk away. Snapping her fingers she stopped and turned around. "I almost forgot…"

Mrs. Hathaway stopped rearranging the bagels and her head popped out from behind the glass display case. "More pastries?"

"Oh, no. I really just wanted to ask you a question." Mrs. Hathaway peered at Pandora expectantly. "Have you by any chance," she began, wondering how to put it. "Well, have you seen anyone *different* hanging around Bedlam?"

Mrs. Hathaway frowned. "Can't say I have. A few tourists, of course. But other than that, it's been dull as dirt around here." Her little nose crinkled in disgust at the nerve of it. "Why do you ask?"

Pandora ignored the question. "Are you sure? This is a teenage boy. He has blond, spiky hair on top, longer in the back. He's about my age."

Mrs. Hathaway's brown eyes sparkled mischievously, just as Pandora knew they would. Letting her think there might be a romantic intrigue in the works appeared to be the price Pandora would have to pay on this particular reconnaissance mission. "Any special interest, dear?"

Pandora shrugged. "I thought I saw someone strange hanging around here. I was worried about you."

Mrs. Hathaway beamed. "You're so sweet, Pandora. I tell anyone who will listen just how sweet you are."

"You're too nice, Mrs. H.," Pandora said, wiggling uncomfortably. "So, have you seen anyone suspicious hanging around?"

The little woman's plump finger tapped the glass as she thought. "I don't— Wait! I remember! Last week a young man came in here asking questions."

"Do you remember what he wanted to know?"

She nodded slowly. "Yes, *yes*! He said he was looking for someone."

Pandora leaned forward, her heart beating harder. "Did he say who?"

Mrs. Hathaway shook her head. "I don't recall him ever saying a name, just showed me an old photograph. I didn't recognize the man in the picture, and I told him so. But it was an awful photograph, so who knows? Maybe I did know the man. I told him that, too." Her full cheeks lifted in a smile, nearly blotting out her crossed eyes. "I do recall he was a very polite young man so I'm sure you have nothing to worry about."

Pandora refrained from adding, "Then I doubt we're talking about the same person." Xavier was far from polite, and far from being a man. She'd better check to be sure. "What did he look like *exactly*?"

"Oh, about this tall." Mrs. Hathaway raised her hand about a foot above her head. "Blond hair, like you said. He had an earring, too. Quite daring, don't you think?" She giggled girlishly.

Definitely Xavier. "Do you know where he went?"

Mrs. Hathaway frowned. "Can't say I do."

Pandora suppressed an irritated sigh. This was going nowhere fast. "Is there anything else you can tell me about him?"

She paused, her eyes peering up at the ceiling as though expecting the answer to come from outer space. "Oh, yes!" She returned her gaze to Pandora's face. "He could put away a bowl of chowder like nobody's business. Anyone who can eat my chowder like that is sane as you and me, rest assured."

Pandora was disappointed. "Okay, well, that's good to know." She held up the two bags. "Thanks for the donuts. Until Sunday..."

"Until Sunday, dear. And I'll be just fine, so don't you fret!" The bell on the front door sounded and Pandora turned to go, but not before catching the eye of a tall, dark-haired teen who'd just entered the bakery. As he crossed the floor to the counter, he kept her in his sights, his heavy work boots loud as blocks on the bright green, tile floor. When he reached the counter, Pandora turned and fled. There was pity in those haunting eyes. And she wanted nothing to do with it.

7

The Dark Side

ON THE RIDE home, Pandora turned her mind to what she'd just learned about Xavier. According to Mrs. Hathaway, he was looking for a man, but he must not know the man's name or otherwise he'd have mentioned it. Pandora wanted desperately to see that photo. She had to know what was going on. Who was Xavier searching for and why was he at Nepenthe Manor? Did he truly belong there or not? The mystery of it all was driving her batty, though she loved every second of it.

Back at the stable, she walked Shadow around the paddock to cool off, then wiped her down, brushed her coat, and picked gunk from her hooves. As it was Monday, she cleaned the saddle and reins with glycerin soap, oiled them, then hung them up on one of the countless railroad ties nailed into the stable walls. She made sure to follow each step Carl mandated, down to the letter, or he wouldn't let her ride Shadow. She'd once spent a miserable week unable to so much as say hello to her horse because she'd missed some grass stuck in Shadow's halter.

Certain Shadow was sufficiently cooled off, Pandora freshened her water and gave her a couple pitchforks of hay and a cup of oats. Patting her on the back, she left the stable, but not before grabbing the backpack where she'd hidden the donuts. On her way out, she said goodbye to Carl, who was now brushing down a horse named Wily. He spit out two squirts of tobacco juice into a bucket, then nodded, all without taking his eyes off his task.

Mind racing as she concocted stories for the posse about what Xavier might be up to, Pandora wasn't aware that someone was standing on the lawn waiting for her until she was only three feet away. Startled at the sight of a shadow looming in front of her, she jerked to a stop, just catching the backpack as it slipped off her shoulder. Yanking it back on, she looked up to see who it was.

Dr. Steele.

The breath went right out of her.

"Hello." His blue eyes, intense as a mesmerist's, peered into hers expectantly. Pandora felt a tremendous urge to giggle, but she fought against it, meeting his gaze directly and soberly. "We met in Director Belfry's office. I'm Dr. Steele."

"Um, hi," she managed to get out. Talking can be difficult when one is biting one's tongue to keep from saying stupid things.

"What's *your* name?" She wasn't sure, but it sounded as though he were talking down to her.

"Pandora."

He frowned. "You're kidding." She shook her head. "You're *not*." He chuckled. She liked the sound of it, rich and full of pleasure. "Now what kind of a person would give you a name like that?" *The person you're now working for,* she thought at him, but didn't say aloud. He rubbed his chin with a hand that had seen the physical side of life—its skin was a warm toffee, interrupted here and there by pale scars, some thin, some thick. "Sorry. I do like your name. I just hope for your sake that it's not a self-fulfilling prophecy."

Pandora wasn't sure what to say to *that* so she kept her mouth shut.

"Who's your doctor?" he asked.

"What?" She took a step away from him. "I'm not an inmate!"

"Of course you're not," he soothed.

She bit her lip. "I'm not lying, nor am I delusional, Dr. Steele. I live here. Not by choice, and yes, I'm a bit, um, different," she felt compelled to add, "but I'm *not* an inmate." She instantly felt like a traitor to the others. But even with a guilty conscience tugging at her, she resolved that for as long as she could, she was keeping Dr. Steele a secret from them. The posse had a way of ruining things, and just this once, she'd like to hold onto something shiny and bright and keep it that way, if only for a few precious hours.

"You're a bit young to be staff." He smiled.

"I'm not staff, either. Could we change the subject?"

He studied her for a moment longer, then nodded, his eyes drifting toward the stable. "Can anyone ride the horses?"

She hesitated a moment before answering. "I guess so. As long as Carl says it's okay. He has a lot of rules you'd better follow or you can kiss your riding time goodbye."

"Do you have a favorite horse?"

"Naturally. Her name is Shadow."

"Ah." He once more turned the full force of his gaze on her and she had to stiffen her spine to keep from shivering. "The Shadow. The dark side of the personality. The embodiment of all our primitive desires, of everything that is unacceptable. The part of our character that sounds bad but can really be something quite good."

Pandora's eyes widened. "How'd you know that's why I named her that? Everyone else thinks it's because she's black." She leaned forward a little and said in a low voice, "And I let them think that."

Surprising her, he threw back his head and laughed. All at once, Pandora began to feel bodily sensations that she'd never felt before. Strange, warm...*urges*. She stared at him, a goofy, very un-Wednesday Addams-like smile curving her lips. "I like Jung, of course," he explained. "But then, I imagine you've figured that out by now. Who, but Jungians and possibly, Darth Vader, would speak so highly of the dark side?"

He was right, she *had* figured him out. She knew everything there was to know about Jung and easily recognized those who shared her passion. It was the way they talked about Jungian concepts—with love and reverence—that gave them away. Pandora, herself, adored Jung's theories.

"The Shadow *is* an important concept to Jungians," she agreed. "But it's more than that that gave you away. I saw through your Persona to your true self. That's how I figured out your philosophy." She looked at him with a challenge in her eyes. Ph.D.s weren't the only ones who knew their psychology.

His eyes sparkled. "You saw through my Persona, hm? I guess I'll have to be more careful in the future. I can't have people thinking they can see right through me." He looked her over. "So what lurks beneath your Persona, Pandora?"

"I don't have a Persona," she announced proudly. "I am who I am, all the time. I wear no masks."

He smiled, crinkles bursting like sunrays from the corners of his eyes. "I expect you are what I see before me...most of the time. But didn't you just say that you let people think you know less than you do? Sounds to me like you present a certain image depending on the audience. I can't see you letting other people think you're dumb when you're so obviously not, unless you get something out of it. People wear masks for a reason and that reason is usually for personal gain or protection."

She tightened her grip on her backpack. He'd caught her out. How very clever of him. "Touché, Dr. Steele."

He shook his head. "Experience, not cleverness, has taught me a few things." Neither spoke for several seconds, Pandora, because she was trying to figure out a good comeback.

"Where'd you get your accent?" she finally blurted out.

An eyebrow lifted. "I'm surprised you noticed it. My mother is from Ireland and I spent the first six years of my life there in a little village near Tralee."

"That explains it," she said knowingly. With that tidbit, Dr. Steele had pretty much raised his attractiveness quotient twenty points, going well beyond anyone she'd ever known. Pandora had a soft spot for all things Celtic.

"So what are you up to now, Miss Pandora?" he asked before she could question him about Ireland.

She paused. The way he'd phrased that. Not, *where* are you *off to*...but, *what* are you *up to*. "I-I'm meeting my friends. What about you? What are *you* up to?" Two could play that game.

He grinned. "Nothing exciting, I'm afraid." He held up a sheaf of paperwork. "Director Belfry had to deal with an incident, so I'm heading back to my cottage to finish these papers and watch the waves crash mightily against the cliffs."

She caught the sigh slipping through her lips. "Do you need any help? I'm an expert at paperwork."

"I'm afraid this is a one-man job, and not a very interesting one at that. The Shadow would definitely not approve of it."

"Oh, okay." She tried hard to stifle her disappointment.

He leaned forward a little, as though about to tell her a secret. "As you probably already know," he said in a low voice, "Jung believed that while the Shadow embodies our dark side, it is also our source for creativity and vitality. While one should be careful to keep one's Shadow in check, one should not stifle it completely for fear of rebellion." He pulled back slightly. "But then, I imagine that you've never had a problem with *your* Shadow rebelling." She stared at him, wondering if he was a mind reader. He lifted the papers in a wave. "Until we meet again..."

"Okay, sure!" she cried, a little too loudly and with way too much enthusiasm. She watched him stroll toward the small gate that led to the cottages, thinking to herself, *Again cannot come fast enough.*

When he was gone, she ran into the manor as fast as she could. Once in the wide-open foyer—the hub of Nepenthe Manor, and from which many hallways branched—she screeched to a stop on the checkered, black and white marble floor. Damn. All the inmates were either in therapy, craft class, or out beachcombing for shells, driftwood, and whatever else washed up on shore to sell via consignment at Shelby's Hall o' Shells in Bedlam.

These character building activities sure get in the way of living life, Pandora grumbled under her breath.

She was about to head to her room to deposit the donuts—she didn't like keeping evidence of her rule breaking anywhere on her person—when Skippy slid around the corner in his slick-bottomed sneakers and raced into the foyer.

"Birdy said you were back!" He skidded to a halt with a double hop only a foot away from where she stood, hanging onto his beret with both hands to keep it from flying off. Pandora pretended not to notice how close he'd come to taking her out. It was the ninja way.

"How did she know I was back? Isn't she supposed to be emoting with Dr. Hannah?" It was an old joke. If Birdy emoted any more, she'd look like a raisin.

"We all called in sick."

"*All* of you?" Crap in a sack. "Don't you think that's going to look a little suspicious? We can't have people watching us when you're going to be embarking on a mission tonight."

Skippy gave a stuttering bark of a laugh. "That's just it. I already went on it."

Pandora gaped at him, exasperated. "Please tell me you went off your meds and are now experiencing delusions of mass proportions."

He shook his head. "Come on," he gestured. "We're meeting at the cemetery. The others are heading there now. Birdy said to bring the donuts."

Pandora sighed. "Fine. But this better be good."

"Oh, it is," he said cryptically.

She followed after him, out the main door, hurrying to keep up. Skippy's long legs and kinetic energy were a combo Pandora couldn't match. Soon they were sprinting across the lawn, Pandora several feet behind Skippy, past the garden where Cracker Jack was still working. Cracker Jack waved, they saluted him, and kept on running.

The wrought-iron fence encircling the two-acre cemetery appeared in the distance. It was, at four feet high, a shorter version of the one that surrounded the property. After reading about Vlad the Impaler when she was ten, Pandora had spent many interesting hours studying the sharp points on the cemetery fence and wondering what they would look like whilst piercing miniature bodies. At last, no longer able to resist, she'd gathered most of her dolls and stuffed animals, along with a bottle of ketchup, and gave it a go. The effect was gruesome. Using Vicki's Instamatic, she'd managed to snap a photo of the entire scene in all its awful glory before Jessie, an obsessively phobic, middle-aged woman, stumbled across the startling tableau. Later, the story went that her screams could be heard for miles, even by lobstermen out hauling in their catch for the day.

Pandora had paid a price for that little escapade. But every hour she had to spend scrubbing pots for Old Corker—a punishment meted out by Nurse Rackett as Vicki was at a conference—was worth the fond memories she'd made. She still took out the faded photograph and studied it dotingly at least once a month. Artistic genius like this could never be appreciated enough.

The gate was open and they dashed into the cemetery, carefully avoiding stepping on graves as they ran. Another minute of bobbing and weaving and they reached the corner of the graveyard where they typically held their outdoor meetings. Birdy, Lucy, and Charles were already sitting on their favorite tombstone—a long, flat stone set on a three-foot high platform. Pandora swiped away dried pine needles that had accumulated since the last time they'd come here, then climbed up to sit at her regular spot—over the name Nepenthe carved beneath a skull and crossbones. The slab was cold and she could feel a chill seeping through her pants. She sat for a moment watching Lucy trace the rainbow that stretched from one sleeve, across her chest, to the other, then glanced around. "Where's Sinclair?"

"He had an episode," Charles replied. "Nurse Rackett interrupted him while he was counting and it threw him all off, and he kinda lost it. You know how he gets…stamping his feet and screeching and banging his head against the wall. It was awful."

"Poor Sinclair," Pandora sighed.

"Poor Sinclair!" Birdy cried. "Poor me! I had to meet with her after he had his fit and she was in no mood to hear about my latest symptoms. I tell you that woman is crazier than you are, Skippy."

But Skippy was in too good a mood to take offense. He bounced on the balls of his feet. "You'll never guess what happened to me!" After a few more bounces, he jumped up on the stone, then crouched down low, all folded up like a bat.

Birdy rolled her eyes. "This had better be good," she said, echoing Pandora's earlier sentiments. "One of these days we're going to get busted and I just can't take that kind of drama."

"Oh, it's good." He grinned.

"You said you broke into the records room?" Pandora prodded.

He nodded. "While Sinclair was having his meltdown. For being so quiet, that kid sure can scream."

"Before I listen to any more of your riveting story, I want my donut." Birdy pulled the ever-present wad of gum out of her mouth and held out her hand to Pandora, who opened her bag and passed everyone his or her donut. The other bag contained her own stash, which none of the others knew about. She figured if she had to risk her neck to fetch the pastries, then a majority of the booty should be hers. Of course, she always ended up giving one to Professor Robertson because he looked so pathetic all the time with his out of control, bird nest hair and wild beard and over-sized glasses, and one to Cracker Jack, who had a wicked fierce sweet tooth, not to mention the fact that sugar soothed his PTSD episodes considerably. Then there was the one she left out for Frank, the security guard, as a diversionary tactic. He always took it without question, as though finding a donut sitting on a plate at the end of a hallway was perfectly normal and safe. He was lucky she didn't drug it. Anyway, he had a habit of closing his eyes while eating it, so whenever she needed to sneak the inmates up to the attic for their weekly Midnight Meeting, she'd set out the donut. She herself could use the secret passages. But the posse, of course, didn't know about the secret passages and Pandora planned to keep it that way.

By the time she'd passed the donuts out, except for Sinclair's muffin, which was carefully stored in a plastic baggie—Mrs. Hathaway always did that for her—Birdy was already finished and licking leftover cream off her fingers like a cat. "Do you have to do that?" Pandora protested as she took a bite of her Bismarck. "You look like you're in heat."

"I *am* in heat, darling," Birdy drawled, batting her eyelashes. Skippy nearly choked on his donut. "Don't you want to know why?"

"No."

"Yes!" Skippy shouted, swiping crumbs off his mouth with the back of his hand.

"I'm not talking to you." She turned her attention back on Pandora. "Who was that man you were speaking to in the front yard? I saw him when we were heading out here."

She'd seen Dr. Steele! Drat, drat, and double drat! "Just some guy," she said shortly and looked out toward the ocean, which was green and choppy today.

Birdy tapped a red fingernail on the stone. "And his name would be…"

Stall, Pandora, stall! "Um…"

Birdy lunged forward. Pandora could smell the exotic scent of her latest perfume, Obsession. The odor was so strong it overrode the briny

briny smell of sea racing toward them on the stiff breeze. She wished Birdy would tone it down when she put that stuff on. "You're keeping something from us. I can always tell!"

Pandora's shoulders sagged. No sense keeping this up. Birdy would find out sooner or later, and she'd be hell on wheels until she knew. She might even track down the man himself and that would be disaster. He'd up and quit before the sun had set.

"His name is Dr. Steele. He's the one replacing Ms. Bombson." She would not reveal that he was a Jungian, not even under torture. That was *their* special secret.

"You don't say..." Birdy pulled her nail across the stone as she relaxed back into her normal posture, which was all spread out like a model for a Titian painting. She popped her gum back in her mouth.

"I only just met him, Birdy, so it's not like I'm keeping anything from you."

"Because of course you were going to tell us..." she needled.

"Yes! As soon as Skippy told us what happened to him, I was going to share my news."

Birdy's green eyes were calculating as she smiled shrewdly. "Of course you were. So...what's he like?"

Pandora focused on the trees. "Oh, he's all right, I guess. Just another doctor."

"Oh, come on!" Skippy roared peevishly. "Enough girl talk. Don't you want to hear what happened?"

Pandora turned to Skippy with relief. "Absolutely! So what did you dig up on Newbie?"

Skippy shook his head. "That's just it. I didn't get anything."

"Nothing?" Pandora cried. "Not even a last name?"

"Nothing!" He leaned forward, grinning broadly. "So here's what happened. I was inside the records room—I knew I didn't have much time so I was moving fast. When I didn't find Xavier's record in the new arrivals file, I had to scan the other shelves looking for the tell-tale pink." All the inmates' records were color-coded by year and this year was pink. "So I'm moving along real well when I came around the corner of the last row and there he was, just standing there!"

"You're fu— You're kidding me!" Pandora yelled. She had totally not been expecting *that* curveball and had nearly dropped the f-bomb. Swears weren't allowed at Nepenthe Manor, a rule which wouldn't normally keep Pandora from saying them, but she had to watch herself around Lucy. That girl was like a parrot. And anyway, no sooner would the word fly out of Pandora's mouth, then Nurse Rackett would be on her like white on rice. Pandora would swear that woman could hear curses from a mile away. Getting into trouble whilst in the midst of instigating a scheme was one thing; getting into trouble for swearing was just plain wrong.

"I kid you not!" He grinned, bouncing up and down like a basketball with feet. "And he said, 'Looking for this?' then held up his file."

"Holy hot damn!" Birdy cried, then covered her mouth, glancing over at Lucy. Luckily the girl was busy trying to untie her Strawberry Shortcake shoelaces, which she'd tangled into knots. "How did he get in there?"

Skippy shrugged. "Beats me. But what he did next was even more totally awesome." He paused and peered around at them. Charles was rapt. Even Lucy looked up expectantly. "He put his file into the shredder. Ripped the whole thing to bits!"

If Pandora was not mistaken, the expression on her posse's faces closely resembled that of admiration, even awe. Crap in a wrap. She had to do some damage control, and *stat*. "Well, that was stupid," she snapped, then groaned inwardly. *That's the best you can come up with? Try again.* "He's going to be in big trouble now." *Okay, just shut your mouth, Belfry.*

The four stared at her reproachfully, then all started talking at once. "He's like a superhero," Charles sighed, absently straightening his cape.

"Or a super hot stud." Birdy snickered.

"Whatever he is," Skippy declared, "I have to admit I'm impressed."

"So he's cute, huh?" was Lucy's contribution.

"Um, hello?" Pandora waved her hand in front of their faces. "He called you guys loonies, remember?"

"With a face like that he can call me anything he wants." Birdy, of course.

"So you didn't find *anything* on him?" Pandora moaned.

Skippy looked a little sheepish. "When I asked him what he was trying to hide, he just laughed. Like James Bond would."

"James Bond," Charles repeated wistfully. "Now there's a real spy hero." He clasped his hands together to look like a gun, which he then aimed at various gravestones and cried, "Bang!" His golden curls bounced up and down with each shot.

Pandora was about to lose her cool. "Listen up, people. He ratted me out. What makes you think he won't do the same to you? Especially you, Skippy."

Skippy finally started to look a little worried. "I suppose you're right." He pulled at the little thingie on his beret. "He did mention something like that. I think he said, 'Don't tell anyone you saw me in here or I'll ruin you.' He totally freaked me out, but what a cool way to put it!"

Pandora felt like she was about to go mental. "He *will* ruin you." She pointed at Skippy. "He'll ruin all of us. I don't know what his game is, but we need to get some dirt on him." She glanced around, then leaned forward, the very essence of someone about to impart top-secret information. "Apparently he was in town, chatting up Mrs. H. He showed her a photo of some guy, but he didn't say a name. We need that picture, got it? We need to bring him down before he brings us down. Because if we're found out, that will be the end of this." She indicated the cemetery and the donut crumbs. "No more secret meetings. No more treats. Nothing. They'll be watching us like vultures for the rest of our miserable lives."

Finally what Pandora was saying sunk in. Vicki was lax about certain things—the straightjacket, keeping doors unlocked, letting the inmates get involved in the running of the farm, but she was lax when it was on *her* terms. She didn't like it when people did things without her permission. She didn't like it when the inmates showed any sort of initiative or imagination. She also didn't like Pandora hanging out with the inmates.

Pandora looked around in grim satisfaction to see that the others had come to their senses. "He might be worth it..." Birdy tried one last time, but Pandora shot her down with a quelling look. "Oh, all right, fine. I'll visit him tonight. See if I can get the picture out of him using my feminine wiles." She kissed into the air seductively, demonstrating what using her feminine wiles might entail.

"No, no, no!" Skippy interrupted, breathing fast and hard, his eyes on her lush, pouty lips. "You can't just ask him for it, Birdy. No way, no way, no way! This calls for stealth. We, um, we need Sinclair. Yeah, Sinclair!" He snapped his fingers. "That's who we need."

It was true. Of them all, Sinclair was the least suspect. Which is why he was their secret weapon, and used only as a last resort. The trouble was, after an episode Sinclair was typically unreachable anywhere from several hours to several days, and they needed him now.

Pandora was worried. Newbie reminded her of the Shadow. He was up to something...something unpredictable, and therefore dangerous. She could feel it in her bones. Or was that just the cold touch of death seeping up from the tombstone and through her clothes? Either way, it was a sinister omen.

The Secret Six would have to do something drastic, and *soon*.

Knock, Knock

8

UNFORTUNATELY, BY THE time the Secret Six decided to disband, they were unable to reach a satisfying solution. It was lunchtime anyway and the inmates wanted to go eat. Not that they'd get any decent food in the cafeteria, but hope springs eternal, even in an asylum. Culinarily speaking, summer was a rare and unusual time for the manor—the one season when the inmates ate decent food. But they had to use subterfuge to get it. Pandora, of course, had elected herself to be the mastermind behind this scheme. Someone had to take charge before Mrs. Corker got her grimy hands on all that fresh, wonderful food and leached out all its flavor as effectively as a bottle of bleach. The woman was so inept in the kitchen she could ruin cereal. It defied belief that she was as big as she was. Pandora was of the opinion that Old Corker was born without taste buds—her olfactory organs were probably defective, as well. Nobody with a working nose could produce that crap and not want to cry.

Not hungry for lunch herself at the moment—a meal at The Shack and one of her donuts usually tided her over until supper—Pandora headed up to her room to think. She climbed up into her sturdy wood bunk, which she'd painted a shiny black, and pulled a faded crazy quilt up to her armpits. Staring at a water-stain that resembled a guillotine, she munched on a powdered donut.

The Newbie was turning out to be more trouble than she'd anticipated. Normally she'd welcome such a challenge, but this time was different. She didn't like this feeling of not being able to control what happened next. The inmates were acting like idiots over the jerk, which left her with only one option—she was going to have to do something to make him look bad. In front of them. If possible, in front of everyone at Nepenthe Manor. And the best place to do that, she finally determined, was the cafeteria.

But what could she do without being seen? Vicki let her get away with a lot, but she had to be careful around some of the staff, who wouldn't. These vigilantes had their own ways of keeping people in line, methods often involving humiliation. And they didn't care that she was the Director's kid. In fact, knowing how indifferent the Director could be about her daughter, they often took matters into their own hands. The old timers had long ago figured out that Vicki didn't want to be bothered with punishing Pandora. They, however, relished it. So Pandora had to be very careful. Knowing she had a propensity for, shall we say, stirring up excitement, the staff kept a close eye on her.

Suddenly, the perfect idea popped into Pandora's mind. She knew exactly what she needed to do, without getting herself into trouble. A slow, villainous smile spread across her face as she licked the powder from her fingers.

Let's see you get out of this one, Newbie!

After some wicked laughter, her mind moved to dissecting her encounter with Dr. Steele. For the next half hour she ran and re-ran through her mind every word, gesture, and nuance that had passed between them. She'd never met anyone so...so *intriguing* in her life and that was saying something, having grown up in an insane asylum. He was smart, he was funny, and he was beautiful, like the Italian statue of the Greek god Perseus showing off the beheaded head of his victim, or Edvard Munch's screamer in *The Scream*. She turned her head to admire the vivid reds, blacks, and blues of her *Scream* poster and sighed enviously.

Such genius.

She'd definitely have to polish up on her Jung now, maybe take a peek at Dr. Steele's application and find out what else he liked. Tonight she'd sneak through one of the underground tunnels that led to the other side of the wrought-iron fence to see if she could determine which cottage he was staying in. Though there were only two places it could be—the one Ms. Bombson had recently vacated, and an empty cottage at the far end of the row. She hoped he chose the one at the end. That would definitely make it easier to spy on him.

With the exception of the Newbie nuisance and her mother refusing to introduce her daughter to the god that walked amongst them, things were looking up at Nepenthe Manor. A fevered buoyancy filled Pandora's body like a hot-air balloon and she basked in the unfamiliar sensation. Content for the moment, she closed her eyes, and tired from waking up before the chickens, soon drifted off. Completely off-guard as she was, it didn't take long for the perfect Freudian nightmare to gallop into her unprotected mind.

Scene: *Her mother standing on the lawn of Nepenthe Manor, looking radiant as an angel. She beckons to her daughter.*

"Pandy, dear, I have some news to share," she called, her voice floating toward Pandora in colored waves. "Such glorious news." Curiosity piqued, Pandora raced toward her mother's distant figure, yet each step brought her no closer than the last. She ran harder, panting and wheezing with the effort, but struggle as she might, she could make no progress.

"I'm coming!" she yelled breathlessly, feeling as though she was running on a treadmill, making great effort but no headway.

"Pandora, you must try harder." It was a different voice now, deeper and more commanding. She looked up to see another figure standing by her mother—a man. He had his arm draped around her mother's shoulders and he was smiling. It was Dr. Steele. Pandora's heart seized in her chest.

Then, without warning, her body snapped forward as though shot by a giant rubber band and she was standing immediately before them, an arm's length away. "Andrew and I have something to tell you," her mother said, her happy voice nearly unrecognizable in its gaiety.

Feeling frightened, Pandora shook her head. *No, no, no!* She didn't want to know what it was, but she couldn't make the words come out of her mouth.

"We knew you'd be happy for us." Dr. Steele smiled wide, his white teeth gleaming. "Your Persona tells me so."

Her mother beckoned again. "Come closer. Come see." Pandora tried to run away, but her feet were rooted to the ground. She looked down at her black boots, which seemed melted into the grass, then up at her mother, jolts of panic shaking her body like a miniature earthquake.

The two figures blurred and wavered like desert illusions, threatening to disappear and leave her all alone. "Wait! Don't go. I want to see!" She blinked and her mother's form sharpened into focus. Vicki was holding something now. A white bundle resembling a large loaf of bread.

She held it out to Pandora. "Look, dearest. Look!"

Pandora promptly changed her mind. She didn't want to look. She *wouldn't* look. But it was like a car accident and she couldn't stop herself. She had to see what was in her mother's arms. A second later she was standing directly over the bundle, even though she hadn't taken a step. Pandora tentatively reached out and pulled a bit of the soft, baby blue blanket aside. At the same moment, her mother thrust the object into Pandora's face.

"We had a baby! Aren't you pleased? Aren't you thrilled? I certainly am! At last I have a child I can acknowledge without shame!" The baby screwed up its face and screamed, its mouth a gaping pit of pink and spittle, its eyes full of evil.

Pandora jerked and sat up, banging her head on the ceiling. "Crap, crap, crap!" She fell backward with a groan, rubbing at the sore spot vigorously, as though that would make the pain go away.

Sweating and shaking, she climbed over the railing and jumped, landing with a thud on the floor. "Go away," she told the image of the horror baby that still had its claws firmly sunk in the pre-frontal lobe of her throbbing brain. "You aren't real."

"I could be," it seemed to whisper.

Pandora frowned, feeling groggy and out of sorts. "Stupid dream," she muttered as she swiped donut crumbs off her black shirt. "Stupid baby. Stupid Vicki."

This was awful. According to Jung, dreams were *prospective*. That meant Pandora thought this event—her mother and Dr. Steele getting together and having a baby—really could occur, and her mind was preparing her for it. She could only hope that in this particular instance—and it pained her to think this—Jung had it all wrong.

Feeling thoroughly miffed by her dream and what it might mean, Pandora glanced at her Swatch watch. A quarter to two. She was mad and she needed to take it out on someone. She paced around the perimeter of her messy room, her fingers thumping ominously against the spines of books lining the built-in bookshelves, a sound that turned to screeching as the flesh of her fingertips dragged along the glass of the two windows that looked out over the estate. She kicked at a ratty old paper bag, stomped on a pile of math homework she'd yet to begin, and growled like a Rottweiler.

At last, growing dizzier with each increasingly rapid romp around the room, it occurred to her just who that someone should be. It was an *aha!* moment that made her shiver with delight. The baggie containing Sinclair's muffin sat in the middle of a pile of driftwood on Pandora's desk, which was an old door sitting on two sawhorses, and she swiped it up. She'd show him good, she would.

Muffin safely stored in her sporran, she hurried through the secret passage down to the Ratched Route to find Sinclair. When she reached the hidden door, she peeked out, her heart pumping with the anticipation of a good and thorough butt kicking about to happen. Public humiliation, though not ruled out, would simply have to wait until dinner tonight. She owed Newbie for ratting her out to Rackett.

But first she needed to stop at Sinclair's room and pass his muffin on to him. If he didn't get it today, he would fret and then his episode would last even longer. Routine meant everything to Sinclair. And although he might be out of it at the moment, he would not forget what was supposed to happen when. Today was pastry day. And he had better get his muffin today or someone was going to pay the price, which, even if it was Nurse Rackett right now, would eventually trickle down to Pandora one way or another. As the saying goes, crap flows downhill. And in this life, Pandora lived at the bottom of the mountain.

Fortunately Sinclair had his own room—it was easier to keep him happy if he didn't have to deal with other peoples' inability to understand the rules of living with Sinclair. She should be able to get in and out quick as a lick and have just enough time to pay a little visit to Newbie. It was nearly two o'clock. Nurse Rackett did her meds rounds at this time, which meant she would have to leave the floor to do so. The Hessian, as the p.a. on duty, stayed on the floor. If she happened to spot anything unusual with her Neanderthal eyes, Pandora knew exactly what to do to distract her. Usually it involved waving something bright and shiny in front of her face.

Staying hidden, Pandora waited patiently for Nurse Rackett to leave, which she did, right on time. From experience, Pandora knew she now had fifteen minutes to do what needed to be done. When the wedge heel of Nurse Rackett's white shoe, the last to be seen of her, disappeared through the doorway, Pandora made her move. As she guessed, the Hessian was using this time to take a little nap. She kept a travel alarm clock in the office for just such a purpose. The nineteen-year-old hulk of a human might be dumb, but like a rat she was good at surviving.

Without knocking, Pandora opened Sinclair's door, slipped inside, then shut the door behind her. The shade was drawn, making the room nearly dark. She sniffed the air. Something smelled good. "Sinclair?" she whispered. "Can you hear me?" There was movement over in one corner. She stepped closer. "Knock twice on the wall if you're awake." While Sinclair was in a state, it was best not to get him talking.

Two knocks sounded. Pandora breathed a sigh of relief. "Good to hear it, buddy. We need you. Newbie's been causing a lot of trouble lately and we need to teach him a lesson." Two more knocks sounded in agreement. Pandora felt hopeful. Sinclair appeared to be recovering from his fit more quickly than usual today. "I brought your muffin from the bakery." She pulled it out of her bag. "I know you don't like it when you miss a day."

Knock, knock.

Wow! Sinclair was on fire. Usually by this point in the conversation, he'd already checked out again, the medication dragging him in and out of consciousness like seaweed on the tide. Maybe Nurse Rackett hadn't needed to use as big a dose this time. Pandora hoped that was the case. She hated seeing her posse drugged to the point of incoherency. That was no life for anybody. Besides, it made them pretty boring.

"I'll set the muffin on your desk, okay mate?"

Knock, knock.

"I'll see you at dinner tonight, right?"

Knock, knock.

"Awesome. Cause I'm going to need you to do your old trick. You know the one. But this time, we're doing it on Newbie. Won't that be cool?"

Knock, knock! This time Sinclair sounded almost enthusiastic.

"Great. All right, I better go now. I have to go talk to Newbie, straighten some things out. I'll tell you all about it at dinner, right before we teach that goober a lesson."

Knock, knock.

"See you then."

Knock, knock...fainter this time. Sinclair was getting sleepy.

Grinning, Pandora let herself out. That had gone quite well. Sinclair was recovering nicely, which was good for him, and great for her. Only he could perform the necessary trick. Only he could pull it off. Everyone else in the posse always ended up muffing it somehow. Not Sinclair. He was a real brick when it came to following directions and not ratting her out afterwards if anything went wrong, which it had a habit of doing.

Squelching a desire to whistle, Pandora scanned the hallway and was further pleased to find it empty. Tiptoeing, she scurried down the hall. When she reached the Newbie room door, she found it wide open. Odd. She peeked around the corner and was surprised to find the room empty and the bed made up tight as a soldier's.

What the heck?

Shaking her head, Pandora backed out of the room, pulling the door to its original position. New inmates typically stayed in this room for at least the first week of their incarceration, giving them time to adapt to their surroundings before subjecting them to the challenging experience of living with another inmate. And since she hadn't heard the Madmobile pull up or any of the other usual ruckus to indicate a new arrival had come, she knew there was no immediate need for the room. Had they released Xavier already? It was possible. Early release happened on occasion, typically with scared kids who had done something dumb, but who weren't really all that messed up. A visit to the local madhouse was often enough to 'cure' them of their troubles.

She frowned, feeling a little uneasy. She should be happy about this unexpected turn of events. So why wasn't she?

Because I didn't get my chance to put him in his place, show him who's boss, humiliate him so badly he'd never recover, she answered her own question.

Ah, well. Such is life. She should have acted faster, is all. It was her own fault. Next time she'd be ready. Next time she'd be the epitome of the Blitzkrieg, striking with a speed and ruthless abandon that would frighten even Hitler. Or, if she was lucky, there wouldn't be a next time.

Feeling a little better, she headed down the secret passage to her room. As she walked, trailing her hand along the smooth paneling, a niggling thought stirred in her mind. There was something odd about what had just happened. Something important she'd missed. But she couldn't put her finger on it.

With a shrug, she entered her room and headed for her desk. She moved last night's dinner tray, which still sat on her desk, over to a growing pile of trays in the corner behind her door, with a mental reminder to clear them out before mice swarmed the place or the rancid smell became too lethal. She then cleared off a space on her desk with a swipe of her arm, picked up her math homework, and sat down to work.

If she got too far behind in her 'classes,' she risked getting sent to public school, even though her mother didn't want her to have anything to do with Bedlam or its inhabitants. But as much as Vicki didn't want Pandora mingling with the townies, a failing child wasn't acceptable for the Director of Nepenthe Manor, who also held a Master's degree in Business. She'd have to do something drastic, like send Pandora off to school on a...*shudder*...school bus.

Vicki had tried to teach Pandora, though that lame attempt had ended years ago, about the same time the topics began to get more difficult. Vicki claimed she didn't have the patience to teach anyone, much less her own daughter. After that came the tutors, one after the other, like cattle to the market. They claimed Pandora was "uncooperative" then "spoiled" and finally "not very bright" and then they quit. Knowing her daughter was quite intelligent Vicki decided Pandora was going to have to teach herself or, her mother threatened, her next tutor would be Frau Folter. Frau Folter lived in Bedlam and was known for her less than kind methods of teaching (her excessive use of a ruler rarely involved measuring anything). Vicki made Pandora follow the curriculum provided by the state, but after that allowed her freedom to use her imagination. Pandora either had to do the work, face public school purgatory, or take on Frau Folter. These choices acted as just enough of a worry to motivate her to get cracking.

Personally, she'd rather stick pencils in her eyes than have to deal with algebra. But the idea of getting out of work through injury, as intriguing as it sounded, was quickly dismissed. The last time she'd made the attempt, her mother didn't even look up to see the bleeding wound on her arm, just told her to go to the infirmary. Pandora was simply going to have to suck it up and do the stupid stuff. If she couldn't figure out a problem, she'd get Sinclair to help her, though the idea of doing that was torturous. Working with him always took forever since he had to repeat everything he said eleven times. One can only listen to equations for so long without wanting to jump off a cliff. On the other hand, they did stick in her mind. Of course, it wouldn't matter, because she'd be dead from jumping off that cliff.

With a sigh and a chewed-up, number two pencil in hand, Pandora settled in to work. It was going to be a long afternoon. And she didn't even have humiliating Newbie to look forward to.

9

That's Called Being a Creep

BY FIVE O'CLOCK, Pandora was ready to eat her homework. She was hungry and she was frustrated. Math was the stupidest invention *ever*. Who needed to know how to figure out the slope and y-intercept? *Who?* No wonder geniuses went insane. It was the only way a person's brain could handle such idiocy.

Defeated, she pushed away a pile of scrap paper filled with equations and awful drawings of evil babies and backstabbing mothers, and stood up. For the next five minutes she stared, hands on her hips, at the ceiling, her mind, no longer distracted by math, racing a mile a minute.

Her mother wouldn't really go after Dr. Steele, would she? He was staff and she was his boss, but other than those easily surmountable obstacles, why not? She was single, she rarely went into town so she didn't meet many men to date, and Dr. Steele, with no ring on his finger—Pandora had picked up on that detail unusually fast—was gorgeous and seemingly available.

The real question here was: Why *wouldn't* she go after him?

Because he's mine, that's why, Pandora thought moodily as she stared at her reflection in the mirror. In the dim light behind the door, her long, pale face glowed like a distant moon, while the rest of her faded into the shadows. She looked awesome. This fact cheered her somewhat, though she did lean in closer to make sure there were no lingering donut crumbs around her mouth. The inmates were ruthless about that sort of thing. They loved having someone to attack, even for such minor things as food on the face. It wasn't cruelty so much as a pecking order/alpha wolf thing, and sometimes just plain boredom. Besides, nobody likes being a victim, and misfits are no exception.

While scrutinizing her shadowed features, Pandora decided that even though Newbie was gone, she'd head down to the cafeteria anyway. Her mother didn't like her hanging out with the inmates and so Pandora had to choose the times she spent with them in public carefully. She often only met with the posse in secret, so hanging with them at mealtimes, when everyone, meaning the staff (the inmates could care less who she hung around) could see them together, was avoided. The one place they could be seen together was in the TV room. Pandora didn't have a TV in her bedroom and the one in their living room only picked up two channels (or three when the weather was good), so her being in the lounge wasn't terribly suspicious.

She leaned closer to the mirror and decided that her make-up needed touching up. She'd begun experimenting with the stuff after watching Michael Jackson's *Thriller* a few months earlier. The awesomely gruesome video was a few years old, but this was the first time Pandora had seen it. While manning the second-floor station, a part-time p.a. had popped a VHS tape of MTV videos his cousin had taped for him into the video player (meant to be used only for mental health training tapes). He was supposed to be keeping an eye on the inmates while Nurse Rackett did her med rounds, but that little fact didn't stop him from wasting the taxpayers' dollars.

Peeking over the open half door, Pandora watched the forbidden music video along with the unsuspecting p.a., enthralled from start to finish. Music videos were forbidden at Nepenthe Manor because Vicki thought watching MTV was like crack for the brain. "Can't you just *listen* to the music?" she'd demanded when the inmates wanted MTV added to the acceptable stations list in the TV room. "Why do you have to watch it, too?" She could be such a downer.

Pandora remembered the video fondly...most especially how MJ looked as a zombie. After some experimentation, she discovered that rimming her eyes with black eye shadow and patting her face with white powder helped her achieve that 'on the verge of death' appearance. She felt it was a good look for her. Her mother hadn't actually given permission for Pandora to use make-up, so she was careful with the effect, making every effort to look as natural as possible. Well...as natural as someone near-dead can look.

After freshening up her powder, Pandora stepped back and studied her reflection. The overall effect pleased her, but she still didn't feel satisfied. Damnit, she wished the Newbie was still around. Sure, that was stupid...she wanted him gone from her domain. But still, she wanted him gone *after* she'd shown him a thing or two.

Feeling out of sorts, she made a gruesome face at herself. She hated it when she couldn't get closure. And in this case, the only way to close this particularly harrowing chapter in her life was to get revenge. Unfortunately, revenge, while tasty sweet, wasn't possible. Her victim had flown the coop.

Of their own accord, Pandora's fingers tightened into fists and she swung at her image in the mirror. Once again, she'd have to push her vengeful feelings way down deep inside her psyche where they would fester like an infected wound. Freud called this repression; Pandora called it survival. One of these days, though, the cork keeping all that emotion trapped inside was going to pop and she'd go berserker on the world's behind. After that, she'd finally fit in at Nepenthe Manor. She might even get her own straightjacket—she'd be sure to ask Nurse Rackett if they had any in black. She'd go on psychotropic meds and talk about herself all day long and never have to worry about anything ever again.

Hmmm…there was something to be said for that.

Still feeling unsettled, Pandora headed downstairs to dinner via the circular staircase, her hand skimming along the smooth, cherry wood banister. The cafeteria used to be the ballroom, which gave their dining experience a luxurious feeling, as though one were about to sit down for an eight-course meal at a four-star restaurant. Which was, of course, a monumental, if not very funny, joke. Meals served in the cafeteria were downright cruel and unusual, and oftentimes, unrecognizable. Old Corker cooked the crap right out of everything, reducing it to mush, like she thought loonies didn't have teeth or something. She should know better after the Stick bit her last year. Seriously…if your food pisses off an anorexic, you ought to leave the cooking to someone else. But Vicki wouldn't fire her and hire someone who could at least boil an egg. Corker worked for cheap.

The atmosphere did go a long way, though, and Pandora enjoyed the rare times when she ate in the grand room, with its two fireplaces, one on each end, and the rose-adorned wallpaper that had managed to survive decades of abuse and food flung at it. She almost felt like she could be normal eating here. Like she was someone else, someone from the outside.

"Hey, Pandora!" Skippy greeted her after she'd gotten her tray and headed to the inmates' regular table. Tonight's dinner was supposed to be turkey, mashed potatoes and gravy, applesauce, and a roll, but looked like a pale dinosaur turd. She sighed and sat down next to Skippy at the long, cafeteria-style table with attached benches for seats.

"Where is everyone?" she asked, looking around. The room was filling up and she returned several waves, salutes, and smiles from the inmates filing in. The smell of disinfectant and grease coated the air, impossible to avoid, and Pandora didn't even try anymore. Metal spoons clinked against plastic trays, laughter and voices mingled to become one.

"I don't know," he said, staring down at the mess on his tray. "I haven't seen Charles since he went to the arts and crafts room to work on his macaroni masterpiece of Superman fighting Lex Luther. I checked the TV room, but Birdy and Lucy weren't there, which is weird cause usually they watch *Bewitched* right before dinner." He tapped the end of his spoon on the table like a woodpecker. "I wonder where they are?"

"What about Sinclair?"

"What about him?"

"Isn't he coming?"

Skippy frowned. "Didn't you hear? He banged his head during his fit and had to be put into the infirmary as a precaution. I think he's okay, though."

Pandora felt a weird, tickling sensation in the pit of her stomach. Behind her she heard Little Gustav, a 77-year-old man with Tourette's Syndrome, shouting, "Fart! Poopie! Turdy, turdy!" The inmates, easily amused, roared with laughter. Little Gustav, his entire body hairless due to having alopecia totalis, grinned and waved in acknowledgement, his lashless right eye blinking rapidly as he bowed to each corner of the room. Luckily the bad words he'd learn as a youngster weren't nearly as offensive as today's curse words.

"When did that happen?" she asked after the laughter died away to a dull roar.

"This morning. Remember?"

"Oh, yeah," she said, feeling more and more peculiar.

"Hey, there they are!" Skippy half-stood and waved. Pandora peered around him and what she saw turned the odd sensation into bile-inducing nausea. *Xavier.* What was *he* doing here? He hadn't left Nepenthe Manor, after all, it seemed. So what...?

Suddenly it all clicked into place like the bones of a skeleton. The niggling thought on the way back to her room—the smell in Sinclair's room. Why hadn't she realized it? Sinclair never smelled sweet. If anything, he smelled of rubbing alcohol or bleach (the laundry staff took special care with his white shirts). And yet his room had smelled like sugary lemonade. Or, to be more precise, *lemon drops.* And his bed had been on the wrong side of the room, too. Sinclair would never have moved it himself. He hated change.

She'd been talking to Newbie the whole time, not Sinclair! Oh crap, she was so busted! What had she said to him? Did she give anything important away?

Feeling slightly nauseous, she watched Lucy, Birdy, Charles, and Xavier get their dinner and make their way over to them. With each step they took, she grew more and more queasy. Xavier arrived first. She leaped to her feet, deciding her best strategy was to go on the attack.

"You vile charlatan!" she shouted, shaking her fist. "You tricked me."

He gave her a smug smile, set down his tray, then grabbed her arm and pulled her away from the table. She saw the startled faces of her posse as she stumbled backward. "Like you were planning to trick me?" he hissed, his head close to hers. She could smell the lemon on his breath. Apparently he was a lemon drop junkie. "I wasn't doing anything wrong anyway," he went on smoothly. "Nurse Rackett made me move in with him. Something about having to prepare the room in case someone else needs it. I was taking a nap when someone rudely barged into our room and woke me up."

"I knew it was you," she tried to cover her gargantuan mistake. "I mean, I thought something weird was going on."

"Listen, Belfry..." he began and she gasped. He knew her last name! He laughed evilly. "Yes, I know who you are...whose *daughter* you are. So if you want to keep your other little secrets safe, you'd better do what I tell you."

It was best to play dumb. "What other secrets?"

He squeezed her arm a little tighter. "You think I'm some kind of idiot? Muffins from the bakery? Sneaking around this place with surprising ease? I'm guessing secret passages. Am I right?"

Yes, playing dumb was definitely the right way to go. She kept her mouth shut tight.

"Yeah, I'm right," he sneered. "I can tell by that dopey look on your face. Okay, so here's the deal. You treat me like a king and I won't say a word."

"Like a king?" she gulped. "I can't do that. The inmates aren't stupid. They'll know you're up to something."

He laughed. "I've got them in the palm of my hand. They've already told me tons about you and I didn't even have to ask them. Birdy has been especially agreeable."

Damn Birdy's eyes!

"Why do you want me to treat you like a king? It would be easier on you if I just ignored you. I'm not exactly the patron saint of Nepenthe Manor, you know."

"Yeah, I noticed. But I need to get out of this place. The faster I can show the shrinks what an upstanding guy I am, the faster I'm history. This works for us both, you know."

She sighed, giving in. He had used the old 'door-in-the-face' technique admirably. "I suppose I can be nice to you. But I won't treat you like a king. I'd rather garrote myself."

"Either way..."

"Funny."

He looked her in the eye. "Okay, you don't have to treat me like a king. But I do want you to stage a meeting with your mom while I'm with you."

"What? Why?" She met his challenging stare with one of her own.

"Cause I need her to see that there's nothing wrong with me."

"But there *is* something wrong with you. You're a psychopath."

He grinned. "You can compliment me all you want, but you still need to act nicey-nicey to me."

"What makes you think my mom is going to be impressed? Did the posse happen to mention that I'm not exactly my mother's favorite person?"

His dark brown eyes narrowed for a moment, then cleared. "It doesn't matter. Since you're her daughter, she's bound to be influenced when she sees how nice I am to you."

Pandora yanked her arm out of his grasp. "If I'm going to have to act nicey-nicey to you, then I need to know what you did that got you landed in here. I'm not that great an actress. I need to understand what my motivation is."

"I didn't do anything wrong," he muttered, looking away, exposing a spattering of blond stubble lining his jaw and a small pimple on his nose.

"Fine. Then you don't need my help. If you're not meant to be here, you'll get released in a couple days anyway."

"That takes time I don't have. Besides, this place gives me the creeps. How can you stand being surrounded by loonies all the time? Birdy actually asked me to marry her and take her away from all this." He shook his head. "She's nuttier than a fruitcake."

Affronted, Pandora reared back. "Seeing as how you're in this place, too, Buster, I don't think you're in any position to be judging the inmates! Just because they probably won't be getting out any time soon doesn't make them any sicker than your sorry behind. At least they're up-front about things. They won't try to trick you." Not all the time, anyway. "They're my friends, you know, and they're good people. You're just some guy who got himself into trouble and who's willing to manipulate innocent victims with serious problems to get himself out of it."

"That's called ingenuity."

"That's called being a creep."

He scowled. "Do we have a deal or not?"

She shook her head. "Not."

He turned toward the rest of the cafeteria. "Hey, everyone!" All heads turned toward him. Anything outside the bounds of normal routine was of immediate interest to the inmates. "I have an announcement to make."

"What are you doing?" Pandora hissed.

He bent low to answer, "Revealing your deepest, darkest secrets." His boa constrictor arm wrapped around her shoulders ensuring she wouldn't be going anywhere fast. "I'm sure your friends will love to know you've been holding out on them."

Pandora's stomach dropped to her toes. "Don't!" she cried, struggling to pull away.

"Pandora here has a secret—" he began, tightening his grip.

"Yes, I do!" she shouted, feeling quite hysterical. "I have a new friend, everybody! This is Xavier, and he's really cool. Treat him nice, all right?"

Everyone clapped and cheered. Little Gustav shouted, "Fumadiddle!" whatever that meant. And Photographer Phil, alias Togs, snapped a photo of them with the ever-present Instamatic camera he wore on a breakaway strap around his neck and which, typically, didn't carry film.

Xavier smiled gloatingly down at Pandora. "You made the right decision, Belfry." He steered her back to the table.

"Yeah?" she muttered. "Well, then why do I feel like I want to throw up?"

"Because you just looked at your dinner?" He snorted with mirth as he sat down between Birdy and Skippy. They both started talking at him, asking him their favorite question: *What are we having for dinner?* He had them laughing as he described his meal, postulating the possibility of innards, dead cats, composted garbage, or all of the above. Lucy giggled when he reached out to squeeze her pom-pom ponytail. Birdy pulled his arm back and looped hers through his. Even Skippy seemed to be enjoying the Newbie's presence, laughing loudly at nearly everything that came out of the serpent's deceitful mouth.

Sitting at the end of the long table, Pandora morosely stirred her food, creating a hole and several tunnels through the sludge. "Not hungry, Pandora?" Charles asked.

She looked up at his worried face. "Oh, I'm fine, Charles. I had some gizzards for a snack and I'm plumb full."

He laughed and scratched the tip of his delicate nose. "Xavier sure is cool, isn't he?"

"Cool as an iceberg," she replied.

"Do you think he'll wanna be my friend?"

Pandora stopped stirring. Charles's blue-tinged face was filled with longing. He so wanted everyone to get along, but mostly he wanted desperately to be liked. "Sure he will. He'd be an idiot not to think you're the mightiest of men and the loyalest of friends."

Charles smiled wide and for one brief moment he was like any other boy, not a delusional kid with a bad heart. "I *am* mighty." He flexed his skinny arm. "And I'm really loyal, too." He nodded a few times as though to prove it, then ducked his head and looked Pandora in the eye. "So if you said not to be friends with him, I wouldn't."

She swallowed hard, fighting the ludicrous tears that threatened to spill. "Oh, Charles. Don't worry about me and Xavier. We're cool."

He sat up straighter, puffing out his puny chest. "Cause I'll take him out if you need me to."

"I know you will." She patted his arm. "But that's what I'm afraid of. He wouldn't stand a chance against you."

"I'm dangerous that way," he agreed. "Sometimes I scare myself."

"Well, there's no need for anyone to be taken out this time, thank goodness. I'd rather have you here than on trial for murdering Xavier."

Charles frowned. "You do like him, then?"

Pandora suppressed a sigh. Sometimes she really underestimated her friends, who weren't as clueless as some might think. She glanced over at Xavier, who was listening to Lucy across the table talk about wanting a new doll, but he had this tension about him that told her he was really waiting to hear what she said.

"I do like him," she replied at last. *Best while boiling in a pot...*

Xavier turned a satisfied smile on her. She returned it, but with her own special twist added. He scowled and turned away, but not before she saw something unexpected peek out from beneath his Persona. Xavier looked scared. But was he scared of her, or something else?

Synchronicity

10

TYPICALLY PANDORA HUNG out with the posse for a couple hours before bedtime, watching TV and goofing around. Not tonight. She wouldn't be able to stand seeing them throw themselves at Xavier like he was some kind of god. Instead, she headed up to her room to sulk. Careful to avoid the secret passages—she'd have to delay her visit to Dr. Steele's cottage until after Newbie was gone—she stomped up the spiral staircase to her room. Once inside, she spotted the rest of her homework in a pile on the floor and was immediately tempted to give it to Lucy to burn. She was sick of trying to make everyone happy. So what if she ended up going to public school? It might turn out to be the best thing that ever happened to her. At last she would be a part of the outside world. She'd make friends and go to parties. She could shop at the mall. Take in a movie. She'd be normal, and her mother wouldn't be able to do anything to stop it.

I'll burn my homework myself! she thought wickedly, and her eyes roamed around the room, searching for her dwindling stash of lighters. She had her own fireplace, where she'd secretly burned a good many things over the years, so what was to stop her?

An image of that teenaged boy in the bakery and his haunting gray eyes, brimming with pity, popped into her mind and she froze. *That's* what could stop her. The town kids' judgments and taunts were bad enough, but their pity was the worst. Nobody pitied Pandora Belfry. Feared her, yes. Pitied? Never.

She promptly decided that public school was not an option, which meant spending the rest of the evening listening to The Police's *Synchronicity* album and crankily working out equations that made little sense to her. She understood enough, however, and drank enough Coke, to complete everything, including typing up a history essay on the Salem witch trials, and then completing with unexpected enthusiasm an English assignment focusing primarily on the Inferno section of Dante's *The Divine Comedy*.

Feeling quite heroic, she skipped downstairs to her mother's office, homework in hand. It was nearly midnight, but as Pandora had guessed, a lamp, its green glass shade casting an eerie glow onto her mother's face, was on and her mother was still working. The door was shut, but two narrow glass panes set in the frame allowed one to see inside.

Pandora was about to barge into the office and throw her work onto her mother's desk with a dramatic flourish when a movement caught her eye. It was a shoe…a man's shoe. She ducked low and peered through the smudged glass. Every night her mother's typical pose was this: the palm of her left hand pressed against her forehead as her right hand scribbled away, making notes, documenting cases, and writing letters asking for donations for Bennington to type up on the computer. By this time of day, her hair was wild and harried as a hunted animal. An ever-present, over-sized coffee mug with the Akmore University golden seal stamped on both sides sat nearby. "Nectar of the gods," her mother would say of her coffee, though Pandora thought it tasted like oil. Even so, she continued trying to develop a taste for it. She needed a better source of caffeine than Coke, and coffee was free. "I could never do this job without it," her mother would add, then swallow a mouthful of the nasty stuff.

Sometimes Pandora would spend hours watching her mother work at night, hunched low and ready to run if anyone came along, though typically it was only Frank, and he was easy to hear coming and slow enough to allow time for escape. From these observations, she'd come to learn her mother's every move, her every gesture and expression. She knew her mother inside and out, and it occurred to her to wonder what she planned to do with this information.

Tonight, to Pandora's shock, Vicki Belfry was acting nothing like her typical self. In fact, she looked like a young girl as she threw back her head and laughed heartily. Her curly hair was brushed and tame, her eyes sparkling and full of good humor. She looked like a different woman. And the reason for this transformation was sitting on the other side of her desk, a packet of papers resting on his lap. Pandora wondered how long they'd been together, talking, laughing, getting to know one another. She wondered if her mother had gotten around to mentioning that she had a daughter and that her name was Pandora.

Anger surged up inside her. If her mother wouldn't claim her, then Pandora would just have to force the issue. She stood and twisted the doorknob hard, pushing the heavy door open with one thrust. It banged against the wall with a sullen thunk.

"Hello, *Mother!*" she called sweetly as she strode up to the large desk. "I finished my homework." She plunked the stack of papers on the desk and smiled demurely, as though butter wouldn't melt in her mouth. She was so furious, though, she thought lead probably would.

Her mother abruptly pushed back her chair and stood, obviously un-comfortable as she tugged at her pale blue blouse with one hand and smoothed back her hair with the other. "Pandy... What an unexpected surprise. You're up awfully late, aren't you?"

Pandora laughed. "Well, it's not like I have school in the morning." Out of the corner of her eye she saw Dr. Steele move, but she didn't dare look at him. Not yet.

Her mother laughed nervously. "Of course not. But you're a growing girl. You need your sleep."

"You stay up late all the time and you manage." She glanced at the clock on the wall, both hands now pointing to twelve. It was the witching hour. How appropriate that seemed.

"We're not talking about me, young lady." Vicki laughed nervously again and looked over at Dr. Steele. "I'm sorry—" she began.

Pandora seized her moment. She swung around. "Oh, Dr. Steele. I didn't see you there!"

The smile he gave her conveyed that he knew very well she was full of it. "I see that we're both night owls." He lifted his pile of papers. "How very good we've both been..."

Pandora smothered the smile she wanted to beam at him in return. He was just so delectable. "So you finished after all."

"My Self requires it of me."

"Your Self or your Persona?" Pandora asked, one eyebrow arched. "Does your Self *truly* want to do paperwork?"

"Does *your* Self truly want to do homework, or is that your *Persona?* Oh, wait. I forgot you don't have one." He was referring to their pre-vious conversation—he'd remembered what she'd said! *Oh, Lord, it's hot in here.* She refrained from fanning herself.

"Of course I want to do it. Without homework, who would I be? How would I learn?"

He grinned. "Touché, Pandora."

Her mother scooted around the desk, her arms folded, a frown on her face. "Am I missing something?"

"Pandora and I had a little talk this afternoon," Dr. Steele told her. He rose suddenly and handed her his paperwork. "It's later than I real-ized, and since I start work in the morning, I'd better get some sleep. I have a feeling this job is going to be my most challenging yet." He nodded at them, then walked over to the door, his stride relaxed. At the last moment he turned around. "Oh, I wanted to ask you some-thing, Director Belfry..."

"Yes, Andrew?" She shook her head and gave a light laugh. "I mean, Dr. Steele."

"I was wondering whether it would be all right for me to ride the horses."

"Ride the horses?" She looked a little confused. "Oh! Ride the horses. Um, yes. That would be wonderful. Pandy rides nearly every day. The horse she takes out is a real beast and I'd rather she didn't ride that one. Perhaps you could..."

Dr. Steele shook his head. "I would not take Pandora's Shadow." He gave Pandora a knowing look. "No, I'll exercise one of the other horses." He lifted an inquiring eyebrow. "Any recommendations, Pandora?"

"Wily might not be too bad," she said after a moment's thought. Wily was an Appaloosa, and though old, he was the most promising of the lot. "See what you can do with him."

"Now Pandy," her mother scolded. "Wily might be more appropriate for you. I don't want you getting hurt."

"Shadow won't ride for anyone but me, Vicki," she retorted. "Besides, Wily's getting fat and needs the exercise and I have too much to do to take them both out."

"Wily it is," Dr. Steele said. "Thank you, Director Belfry. Good night and pleasant dreams." Before turning to go, he gave Pandora a conspiratorial wink, then slipped out the door without looking back. She stared after him, startled. He couldn't possibly know about her dream starring him and her mother, could he? She shook her head. No. He was just being a good Jungian.

"Are you wearing make-up?" her mother asked after he was gone. Pandora turned slowly. Her mother's arms were still crossed—a bad sign.

"A little."

"Where did you get it?"

Pandora shrugged. "One of the inmates was getting rid of all her old stuff. She decided to go a different direction with her look." That was true. Before Marilyn Monroe, Birdy had tried Madonna. It was not a look that worked for her. With her figure, she looked more like a bag lady than a sexpot.

Her mother sighed. "Well, don't overdo it. Personally, I think you're wearing too much powder and eyeliner. You look like death."

Pandora nodded, satisfied. Mission accomplished. "I'll keep that in mind" she said, meaning just the opposite. "So I guess Dr. Steele now knows you have a kid, huh? Sorry to blow your cover."

Her mother, who'd been heading to her chair, jerked back around. "I wasn't trying to cover anything. I just thought you could introduce yourself. You're always complaining that I don't let you do anything. Well, I gave you your chance and you didn't take it."

Pandora scowled. "I just thought you'd want to publicly acknowledge me to the new doctor."

"I publicly acknowledge you every day, Pandy. What more do you want?"

"Nothing," she mumbled. *Your love*, she thought in her head, *maybe a dang hug once in a while, perhaps share a meal together a few times a week.* "So what's the new kid in for?" she tried, hoping to catch her mother off guard.

"I can't talk about the residents with you," her mother warned. "You know that. Now off to bed." She made a shooing motion with her hand.

"I was just wondering why he's in here. He seems pretty normal to me."

"Yes, well, he did something stupid and—" She stopped, then gave a long sigh. "Just leave him alone, all right?"

Pandora ran her finger along the edge of the desk. "I just thought I should try to make him feel welcome. He seems like a nice kid."

Vicki's eyes sharpened like a predatory bird. "What do you mean?"

Pandora peered more closely at her mother. She looked odd. "I don't know. I'm bored. Can't I have *any* friends here?"

It was a sore point between them. "You can have friends, just not the residents."

"And not the town kids, either. Which leaves me with—hmmm…the staff? Should I hang out with the p.a.s? Dr. Steele?"

Her mother drew in a quick breath. "I'm sure you can find plenty to do to keep you busy without mixing with the staff. Why do you need friends anyway?"

Pandora gaped at her. "How could you even ask a question like that? Just because you don't have any friends doesn't mean everyone else wants to live that way." As she so often did, Vicki remained mum on the subject of her pathetic social life. "Besides, I like Xavier," Pandora poked, feeling spiteful. "I think he's pretty cool."

Her mother sat down hard. "Xavier is off-limits to you." She looked even worse now, her eyes darting back and forth between the papers on her desk and Pandora. "As for Dr. Steele, you know the rule."

"Leave the staff to do their work." Pandora sighed. "All right, then. Tell me why I can't hang out with Xavier and I'll stay away from him."

"You can't hang out with Xavier because I said so. That's non-negotiable."

"Good argument, Vicki. I guess I'll tell him that, then."

Her mother suddenly stood, as though snapping to attention. "You'll do no such thing, Pandora Cole Belfry!" She pounded her fist on the desktop, making a pen jump. "You give me enough trouble as it is. I won't take any more!"

Pandora drew back, her eyes filling with tears of frustration. She immediately swung around to hide them. *I'll show her*, she thought to herself. *I'll make her regret ever giving birth to me...well, I'll make her feel* more *regret*.

"Fine," she said aloud. "I'll stay away from him."

She scurried out of the room before her mother could say another word. It wasn't until her feet were flying up the steps that something occurred to her. The only time her mother threatened her was when she was afraid something bad was going to happen.

What, she wondered, was her mother afraid of, and did Xavier fear the same thing? The answer to that question just might be what Pandora needed to get back at her mother. Because this time Vicki had crossed a line.

This time *Pandora* had had enough.

11

Et Tu, Birdy?

PANDORA SPENT AN awful night filled with angst. First she couldn't fall asleep, then, when she finally drifted off, she dreamt bad dreams, none of which she remembered when she woke way too early in the morning, but all of which left a sour taste in her mouth and an anxious throbbing in her bones.

The first thing she did after climbing down from her bunk bed was head to her closet and open a bottle of Coke. Her stash was getting low, she noted, and as she chugged the fizzy drink wondered vaguely when she should sneak into town to replenish it.

After releasing a tremendous burp that burned her windpipe, she wiped the back of her arm across her mouth and recapped the bottle. Urgh. That certainly had tasted better going down. She didn't like warm soda, but she couldn't keep it in their fridge—her mom would see it. They lived in a suite of rooms on the third floor, South Wing, their bedrooms separated by a rarely used living room and kitchen, and a tiny bathroom. A few of the staff lived on the third floor of the North Wing—a couple full-time p.a.s (like the Hessian), one nurse, and Frank, the security guard, along with his son, Beetle, a gangly, pimply, twenty-something dork, who sometimes filled in for his dad when he wasn't working at the Bedlam Garage or hanging out at the mall with his equally dorky buddies.

The rest of the staff lived in town, like Mrs. Corker and Nurse Rackett (thankfully). Most the p.a.s were college students, typically psych majors, attending Akmore University, about twenty minutes away. For the most part, the counselors lived in the cottages. That way, in case of an emergency, they could reach Nepenthe Manor in a matter of minutes. One exception was Dr. Weisenhammer, the sex therapist. She only visited the manor twice a month, typically for group sessions, though she worked one on one with the occasional inmate who might be struggling with such scintillating issues as, "Why don't people want to see my twigs and berries?" and "Even though I'm quite manly, I seem to be addicted to wearing ladies underwear."

Pandora staggered into the bathroom and took a long, increasingly cooler shower as the hot water supply dwindled, trying to wake up. After twenty minutes, she accepted the fact that neither her brain nor her body wanted to be awake. It would be far easier to crawl back into bed, pull the covers over her head like a giant cocoon, and go back to sleep.

Unfortunately, she had work to do. Now that she couldn't help Xavier the way he wanted her to, she was going to have to repair the damage he'd done to her power over the posse. She needed to get them back on her side, and pronto. Besides, she missed them, missed spending the evening hanging out, laughing and making fun of whatever was on television, much to Mrs. Johnson and her crony, Mrs. Bodkin's, annoyance. The two ladies took their television watching very seriously, and woe be to those who mocked it. Their prissy attitudes, of course, made those hours before lights out all the more fun.

Pandora closed her eyes for a moment, scenes from a typical night filling her mind. During commercials, Lucy liked to spin in circles and her short legs were always covered with bruises from banging into the furniture. Pandora had instituted a red-light/green-light rule to cut down on the damage and to keep her from blocking the TV. Skippy often drummed the tables and chairs with his drumsticks. Birdy would paint her fingernails yet another color, the smell of polish remover adding a chemical bite to the stale air. Charles worked on his drawings for the superhero comic strip he was creating, brows pulled together and the tip of his tongue protruding from between his purple lips as he worked feverishly, pencil tip tapping. He was a really good artist and Pandora often both praised and envied his work when he showed it to her. Sinclair quietly counted things as he rocked back and forth, or on days when he felt most anxious, practiced sitting very still. Pandora watched them all in her mind, reveling in the normalcy of their actions.

Pulling on black stirrup pants and a black, long-sleeved t-shirt with a glow-in-the-dark skull on the front, she rehashed what her mother had said to her about Xavier—that she was to stay away from him. The *or else* was pretty much implied. Vicki's threat ruined any chance Pandora had of being seen with him, and therefore fulfilling her half of the bargain. It was a major blow. But still, while she couldn't show her mother what an upstanding guy he was—*gag*—she had pointed out to her that he didn't fit the norm for Nepenthe Manor. He was an outlier; he did not *truly* belong here.

Like me, she thought.

Well, not exactly like her. He could easily enter the outside world, knowing its rules and mores; she couldn't. Not so easily, anyway. Not like she wanted.

She quickly shoved that thought away and yanked on her black sneakers, lacing them tight. She wished she owned a pair of black riding boots, instead of just her old work ones. They would look so cool with her stirrup pants. She was saving up her measly allowance to buy some, but her Coke habit kept setting her back.

At the small round table in the kitchen, she ate soggy Cap'n Crunch and went over what had happened in her mother's office last night. She wondered why Dr. Steele hadn't said anything to her mother about not introducing her daughter to him. Was he being polite? Was he being savvy? It wouldn't do, she supposed, to piss off your employer before you've even started work. Or was he simply being kind by not bringing up a touchy subject?

It was a strange idea, someone being kind, that is, and Pandora quickly dismissed it as a viable theory. He was just being smart, she decided, though she didn't feel very good about concluding that. It made him look bad. She should know better than to think so highly of him, though. She knew from experience that Nepenthe Manor was the wrong place to look for saints.

After rinsing out her cereal bowl under the tap, she set it in the plastic dish rack, dried her hands on a grungy, pink and white flowered dishtowel, and headed back to her room to put on her make-up. When she was satisfied that she looked as much like the warrior of death as a fourteen-year-old girl could, she pulled on her sporran and headed downstairs to find her posse. They should be eating breakfast in the cafeteria and would not be expecting her. She would have the advantage.

Once on the main floor, she drifted down the long, dusty hallway, inhaling the smell of old house that never quite went away as her finger bumped along the cherry wood wainscoting. Whistling softly, she rounded the corner, then immediately pulled back, startled. The posse was already coming out of the cafeteria, and in the middle of their close formation, was Xavier. He looked like a movie star surrounded by his entourage. She hated him.

Taking a deep breath to steady her nerves, she was just about to confront them when she heard Birdy laugh riotously, like some kind of jungle bird. "You're totally right, Xavier. Pandora is as bossy as they come. To be honest, she can be a real pain sometimes."

Et tu, Birdy?

"And her mom?" Xavier asked, his voice getting closer and closer to where Pandora stood. She backed up, feeling Cap'n Crunch rise up her gullet, scratching it. She swallowed hard, forcing the cereal back down.

"Oh, the Director's all right. Pandora is always causing her trouble. I sort of feel sorry for the woman, actually."

The group rounded the corner. Lucy was the first to spot Pandora. "Hey, Pandora Pancake! We were looking for you."

"I'll bet you were," she growled. She glared at Birdy, then at Xavier. He quickly unlooped his arm from Birdy's, who scowled at him, then at Pandora.

Sinclair, whose right brow was covered in a white bandage, had returned to the fold. He did not acknowledge Pandora. In fact, he didn't even seem to see her. His rust-colored eyes were filled with Xavier. He couldn't look away. The Newbie had hypnotized him!

Behind Sinclair, Skippy was doing his best not to look at Pandora, either, focusing instead on cleaning his glasses with his *Give Peace a Chance* t-shirt. If he scrubbed any harder, he'd put a hole right through the glass.

"What's the matter, Pandora?" Charles asked when he saw her. "You look sick."

"How could you?" she accused, pointing at all of them, but her eyes were focused mainly on Birdy. "I thought you were my friends! But you're traitors. All of you!"

Her incendiary comments hung in the air like bodies from a gibbet as she dashed down the hall toward the foyer. Footsteps thudded after her. "Just leave her," she heard Xavier call, his voice calm. Her pursuer skidded to a stop, his shoes screeching on the foyer's marble floor.

Standing at the main door, Pandora peered back at the posse one last time, wanting to sob, and trying desperately not to, as she scanned each of their faces. Charles looked confused, his blond curls swinging as he glanced back and forth between Pandora and Xavier. Lucy was tap dancing on the squares, oblivious to the tension. Xavier looked smug, yet again, and Skippy, who was halfway across the foyer, had yet to look at Pandora even though it seemed he was the one who'd been chasing after her.

But it was the expression on Birdy's face that drove home the final thrust. She looked furious, as though Pandora were at fault! As though Pandora was the one who'd done something wrong. The pain in her gut burgeoned like heat in a forest fire and she turned and ran out the door, toward the stable. She had to get away!

"I hate them!" she sobbed as she saddled up Shadow, her trembling fingers slowing her down. Lucky for her, Carl was out plowing the field in preparation for planting. He would never have let her ride in this condition. "They are dead to me!" She tightened the cinch with a jerk and Shadow skittered backward. Pandora patted the horse as she fought the emotions jerking about inside her.

Must get away, must get away!

She hauled herself into the saddle and with a "Yah!" and a tapping of her heels against Shadow's flanks, they galloped out of the stable toward the sea. The day was overcast, the dark clouds flying fast overhead in a treacherous breeze that blew out of the northeast. Pandora took it all in with a quick glance at the sky and dismissed any forebodings she might feel about the weather. If the rain came, Shadow would just have to put up with it for once!

The wrought-iron fence cut off the way to the ocean for most Nepenthe Manor residents—only a few members of the senior staff possessed a key to the large, ornate gate that led down to the sandy beach. Pandora, however, had her own ways of getting down to the seashore. Unbeknownst to her mother, the gate that allowed Pandora to escape to Bedlam wasn't the only one along the seemingly endless fence. There was another such gate, hidden in a tangle of vines and opened by the same key as the other one. As luck would have it, a stand of white spruce hid the spot from prying eyes.

Pandora dismounted and led Shadow around the trees and through the gate. Once on the other side, she locked the gate, climbed back in the saddle, and headed toward the rocky trail that meandered down to the beach.

Standing on the cliff for a brief moment before heading down, she noted the wild, blue-gray water churning about and smashing against the rocks. It looked like what she felt inside.

She breathed in the cold, sharp air, taking in the electrical currents of an impending nor'easter with it, and smiled grimly. This was the perfect weather for her mood—dark and threatening and dangerous. It also meant no one else would be coming down to the beach any time soon. Her mother deemed days like this too risky for the inmates to be near the ocean. So they would not be collecting shells today, and would not be witness to her mad ride.

The tide was coming in, though an hour or two remained before the beach would be entirely swallowed up. When Shadow's hooves touched the packed sand, Pandora let out a whoop and the horse took off at a full gallop. Sand crystals flew into the air as they raced down the beach. Pandora glanced briefly up at the manor. From this perspective, the giant edifice looked eerily condemnatory with its blank window eyes staring down at her like a hanging judge.

Further on, high up on the cliff, the cottages appeared. All eight of them were painted white with ocean blue shutters. Dormant vines spread their tentacles over the front and sides of the buildings like cracks in old china. As Pandora neared the assembly of cottages, she spotted a lone figure standing at the edge of the cliff looking out over the ocean. *Dr. Steele.* Her heart sped up to match the drumming of Shadow's hooves on the sand. As she hoped, he'd chosen the last building in the row, separated from the other staff cottages by a good fifty yards.

He spotted her and raised a hand. She pulled on the reins and Shadow reared up before returning to earth with a shuddering thud. Pandora, used to her tricks, maintained her seat, though barely. With a single glance up at Dr. Steele, she whirled the horse around and prodded her flanks with her heels. Shadow bolted forward and the two sped away, leaving Dr. Steele staring after them.

Holy crap, she hoped that looked as cool as it felt.

Pandora wasn't sure why she felt it necessary to snub Dr. Steele, but thought it probably had to do with the fact that he hadn't called Vicki out on not introducing her daughter to him. Or maybe it was because he'd made Vicki act like a gushing schoolgirl the previous night. Witnessing her mother behaving so indecorously had been very traumatizing for Pandora. For these infractions, Dr. Steele most definitely deserved to be punished.

Much too quickly, she reached the part of the beach where an impressive gathering of rocks called Pirate's Teeth, but which she had rechristened, The Fangs, tumbled out into the sea. She yanked on the reins. The incoming tide had already cut off access to the beach on the other side of the pile. Damn. Even though that part was off-limits, Pandora wanted to keep going. She wanted to ride and ride until she collapsed from fatigue, soaking wet from ocean spray, and near death. Dr. Steele, being the last one to see her, would be the only person who knew where she'd gone. Upon hearing she was missing, he most certainly would race to her rescue, and after finding her limp body slumped over Shadow, would carry her to the safety of his cottage where he would nurse her back to health.

Dwelling on this enticing scenario, she whipped Shadow around. Though she wanted to go at a hard gallop, she couldn't exhaust the horse and had to settle for a trot. When she finally reached the row of cottages, her eyes scanned the cliffs, but Dr. Steele was gone. Double damn. Once more she pulled Shadow to a stop, wondering what to do next. Maybe he was coming down to talk to her. Maybe he wanted to find out why she'd spurned him. With visions of a daring tête-à-tête dancing in her head, Pandora trotted Shadow back and forth along the three-quarters mile beach, until, finally, the incoming water forced her to leave.

He obviously wasn't coming.

Her hopes crumbled like bits of the cliff in front of her and all her romantic fantasies flitted away like deluded butterflies. "The curse has come upon me!" she shouted hoarsely as she directed Shadow back up the narrow path. "*I have crack'd from side to side!*" she purposely misquoted Tennyson's poem.

Angry and still hurting from her friends' betrayal, she shook her fist at the heavens as she and Shadow navigated the rocky cliff, daring the wild elements to do their worst. At that moment, Shadow's back hoof slipped on a loose rock, forcing Pandora to tighten her grip and her focus.

Not cool.

If she was going to die in a tragic accident, it wouldn't be falling off a cliff with her horse landing on top of her and smashing her flat. As much as she adored a gory demise, that sort of pathetic ending belonged to other people. She wanted her death to look good—*she* had to look good. No guts, no bulging eyeballs, no missing limbs. Simply her wearing a long, white dress, hair loose and flowing about her. Eyes closed. A faint blush to her pale cheeks and bold red lips to contrast with her blood-drained skin. Looking like death while alive was one thing. She certainly didn't want to look like that when she was dead.

"What a beautiful girl," she could almost hear the mourners whispering to one another. "Such a tragic loss." The crowd gathered around her grave would sadly murmur their agreement. There'd be crying and lamenting and teeth gnashing. Certainly lots of wailing.

The inmates would be devastated. Lucy would be lost without Pandora, Charles inconsolable. Birdy would threaten to kill herself, though since she did that at least once a week, no one would really pay much attention. Skippy would sink into a deep depression. A never-ending fit would seize hold of Sinclair. The poor things wouldn't know what to do without her.

Well, Pandora thought huffily, *serves them right for betraying me!*

But of course, since she didn't plan on dying any time soon, much as she felt like she wanted to at times, nothing would come of her fantasy. But she wouldn't mind if others died. Like Xavier. And that traitorous Birdy. Or, at the very least, they should suffer.

And she knew just how to make that happen.

12

WHILE PANDORA WIPED down Shadow's glistening coat, she worked out the details of her plan. This time she wouldn't rely on the posse to get revenge on Xavier—they'd just let her down like they always did. No. She could only depend on herself. She was on her own.

"I am a rock; I am an iii-i-island," she sang softly into Shadow's ear.

Her plan was simple. While the inmates were eating lunch, she'd sneak into Xavier's room and find that photo. Once it was in her possession, she'd finally have *something* to hold over his inflated head. She would bet her extensive arrowhead collection that he hadn't told the inmates anything about himself, even though he ruthlessly pumped them for information. If she could prove that he was only using them while he searched for the man in the photo, he was as good as dead to the inmates. Once they turned on him they would beg Pandora to make things right. And she would. She'd toss out the usurper and regain her throne. She'd rule Nepenthe Manor once more, and she'd get her friends back, even if they were traitorous little buttheads.

Except Birdy. She had another plan for *her*.

Outside the stable, the growing wind knocked against her like a battering ram as she ran toward the manor in slow motion, fighting the gusts that battled to keep her away. Despite her ducked head, she spotted a strange car blocking the wide, front steps while still a hundred yards away. It was hard to miss. Built low to the ground, spotless and a bright cherry red, it was quite the sporty vehicle. Pandora, herself, would have preferred a hearse like the one Harold drove in the movie *Harold and Maude*. A hearse had lots of space to carry…*things*, it was virtually indestructible, and people made way for you when they saw you coming. She'd be like Death on Wheels.

As she climbed the steps, Pandora glanced back at the car several times, wondering whose it was. She had a bad feeling about it, and when she entered the building, she discovered why. A man inside her mother's office was shouting furiously.

"I want to press charges!" Mayor Daft hollered, belligerent as a charging rhino.

"Please calm down, Daft," her mother ordered in her most patronizing voice—the one she reserved for politicians, government officials, and snotty kids. "This is a mental health institute, not a zoo. And right now you're acting like you could be in either one." Pandora nodded appreciatively. It was an excellent comeback.

"Don't you tell me what to do, Director Belfry. I'm the mayor of this town!"

"Well, you're setting a bad example, *Mayor*. Bennington, could you please shut my door?"

Before Pandora could slip inside, the door shut in her face. Crud.

"Hello, Pandora." The voice was quiet, nearly flat, except for the slight menacing note that occasionally surfaced like the fin of a man-eating shark.

She peered into the shadows, then quickly pulled back. There, in the dark corner of the hall, stood Douglas Daft in all his smarmy creepiness. At sixteen, he was not very tall for a boy, only about 5'7", but he had a way of taking up space...once he decided to make his presence known, that is. Douglas was a lurker. Like the trap-door spider, he hid himself with whatever camouflage was available—waiting, patiently waiting, until a victim strolled along, completely unaware of their impending doom, and then he'd pounce. He was patient, could stand as still as a statue, and he seemed more interested in Pandora than she thought necessary.

Wearing his Hadley private school uniform—a pink polo shirt with upturned collar, navy blue blazer and slacks, and penny loafers, he looked ridiculous, like a child pretending to be an adult. At first glance, Dougie didn't look old enough to be sixteen—more like twelve—but when he turned his pale blue eyes on Pandora, she could see an ancient evil skulking below their milky surface. Adults loved him, though. Probably because to them, he was polite to the point of obsequiousness. He got all A's in school and participated in all the town events. He even looked adults in the eye while addressing them, something Pandora personally found unnerving when he did it to her. To adults, he seemingly did no wrong.

Pandora wasn't fooled. She didn't like Dougie Daft, not simply because of what she saw in his soul, but because she knew something about little Dougie that most adults didn't. He liked to torture animals. Four or five summers ago, she'd caught him kicking at a stray cat on a back street in Bedlam. She sent him packing, to be sure, but only after beating the crap out of him, then threatening him with a lobotomy followed by repeated electro-shock treatments until he peed his pants. One would think what she'd done to him would make her his sworn enemy, but apparently he was a masochist and liked it when people mistreated him. Or, more likely he was intrigued that she, a little scrap of a girl, had stood up to the mayor's kid.

After picking himself up off the ground, he had told her in his dead voice, "Nobody messes with the Dafts." He wasn't lying. The Dafts had founded Bedlam in 1736, and since then had made sure to stick their vile little fingers into virtually every kind of pie in town. They held a lot of power in Bedlam and made sure to abuse it at every opportunity.

"Well, then you'd better start calling me Nobody," she'd retorted. With that and one last shove, she'd walked away without looking back. Ever since that fateful day he'd done everything he could to ingratiate himself with her. It hadn't worked. In fact, she despised him now more than ever.

"What's your dad up to now?" she hissed.

He shrugged. "I believe he's demanding justice." A small smirk lingered around the corners of his wide mouth. He was a pale boy all around, but his lips were always an eerie shade of red. At one time Pandora had herself convinced he was a vampire, and not the good kind. Actually, she still kind of thought he was one.

"For what?"

Another shrug. "I'm not at liberty to say." He took a step closer, then another, until he was standing less than two feet away from her. She saw that he had a black eye and a scrape on his right cheek, and she could hear him breathing, slow and deep like an underwater diver. Outside, the rain began, light at first, then hard, dashing itself against the windows as though fighting to get inside. "I haven't seen you for quite some time," he said in a low voice, hard to hear over the increasing rain and wind. His voice was always muted, as though he expected someone to be eavesdropping. "What have you been up to?"

"I'm not at liberty to say."

The smirk grew into a cold smile and his hand reached toward her, hovering in the air, wanting to touch her. She stood her ground, but it wasn't easy. She felt like a rabbit frozen in fear while a boa constrictor snaked its way toward her. "I like your spirit, Pandora. It would be quite a challenge to break you." He paused. "Much like your horse. How is she, by the way? Have you claimed her spirit yet?"

"She's like me," Pandora ground out, fists clenched. "There is no breaking her. I simply put up with the way she is, and we get along well enough."

"Too bad," he murmured, and then he did it. He touched her hair, letting his fingers ride down her braid, his palm bumping over the separate strands. She jerked away, but his grip tightened so that his hand caught her hair. She pulled again, more violently, freeing herself this time.

"Shouldn't you be in school?" Her scalp stung but she refused to let on. Dougie took great pleasure in witnessing someone else's pain.

His dull eyes were bland. "I'm taking a short leave of absence."

"For what?"

"Emotional suffering." He grinned at her, but though he meant it to be engaging, it only looked unnatural.

"I thought one had to experience emotions before they could actually suffer from them."

He nodded. "That's true."

"So you lied?"

"I needed a break from the endless politics of education. Father presented me an opportunity to have one. I, of course, took it."

"Listen, Dougie…" He winced. He hated that name. "Stop playing games. Why is he here, and why does he want to press charges? And don't shrug at me and say you're not at liberty to say. I've perfected my snake bite technique," she lifted her hands into position, "and I'm not afraid to use it."

Douglas looked amused. "As much as I would like that, Pandora, I've decided to tell you what happened. One of your loonies attacked me."

"Who? Nobody can get out of this place. You know that."

"He wasn't yet—how do you put it?—processed."

Pandora's heart seized and her hands dropped. "You mean, Xavier?"

"If he has spiked, blond hair, an earring, and a bad attitude? Then yes."

"But why would he attack you?"

Douglas tried his best to look puzzled. "I can't imagine."

"This is good news," she mused, unfortunately out loud.

"You think so? Just remember who told it to you." He reached out to touch her again, but when she glared at him, he pulled his hand back until it stopped against his chest and curled into a fist.

"So your dad wants to file charges against him? I mean, it looks like he barely touched you." Now she knew why Xavier was afraid, and why her mother wanted her to stay away from him. Xavier was a delinquent, a thug, not someone Vicki would want around her daughter. The idea was rather appealing.

"Barely touched me?" Dougie looked disgusted as his hand drifted up to his puffy, purple eye. "First he kicked me, then he punched me and knocked me to the ground. Luckily Officer Riley happened to walk by at that moment and pulled him off. The boy started screaming and swearing at him and then he threatened to kill me."

Pandora often felt the urge to do the same, but even she knew enough not to threaten anyone when there were witnesses, especially one who was an officer of the law, and also firmly entrenched in Mayor Daft's back pocket. "Okay, so he kind of lost it. So? He's just a kid. Kids do stupid stuff. Why would your dad care enough to press charges?"

Dougie's red lips twisted. "Normally my dad wouldn't care what happened to me, but he wants this place closed down and that boy gave him an opening to do it."

Pandora gaped at him. "Why does he want to close down Nepenthe Manor?"

Dougie's good eye wandered around the foyer. "This place is bad for Bedlam. Nobody wants to come to a town with a bunch of violent, unpredictable loonies living just down the road. Not businesses, and certainly not tourists."

"Stop calling them *loonies*."

"Does that word bother you, Pandora?" His lips caressed each syllable of her name.

She looked him straight in the eye. "You know who the real loonies are, Dougie? The ones who pick on those who can't defend themselves. The ones who watch it happen and do nothing. And the worst? The ones who hide behind a mask because they're too chicken to be themselves."

"You aren't implying that *I'm* one of these people?" He shook with mirth, his lips pressed tight to keep it in. "I think I'm very upfront with people. Don't you?"

"I think this conversation is over."

The door flew open. "Come on, Douglas!" Mayor Daft snapped. "That woman is as crazy as the loonies she's supposed to be supervising."

"Are you talking about my mother, Mayor Daft?"

He pulled up short and glared at her. "Who are you?" He hadn't even seen her standing there. Mayor Daft never noticed anyone who might be beneath him…and in his opinion that was a lot of people, practically everyone he met, actually. Unfortunately, the good citizens of Bedlam couldn't recognize an elephant covered in mud, so he had them fooled. Not all of them, perhaps. But enough to get the vote time and again.

"Well, if you did the math, Mayor Daft, you'd realized by my question that I am, in fact, the Director's daughter."

His bloodshot eyes, rumored to come from excessive time spent with his good buddy, Jack Daniels, passed over her and he snorted. "Should've known." He stormed toward the door, his perfectly polished, brown leather dress shoes clacking over the tiles. "Move, Douglas!"

Dougie turned to face her. Like a soldier, he held his arms stiffly at his sides, his heels on the verge of clicking together. Like a *Nazi* soldier, she amended. She stifled a shudder. She refused to let on that he disturbed her. That would be like handing the ax to an ax murderer. "Until we meet again," he murmured. "Which will hopefully be soon. There's something I want to ask you…"

But before she could demand to know what it was he wanted to ask, he spun on his heel and walked away. She watched him creep across the foyer in his perfect outfit with his white-blond, slicked back, perfectly coiffed hair. He stopped at the exit, looked back to see her watching him, and gave a satisfied smile before disappearing out the door and into the wall of rain.

Holy Psychopath, Batman.

"Are they gone?" Pandora turned toward the office door to see her mother peeking out. She nodded. "Good. That man is a nuisance."

"What did he want?"

Vicki rubbed her eyes. "Nothing important. Have you eaten lunch?"

Pandora shook her head, feeling suddenly generous. Her mother cared enough to want to protect her from the violent Xavier! "I was just about to go find something. What about we get—"

"Good," her mother interrupted. "I don't want you skipping meals."

"I never skip meals."

Her mother actually looked at her this time. "You could've fooled me. You look like death."

"It's a façade, Vicki," Pandora, painfully disappointed, replied in her best, *whatever*, voice. "Used to reflect my inner state of turmoil."

"Yeah, yeah. All that psychobabble gives me a headache." Vicki Belfry, Director of Nepenthe Manor Insane Asylum, had a terrible secret. She thought the entire field of psychology bordered on something akin to hoodoo voodoo. She started to shut the door, then stopped. "Oh, and Pandy?"

"Yes?" Hope surged up again.

"Remember what I told you about Xavier."

"Yes, mein Fuhrer," she grumbled. But her mother didn't hear, having already shut the door.

Pandora fled to the cafeteria—the inmates would be heading there themselves right about now. She planned to be extra careful this time. They'd surprised her this morning by coming out earlier than she'd expected; she couldn't let that happen again. Xavier was just wily enough to mix things up and keep her on her toes. He'd better watch out, though. The inmates didn't like changes in routine, especially Sinclair. You might as well start shooting rubber bands at his head.

She quickly found a place to watch for their arrival and squatted down. As she waited, she pondered over the two bits of news she'd just acquired. First...Xavier had attacked Dougie Daft and threatened to kill him. She twirled the end of her braid and smiled wickedly. With this juicy tidbit and the photo in hand, she'd rule Newbie.

Regrettably, the second piece of information was more worrying. Dougie had said that Mayor Daft wanted to close down Nepenthe Manor. But surely that was just an empty threat...

Or was it?

13

A Strange Man

TWENTY MINUTES LATER, and running behind schedule, the inmates, led by Xavier, filed into the cafeteria. No one looked very happy, an observation that pleased Pandora immensely. Lucy's lower lip stuck out like a fat worm and she kept stepping on Xavier's heels, nearly taking his shoes off several times. By now he had graduated to normal street clothes—no unbelted robe and non-skid slippers for him anymore. He bore Lucy's behavior with seeming patience, though his face was taut with barely repressed annoyance.

Birdy was talking at him a mile a minute, her heavily mascaraed lashes blinking furiously in an attempt to look coquettish. Skippy tagged behind them, watching Birdy intensely, dark circles weighing down his eyes. His fingers twirled one of his drumsticks around and around like a baton. Charles was a good ten feet back from them, dragging his feet. His Superman cape was twisted about so that it covered his left arm entirely. Next to him, Sinclair's eyes darted around the hall and his thin fingers plucked at his argyle sweater vest like hungry baby birds.

Taking it all in, Pandora no longer felt so pleased. What was happening to her posse? They all looked terrible, like little lost puppies. She bit her lip, feeling determination building in her. They might have betrayed her, but they hadn't meant to. Xavier was like a magician, tempting them, tricking them. Every member of the posse, with the possible exception of Skippy, was like a child, forever stuck in the early stages of psychological development, unable to work through the tasks necessary to form a healthy ego. They were vulnerable to charlatans like Xavier.

Her posse needed her, and Pandora felt up to taking on this monumental responsibility. She would rescue her friends. And after she saved them from that monster, they would recognize her as their supreme leader, though she'd settle for just plain leader. Xavier could go flush himself down the toilet for all he'd be worth after she was done with him.

But first she must get that photo. She needed to prove that Xavier, a loose cannon who cared nothing for the posse, could threaten everything the Secret Six had worked so hard to build. But to make her case, she needed more leverage to use against him. She'd already decided that merely knowing he'd attempted to beat up Dougie wasn't going to win over the posse. In fact, they knew enough about Dougie Daft and his nasty dad to think the little creep deserved it. And while Pandora agreed that Dougie did deserve a good thumping, she would still keep what Xavier had done tucked in her back pocket in case she needed it. Hopefully she wouldn't.

Growing increasingly jittery, she waited until the posse had been inside the cafeteria for five minutes before heading to the secret passage. Nurse Rackett and the Hessian would be on duty, but today Pandora didn't care. If they caught her sneaking about in the boys' section and asked what she was up to, she'd saucily tell them that she was doing something for her mother. It wasn't *exactly* a lie. If Xavier was up to something that could bring down Nepenthe Manor, then exposing him would be for her mother's sake.

When it came down to it, Pandora was actually doing *everyone* at Nepenthe Manor a favor. She wished they'd just let her get on with it without always having to ask questions and point fingers and basically stick their noses into places they didn't belong. Everything she did was always for the greater good. But did they get that? Never.

Taking a deep breath, she pushed open the secret door and stepped into the hall. The passage was silent—all the inmates were either in therapy or at lunch. She leaned forward slightly. Nurse Rackett and the Hessian were inside their office, eating their own lunches, backs to the hallway. Neither were big talkers, but the Hessian was a loud eater. She could make eating noodles sound like a dog at a bone, slobbering, smacking, and panting like she did. Pandora hoped it would be enough racket to cover any noises she might possibly make. She might be agile as a ninja most of the time, but at fourteen, she occasionally tripped over things...like her own feet.

She reached Sinclair's door without incident. The maintenance crew kept his door hinges well-oiled, as per Nurse Rackett's instruction. Sinclair didn't like squeaks. They made him think of rats and vengeful spirits, both of which he feared most intensely. Forcing himself to attend their Midnight Meetings in the attic spoke to his strength of character, and perhaps to an even stronger motivation: his desire not to get left out. The boy might be quiet, but that didn't mean nobody was home.

Once inside his bedroom, she flipped on the light. The shades were still drawn, creating a sort of never-ending gloaming effect inside the room. Sinclair would not like that. He preferred bright light so that he could see what was coming, search out what hid in corners, spot what might be lurking under his bed. For Sinclair, the world was filled with peril. His best defense against such threats was for him to find them before they found him.

Pandora marched over to the windows, pulled down the shade, then released it. The white vinyl slid upward, slowly revealing the rain-washed glass and the turbulent ocean down below. She no longer cared if Xavier knew she'd been in his room. In fact, she wanted him to know it was her. She welcomed his accusations, and was rather spoiling for a fight.

A thorough search of the room revealed nothing of interest and certainly no mysterious photo. Over the years, Pandora had explored this building inside and out and knew all its hiding places, not that there were many places to hide things in the inmates' rooms. There was very little furniture—two narrow beds, two dressers, two desks. But some rooms had loose floor boards or hidden panels in the wall and/or closet.

After looking in and under and over everything, Pandora plunked down on Xavier's rumpled, unmade bed—a stark contrast to Sinclair's twin (which was where it had always been), blankets and sheets pulled so tight a quarter would bounce on them. Pandora would know—she'd tried it once.

She checked Xavier's pillowcase again, then ran her hands under his blankets. She found his stash of powdery lemon drops in a baggie under his pillow, but nothing else. She took one out of the bag and popped it into her mouth, then settled in to think, which wasn't easy with the howling wind outside. What if Xavier hadn't brought the photo with him? Or what if the nurse or p.a. on duty had confiscated it when he arrived? A more troubling thought—maybe he'd left it wherever he was staying in Bedlam.

Come to think of it, where had he been staying? Not too many places would allow a sixteen-year-old without parents in tow to get a room on their own. Which brought up another issue. Where were his parents? Wouldn't they notice their child was missing? One would think so, but Pandora had met more than her fair share of parents who'd just as soon forget they had children. Her own mother came to mind, but Pandora had seen worse. Several of the inmates had no one visit them on Visitor's Day, which was every other Saturday from ten to two. Visitors could come any day, any time between the hours of nine and four, but Vicki said people were more likely to come if they had the proper incentives to do so—guilt and shame being the two best. If you couldn't manage to make it to Visitor's Day, she believed, everyone would know you for the terrible parent you are. Guilt and shame worked on some of them, but obviously not all.

Maybe it was just as well that some of them didn't come. Many of the posse's parents were more screwed up than their children. Lucy's mother, Mrs. Landry, was okay—quiet, mousy, easily frightened, and simply unable to deal with Lucy, but she tried to come to every Visitor's Day and a few times in between. She had six other children, all younger than Lucy, and a lazy husband who couldn't hold down a job, so she did her best. Charles's parents were dead, killed in a car accident when he was two. His grandma had tried to raise him on her own, but the elderly Mrs. Pippen didn't know how to handle a sickly boy with a too-vivid imagination when she herself was agoraphobic and never left the house.

Skippy's mom was a heroin addict and often forgot his existence, as well as her own. When Skippy was only six, his father, Mr. Stone, left them to build houses or huts or whatever building they lived in in remote Africa. Birdy's mom, Delilah Peacock, was worse than Birdy in the vanity department and always made every visit about herself. If Birdy had a symptom, her mother had it, too, if not worse. Birdy's father, George, was a fat, little man who thought the world of Delilah. He was okay, but his self-esteem was in the gutter. Sometimes Birdy's older sister, Jessica, came, too. Pandora actually kind of liked Jessica—well, she liked looking at her anyway. The complete opposite of the rest of her family, she wore long, black dresses, had awful piercings all over her face, and never spoke. Birdy said Jessica refused to go by their last name, preferring her mother's maiden name, Laroche. Pandora didn't blame her.

Sinclair's parents, a Mr. and Mrs. Prim—nobody knew their first names—were emotionally distant, stiff as a board, germaphobes (they tried not to touch anything, including Sinclair, while at Nepenthe Manor). They reminded Pandora of cyborgs. Sinclair was always worse after they visited, upping his rituals to the point of insanity, and sometimes Pandora wished they wouldn't come at all. But they did, once a month, rarely on Visitor's Day—too many riff-raff—and only for exactly one hour. They claimed their jobs as accountants for a major pharmaceutical corporation (Mr. Prim) and for the town of Bedlam (Mrs. Prim) demanded they be accessible at a moment's notice. This was some small mercy for Sinclair.

So what about Xavier's parents? Did they kick him out? Knowing what he was like, she would have to cast her vote for that theory.

Though he might have run away, too. She had run away several times herself, though the last time was when she was twelve. *Ages* ago.

Growing frustrated with the lack of answers, she exhaled through her nose like an irate dragon and stood up. That boy was entirely too mysterious. She needed to know what he was playing at, and soon, before he destroyed the posse. Pacing back and forth, her eyes roamed around the room, searching for a sign of anything that might be out of place. That's when it hit her. The photo had to be at Nepenthe Manor—he would never have left something so precious behind. And if the p.a.s had taken it from him upon arrival, he would have retrieved it from his file that night Skippy found him in the records room. Of course Xavier wouldn't have hidden it in his own room. He'd already proven he wasn't entirely brain dead, knowing anyone could get in and snoop around, so he'd have hidden it somewhere else, either in someone's room or in a common room. The down side was that Nepenthe Manor was huge, which left a lot of places to cover. But, Pandora reasoned, it would have to be somewhere he could get to easily and without being seen when he went to retrieve the photo. Where would that be?

She paced back and forth six more times when she stopped suddenly and stamped on the floor with delight. Of course! He'd hidden the photo in the bathroom across the hall. It was so obvious she wondered why she hadn't figured it out instantly.

Pandora flipped off the light and quietly opened the door. She peeked down the hall. Rackett and Hessian were still eating. Hessian looked immensely bored as she chewed. Rackett had started doing paperwork, her neck bent at a forty-five degree angle as she made neat notes in a file. It was safe to go.

While tiptoeing across to the communal bathroom and shower room, Pandora wondered when the staff would discover Xavier's missing file. Then she wondered how they could have missed its absence this long. In the early days, inmates were closely watched and notes were assiduously taken. So what was taking so long for someone to sound the alarm?

Unable to figure it out, she pushed on the bathroom door, which closed on its own if you just left it alone, stepped inside the damp room, then gripped the handle so that the door would close quietly behind her. There were no windows in the bathroom, which was why special lights had to be installed that could never be turned off. It was hard enough having a mental illness. The inmates didn't need the added trauma of being trapped in a pitch-black room, especially while sitting on the pot, when another inmate absently, or purposely, turned off the light upon leaving.

Once Pandora entered the dank bathroom, she didn't waste any time. She knew exactly where to go. A locked, metal linen closet, which housed bleached-white towels, sat in a corner close to where the showers were located. She went straight to it, and sinking to her knees, started to feel around in the narrow space between the back of the closet and the wall.

For the first couple minutes of her search Pandora found only cobwebs and bug carcasses. With a crick developing in her neck and a cramp in her wrist, she was on the verge of admitting defeat when the tips of her reaching fingers touched something with a paper-thin edge. The photo. It had to be. She'd found it at last! But a glance at her watch told her twenty minutes had passed since she'd come up to the second floor. Lunchtime would be over soon, if it wasn't already. She had to move quickly.

Centimeter by centimeter, she scooted the rectangular object in her direction by turning it over and over. Moving a thin piece of paper when she could hardly bend her knuckles wasn't easy. Sweat accumulated, making her skin itch, and her fingers grew trembly with fatigue. Someone—anyone—could come in at any time. The boys did not like a girl in their bathroom and made sure everyone within a two-mile radius knew about it if they found one. Or a p.a. might come in. Or Frank. Even Nurse Rackett popped her head in on occasion to be sure no monkey business was going on.

And what a lovely position she'd find me in, Pandora groaned as her increasingly slippery fingers, which were starting to cramp, worked desperately to get that photo out and into her possession. *Half-stuck behind the cabinet, with my butt in the air.*

A door out in the hallway banged shut. "Baby Ruth! Ruth Baby!" Skippy hollered down the hallway in his best Sloth Fratelli voice.

Pandora froze. They were back! She jerked on the photo one last time and it flipped into her waiting hand. Yes! She had the photo, but still had to get it, and herself, to safety. She pushed herself to her feet and scanned the room, her eyes lighting on a bathroom stall. Knees stiff from kneeling on the hard tiles, she hobbled across the floor. The outside door started to open. She flung open the stall door, quietly closed it behind her, and slid home the latch. At the last second, she climbed up onto the toilet so no one could see her sneakers.

"I've got plans, baby!" Skippy shouted, his voice echoing. Then he sang in a falsetto reminiscent of the Bee Gees, "Newbie's going down.

Newbie's going down!" He banged into the stall next to her and she could hear the metallic zip of his zipper heading south.

Before he could begin something she didn't want to hear, Pandora rapped on the metal wall with the hand she was using to keep from falling off, or into, the toilet. She quickly returned the hand to its place. "Skippy!"

Silence. "Yeah?" he asked cautiously.

"It's me. Pandora."

The zipper flew back up. "Pandora! What the hell are you doing in here?"

"I'm on a mission."

"Oh." There was a pause. "Does it involve Xavier?"

"Yep."

"Good," he exhaled noisily. "Cause I'm in."

Pandora pondered this. "I thought you thought he was cool."

"I changed my mind."

She didn't bother pursuing his reason; she didn't have that kind of time, but had a suspicion it had to do with Birdy. "Most excellent. I need your help."

"In the bathroom?"

"*No.* I found something that he hid in the bathroom."

"Oh, good," he replied, sounding relieved. "What did you find?"

"Remember I told you he was showing a photo around town?"

"Yeah?"

"Well, I've got it in my hands." As she said this, she realized she hadn't even looked at it yet. She glanced down. Gripped tightly in her hand was a smudged, birthday card-sized envelope, unsealed. Balancing herself with an elbow, she opened it and pulled out its contents—a black and white photo of a strange man—and studied it.

It was hard to get a firm grasp on what he looked like. The fedora he wore pulled down low cast a shadow over his face. Stubble covered his square chin and jaw like a shag rug. He looked a little uncertain as he stared at the camera, but kind enough. Pandora had been hoping he'd look more sinister, like a member of the mob, or something. She flipped the photo over. Written in flowing script at the bottom was the word, Bedlam. Well, that explained why Xavier was snooping around in town.

"Do you know who it is?" Skippy asked.

"No idea. The sun is right behind him so it's not the best photo." She peered more closely, noting some dark shapes—possibly trees—behind him, but his features remained elusive.

"Hand it over," he said. She grabbed the toilet paper dispenser, leaned over, and slipped the photo under the stall wall. "What do you think?"

"I don't recognize him, either," he concurred.

"He kind of looks like Indiana Jones, doesn't he?"

"It's the totally rad hat he's wearing." Skippy sighed enviously. That boy experienced hat envy entirely too often.

"Probably...and the stubble, too."

"Not much to go on, is it?" he said. "We really need to see Xavier's files and I really need a hat like that."

"I was just thinking about that—well, not the part about the hat. Don't you think it's strange that we haven't heard anything about his file going missing?" The inmate gossip network could not be beat. They would have started blabbing the moment word went out.

"You know, you're right," he said thoughtfully.

"I don't think he really shredded it. I think he just pretended to do it to throw us off."

"You mean, like a fake? Hot damn, he's good! I'll bet he can pick locks, too. That's how he got into the records room." He chuckled. "Boy, if I didn't hate his guts right now I'd want to go out and shake his hand."

"Just remember, Skippy," Pandora said, attempting to sound like Vicki in full Director mode, "he isn't good for us."

"Yeah, I know." He sounded disappointed. "We have to do something about him."

"You need to go back into the records room and see if you can track down his file."

"I will! Tonight after shift change. But what do we do in the meantime?"

"I'm going to make a copy of this puppy and you're going to return it to where I found it behind the towel cabinet." She pulled up the bottom of her turtleneck, slipped the photo into the waistband of her pants, and pulled her shirt back down. "Can you make sure no one's coming while I flee the scene?"

"Sure. Do you want me to set off a smoke bomb? I've got a few left over from that stash Beetle sold me last Halloween. Oh...I know! Let me blow a circuit, then yell, *fire!* That should clear the way!"

"Whoa, big guy. Pull back. Let's KISS, okay?"

He groaned. "I hate it when you say that."

"Skippy..."

"Yeah, yeah. I got it. Keep it simple, stupid."

"I'll meet you at the door in ten minutes, okay?"

"Okay. But I still have to pee. Close your ears so I can go." He paused. "Did you cover them?"

Pandora didn't answer, figuring that was the best thing to do in this instance. She wasn't letting go with both hands to cover her ears. Satisfied, Skippy did his business and after flushing, left his stall with a skip in his step. A moment later, the heavy door swung open and he ran out into the hallway. Twenty seconds after that, he bellowed, *"Heeey, youuu guuuys!"* Footsteps thudded down the hallway past the bathroom, heading in the opposite direction of the exit door. The inmates all knew that Skippy, while in the midst of a manic high, was good for a show.

Pandora inched the door open. The inmates had followed after him, even Xavier had come out to see what was going on. His back was to her as she tiptoed out and down the hall. When she was at the exit door—Nurse Rackett and the Hessian had already returned to their lunches after discerning that nothing bad was going on—Pandora stopped and looked back.

Xavier had turned around. Arms folded and eyes squinting suspiciously, he watched her go. She flipped him a wave. "Later, loser!" she mouthed. Then she slipped away down the stairs, giddy with triumph. She'd won this round, and very possibly the war.

Newbie was going down.

WHEN PANDORA ENTERED her mother's office, there was no one there. No mother, and no Bennington. This was a first. The office was never left unattended and/or unlocked. *Never.*

Not one to question good luck, she scurried into Bennington's office through the connecting door, which she closed behind her, leaving a narrow crack so she could hear if someone was coming.

Moving quickly, she made two copies of the photo. Once the light flashed twice, she lifted the cover, snatched up the original, and stuffed it back into its envelope. She was about to pick up the copies when she heard the door to Vicki's office, which had its own special creak, like a groan, swing open. She froze in mid-grab.

"Come on in, Dr. Steele," Vicki invited, her voice unusually carefree. Pandora's legs turned all wobbly and she leaned hard against the copier. Of all the rotten timing... "I just ran to the cafeteria to get a fresh cup of java. Boy, did I need it." She laughed lightly. "Mayor Daft, whom you'll be unfortunate enough to learn all about in your time here, stopped by earlier."

"Not your favorite person?" he mused.

"Not exactly. Sit down." Her mother's old-fashioned office chair squeaked as she sat, and she gave a nervous laugh. "I really have to get those springs oiled. I think this chair is about two hundred years old." More squeaking, then a quiet followed, which seemed to go on forever. "So how can I help you?" Vicki asked at last.

"I met with Xavier Carlisle this morning." Xavier *Carlisle.* Pandora wanted to jump for joy. She had a last name. Now maybe she could get somewhere!

"Ah, yes. What did you think of him?"

"I don't think he needs to be here."

There was a moment's silence. "Yes, well, about that. I think he needs to stay."

"I have to disagree. He made a mistake, and he has a bit of an attitude, but he's generally a well-balanced kid. There's little that can be done for him here. In fact, I think staying here any longer could be damaging for him."

"I understand that, but I have my reasons for keeping him here a little longer."

"I hope they're good," he said smoothly. "It's costing the taxpayers a fair amount of money to care for a boy who doesn't need it."

"Listen, Dr. Steele…" Vicki began. Her voice was cool and calm, but with an edge sharp as a knife, and Pandora braced herself for the attack. Whenever her mother took that tone, whoever it was directed at had better look out. "There are things you don't know."

That's it? Pandora deflated, immensely disappointed. She wanted them to fight.

"Enlighten me."

A moment's hesitation. "I'd like to, but I can't."

"So you're going to override my recommendation."

Vicki's pen started tapping on the desk like an overzealous woodpecker. "For now."

"I really wish you'd confide in me, Director Belfry. I think I have a right to know." This, Pandora had to hear. Vicki was all for cutting costs and saving money, so why not dump Xavier? She leaned forward to hear her mother's response and accidentally knocked a book sitting on a small table near the copier to the floor.

A heavy silence nearly made Pandora pass out, then, "Bennington?"

"It's just me," Pandora called in a loud voice, while trying to keep it steady as she pushed the copy button. The machine roared to life. "I was making copies for a project I'm working on," she improvised, sticking to the truth as best she could. She didn't want to get caught, yet again, in a tangled web of her own weaving.

Footsteps clacked across the hardwood floor, then her mother appeared in the doorway. Her eyes swept the room, before settling on Pandora. "I didn't know you were in here."

"I didn't know anyone was out there." Pandora widened her eyes and slapped her chest a few times. "You really startled me. This dinosaur of a copier is so loud!"

Her mother paused to consider this, then said, "I thought you were going to lunch."

Pandora waved at the copier. "After we talked I remembered something I meant to finish for my homework. I didn't want to forget my idea so I ran upstairs and made amendments, then came down to make copies of it."

Her mother stepped forward. "Can I see it?"

"Um, sure. But it's only the proposal." Dang. Now she was going to have to actually do something.

"Right now." Her mother held out her hand.

"Absolutely." Pandora made as though to turn around, then swung back. "You know, I thought it was strange that your door was unlocked, but no one was in here. I know it's your policy not to leave your office unlocked and unoccupied, so I thought I'd better stay until someone came back."

Her mother slowly lowered her hand. "Oh, yes. Bennington's out on errands and I ran to the cafeteria for a coffee. I must have forgotten to lock up behind me." She frowned. "That's so unlike me."

"Well, don't let me keep you," Pandora rushed to say. "I really have to eat something soon or I'm going to pass out. I'm starving." She hustled toward the door, forcing her mother to back up to avoid getting trampled. "Oh, hello, Dr. Steele," she greeted breathily as she darted into the office. "I can't stay. I'm off to lunch."

"Hello, Pandora. I saw you on the beach earlier. I waved..."

"Did you?" She whisked past him, toward the door. As much as she'd like to stay and banter with him, she had to escape now or risk her mother seeing the envelope in her hand. Before anyone could stop her, she was out the door and across the foyer, heading toward the side stairs that led to the inmates' sleeping quarters, all the while congratulating herself on her successful escape.

Her feet flew up the steps, two at a time, but instead of finding Skippy's face peering through the tiny, chicken-wired window in the door, she found Xavier's. *Chicken butt.* She stopped three steps down with her hand on the wood railing, grateful she'd slid the envelope back into her waistband.

He swung open the door and peered down at her. "What are you up to now, Belfry?"

"What makes you think I'm up to something?" She tried to look innocent by fluttering her eyelashes and smiling sweetly.

"Cause it seems to me that you're always up to something." His fingers tapped on the doorframe impatiently. "Will you stop doing that weird thing with your eyes? And that smile is just plain creepy." Pandora stopped fluttering and smiling. "So when are you going to do what I asked? I'm ready to blow this joint."

Pandora studied him. He really did want to get out of here...was itching to. She couldn't blame him, but still, his urgency was telling; it could only mean he had something to hide.

"I can't be seen with you," she told him.

He looked surprised. "Why?"

"I was trying to help you out, put in a good word for you, but my mother warned me away from you. Any idea why she'd do that?"

"Because I'm so terribly good looking?" he hazarded, though he seemed uncomfortable, his eyes fixed on the wall over her head.

"I think they can safely add delusional to your list of symptoms, but nice try." She folded her arms and waited. "I have all day."

"So do I," he retorted, copying her movement.

"Oh, come on, Xavier. I know what you did."

His eyes flashed. "Of course you do, snoop. So you'll know I was provoked."

"I can understand that." Pandora let a couple seconds pass before she delivered her blow with the skill of a boxer. "Though the mayor, whose son you attacked, isn't as understanding as I am."

"The *mayor*?" He shook his head. "Son of a bi—"

"Ah, ah, ah!" She held up her hand. "No swears."

"Screw that," he snorted, though she noted he didn't drop the more impressive F-bomb like he could have. He was learning the ways of the asylum.

"I did talk you up to Vicki, but I just don't think she's going for it. Actually, I don't think she was even listening."

Xavier stared at her. "What did you just call the Director?"

"Um, her name? Vicki?"

He frowned. "You call her Vicki?"

"Got a problem with that?"

"You really call her Vicki?"

She sighed. "That's her name." People who shouldn't care that she called her mom by her first name often were the most judgmental about it. "So get over it. How's it going with the posse?" she asked, tired of the subject.

He groaned. "I don't know how you can stand them. Birdy never stops talking. Lucy keeps trying to take my shoes off. Charles looks at me with those mournful eyes of his, like I just killed his best friend. Sinclair makes this weird, keening noise whenever we're in our room together. Skippy's about the most normal of the bunch, but I'm not sure he likes me."

Pandora's lips clamped down on a triumphant smile. "Well, good luck with them. They're just getting started."

He paled. "What do you mean?"

"The more comfortable they are around a person," she explained, "the more they relax and show their true selves."

"You mean, they're going to get even more bizarre?"

"Listen, *Carlisle*. You made your bed, now it's time to lie in it." She paused. "Speaking of beds, you should make yours. That's why Sinclair is keening. He hates disorder."

"How'd you know my bed wasn't made?" He took a threatening step toward her. "And damnit, how'd you know my last name?"

"Tsk, tsk. Language!" She took a step backward, her grip firm on the railing. Xavier was looking mighty peeved, and *scared*. Probably because she had him by the short hairs, which was just the way she liked it.

"All right, Belfry," he growled, "the bargain is off. I'm telling anyone who will listen what I know about you."

"Are you sure they'll believe you?"

"Of course they will," he replied smugly, then his dark blond eyebrows nearly crashed together as he frowned. "Wait, what do you mean?"

"I mean that the longer you stay in this place, the less credible you seem. It's like the criminal who didn't commit the crime he was arrested for. No one is going to believe he didn't do it because he's a criminal. All criminals claim they're innocent."

"You're saying people are going to think *I'm* a loony?"

"You were brought to an insane asylum in the Madmobile. You've been here longer than twenty-four hours. I'd say your chances of becoming one of us increase with each hour you stay here."

His eyes grew frightened. "You're lying."

"Think about it, Carlisle. If you knew someone who'd gone through what you're going through, would you think they were normal? Would you believe them?"

"Maybe," he said slowly. "If they seemed believable."

"Oh, stop kidding yourself. You'd always have a doubt about them."

"No, I wouldn't!"

"Yes, you would! You already have this fear of loonies, yet you've probably never met one before you came here. It's a societal thing. You believe what you've heard about the mentally ill—that they're violent and aggressive and will attack you in your sleep. And anyone painted with that brush is suspect, right?"

This time, instead of moving toward her, he took a step away, back up the stairs. "That's not true." But it was. She could see it in his face.

"Just leave me and my posse alone, Xavier. We're only trouble for you."

"You're trying to trick me into giving up my hold over you."

"I'm trying to help you, idiot."

He laughed. "You've tried to help me before, remember? You're as bad as the rest of them, Belfry. I've heard what they call you in town, though I didn't realize until Birdy told me who you were that people were talking about you."

"You mean the name, Bats?" she said casually.

"Yes!" he barked. "As in, 'she has bats in her belfry.'"

"And?" she retorted saucily.

"So if all those people think you've got problems, then you *must* have problems. I'll bet you're just as crazy as the inmates. I shouldn't believe a word you say."

"And yet you know I'm right." She was the one to take a step forward this time. She pointed a finger at him. "I'm on to you, Carlisle. I'm going to dig up your dirty little secret and when I do, I'll expose you to everyone."

"And I'll tell them all about—"

"About what? That there are secret passages? That I sneak into town?" She laughed. "They already know all that!" She was bluffing, but it was all she had. She laughed again, just for good measure.

"They do not. You were scared about me telling on you before. You agreed to my threat."

"I agreed because I thought it was the best way to get rid of you. I was wrong." She took another step forward. "Look, Carlisle. We want the same thing—to rid Nepenthe Manor of your heinous presence. We should be working together to achieve that glorious goal."

He stared at her for several long seconds, taking in her confident pose, her cocky smile. "I'll think about it," he finally muttered and looked away. "I have to go now. It's time for my craft class."

He let the door shut in Pandora's face, and she let out a long breath. *That went well.* She was about to head back down the stairs when the door swung open again. *Now what?*

Skippy stuck his head and one arm through the narrow space. "Quick. Give it to me." She handed him the envelope. "Mission accomplished?"

She rubbed her hands together like a mad scientist. "I have him on the run."

"Are we having our Midnight Meeting tonight?"

"Of course. It's time the Secret Six reunited."

"Are you still mad at Birdy?"

Pandora's hand flew to her chest and she fluttered her eyelashes. "Who, me?"

"No, your mama," he snipped. "Yes, you. She turned on you. You'll probably want revenge, won't you?" He looked worried.

"You know how you say Dr. Malik likes to bring up Karma in his sessions? That he believes what goes around, comes around?"

Skippy gave a reluctant nod. "So what are you going to do?"

"Birdy needs to learn the facts and she needs to learn loyalty. I am *not* bossy and my mother is the enemy."

"And how are you going to teach her that?"

"All in good time, my friend," she whispered, "all in good time."

He frowned, then backed away, letting the door close nearly shut. "Just don't hurt her, okay?" he said through the crack. Only his eyes, nose, and mouth showed.

"Why do you care?"

"I don't. It's just that…well, Xavier isn't being very nice to her."

Pandora pretended to stagger backward. "And he's being nice to me? You guys abandoned me to hang out with him. I should be teaching *all* of you a lesson."

"Yeah, I know." The nose sniffed. "Sorry about that."

"I get the sense that you're not *truly* sorry, Skippy."

"I am, Pandora. You can't imagine how much."

That sounded better. If Skippy turned on her, all would be lost. "Oh, all right. I'll go easy on her. But I'm still going to do *something*."

The nose and mouth bobbed up and down. "Fair enough."

"Now go, my noble fellow, and carry out your noble deed. I'll be expecting your report tonight."

"Yes, my liege."

"Xavier's last name is Carlisle, by the way."

Skippy's nose and mouth looked impressed. "How did you find that out?"

She shrugged. "I have my ways. Now remember to let the others know about the Midnight Meeting in the attic. Oh, and remind them to keep quiet about it. We can't have Newbie finding out."

"Got it, Cap'n." He saluted and then he was gone.

She nodded, feeling quite satisfied. The throne was in her grasp.

15

A Slippery Sucker

FOR PANDORA, WAITING for their Midnight Meeting was like waiting for Christmas—endless and painful. She decided to stay in her room and lay low until the meeting, but it wasn't easy to stay put and do nothing. Bored out of her skull, she actually resorted to doing more homework, starting the project she'd made up for her mother's benefit in Bennington's office. The only agreeable thing about having to make good on her lie was that she actually did need to do a research project for her science credits.

After paging through her biology book for half an hour, she decided she was going to do her research on pheromones, those wondrous chemicals that animals and humans excrete to attract a mate. Where before the word 'pheromone' had barely registered on her radar, the whole topic now suddenly seemed infinitely attractive to her. Vastly useful, too. Just imagine what she could do if she could determine what attracted who. The possibilities for nefarious schemes were endless!

For the next hour, she struggled with exactly how she was going to research something that was invisible. In the end she decided to collect specimens from the armpits of the males and females of Nepenthe Manor. Phase two would involve having her subjects do a sniff test of said specimens to see which scents attracted them. The experiment probably wouldn't be the most controlled of studies, but it would certainly be interesting making the attempt, especially if she could get Dr. Steele to participate. Collecting a sample from him, preferably after he'd had a good workout, definitely would make the top of *Pandora's Ten Most Amazing Life Moments*.

Once she had her agenda firmly mapped out in her mind, she spent the next couple hours typing up a proposal and creating a brief questionnaire on her computer, being careful to follow procedures to maintain confidentiality. She hated these types of restrictions in research, but made sure to follow all the rules, down to the last letter, for running a valid study. She actually liked learning the outcome of her research, and the more controlled the study, the more reliable the results.

But even if the study was a bust, at the very least she could determine who Dr. Steele found attractive. Nurse Burns was a likely candidate. If

Pandora could get her to participate, she'd save a lot of time and energy. Because if the goddess were a threat, then Pandora would use all her wiles to drive her away from Nepenthe Manor. If not, well, then Miss Burns was welcome to stay, and no harm done. Too bad Pandora couldn't get rid of her mother that easily—not legally, anyway. But she wondered if she should include her in the study. Collecting her mother's sweat would be one of the more repulsive things she ever had to do, but it might be worth the effort and sacrifice to know definitively about Vicki and Dr. Steele's love connection.

After adding one last question, Pandora leaned back and stretched. She was exhausted and hungry. The cafeteria closed in twenty minutes and if she wanted to eat she'd better get moving. She printed out the proposal and questionnaire and took them with her as she headed down to the cafeteria for her supper. After getting her food, she would make copies of her proposal and give them to Vicki. Providing proof to back up her necessary fudging should once and for all allay Vicki's suspicions about what her daughter had been up to in the copy room.

Ordinarily Pandora wouldn't make any effort to avoid trouble, and in fact, would be curious to see how Vicki would handle the whole situation. Would she continue to ask for the proposal, or would she forget all about it, forcing Pandora to push the issue? Pandora often couldn't resist provoking her mother this way, which, according to some theories, was perfectly normal behavior. Getting negative attention is better, or so the idea goes, than getting no attention at all. Most of the time Pandora heartily agreed with that concept. She, like countless others, liked attention any way she could get it. But today she had an important mission to carry out. She must sacrifice her own needs to save her posse from the enemy. It wouldn't be easy to go without attention, but doing so was essential.

Pandora zipped into the cafeteria singing boisterously, "Come 'n listen to my story 'bout a man named Jed..." The room was nearly empty and she headed straight for the serving line where women dressed in white stood behind a long, stainless steel counter and dished up meals with the precision of a zombie assembly line. Today there was only one worker. The rest were no doubt back in the kitchen scrubbing giant pots and scraping blackened grills while Old Corker finished off any leftovers.

"Hey, Gladys!" she greeted the old woman who'd worked the line for as long as Pandora could remember. Rumor had it Gladys's mother had been housekeeper for the Nepenthe family back when they still owned the manor. "This actually looks kind of good," she commented as she peered at the offerings of pork chops and corn and mashed potatoes with gravy. "Old Corker pass on?"

Gladys snorted and loaded up Pandora's tray. Gladys never said much on account of having lost all her teeth years ago, but her toothless, weathered face spoke volumes. Today the expression said, "Lord, I wish it were so."

"Thanks. Any dessert left?" Gladys shook her netted, gray head. "Ah, well," Pandora sighed. She was in serious need of a sugar fix after doing all that homework. "I guess I'll just grab a few sugar packets on my way out."

Gladys glanced to the left, then to the right, then reached under the counter and pulled out a white plate upon which sat a generous slice of apple pie. She put an arthritic finger to her lips and Pandora nodded, quickly grabbing the plate and setting it on her tray. Without being told, she unfolded her napkin and covered the pie.

"You're the apple of my eye, Gladys!" she said happily, and Gladys nodded her head. She knew this quite well. "Good luck with the ogre." Then, shoulders hunched over her tray, Pandora hustled out of the cafeteria. She couldn't wait to eat that apple pie. Gladys made pies on occasion, using an old recipe of her mother's, and often shared a piece with Pandora. They were de-lish.

Before heading up to her room, Pandora dashed into her mother's office to make her copies. Mother wasn't at her desk, but Bennington was, busily typing on her computer. Pandora set her tray on one of the visitor's chairs and headed into Bennington's office.

"Hi, Benny." Though she was only twenty-eight, Bennington played the role of director behind the Director. She made sure everything ran smoothly…ordering supplies, doing payroll, typing up reports. As long as the tiny Korean woman didn't have to talk to people she didn't know, she was happy to stay at Nepenthe Manor and do her work with little reward beyond an undoubtedly measly salary. Pandora both admired this trait in the secretary, and scorned it. Really, Vicki took frightful advantage of poor Bennington and poor Bennington did nothing to remedy it.

"You up to trouble, Dora-ora?" While Bennington might be shy around other people, she had no trouble bossing Pandora.

Pandora blinked innocently. "Thou hast besmirched me, Benny. I'm making copies of my homework to give to my mother." She never called her mother Vicki in front of Bennington. Koreans held their elders in great respect, and there were just some things Pandora didn't mess with. Not to mention the fact that the normally reserved Benny had jumped all over her the first time she heard Pandora make the attempt. It wasn't savvy to invite that kind of bad mojo into your life.

"You up to trouble, and you in trouble, too." She shook her head and tsk-tsked.

"What do you mean?"

Leaning forward, Bennington pushed up her oversized glasses, ones that nearly overwhelmed her petite Asian nose, and placed her elbows on her neat as a pin desk. She was wearing her typical outfit of high-waisted, navy blue slacks and navy blue flats, white blouse heavy on the ruffles, and a wool cardigan of varying colors. Today it was turquoise. A pink, flower-shaped brooch, one of an assortment that Bennington wore daily, sparkled from its exalted position over her heart.

"Your mother, she find something that make her mad." She used her hands to demonstrate what her mother looked like while angry. Pandora had the impression of sparks shooting out of her mother's head.

She took a step forward. "What did she find?"

Bennington shrugged, looking more than a bit disgusted. "I don't know. She tell me nothing."

Pandora frowned. "Hm. That sounds serious. I guess I'll just make my copies and blow this joint before I find out what's chapped her, um, behind."

Bennington nodded in agreement. "You do that. I keep eye out."

With Benny on lookout, Pandora hurried over to the copier and opened the lid. The lifting motion triggered a memory, and when it came back to her, she felt an urge to stick her head inside the machine and copy herself to death. *The copies.* She'd forgotten to grab the copies of Xavier's photo! This was bad. Really bad.

Even so, she had to stay calm, think this through and interrogate Bennington. Taking a deep breath, she inserted her proposal and questionnaire into the copier and pushed the correct buttons to make two copies of each. "So," she said casually over her shoulder. "What was my mother doing when you realized she was mad at me?"

"I brought her copy of daily report. She read it, she start swearing." A couple seconds of tsking followed that statement. "Your mother, she know I don't like potty mouths."

"And my name came up while she was shouting?"

"Many time."

Crap.

"Okay, thanks, Benny." The copying job complete, Pandora grabbed the papers and turned to face Bennington. "Where is she now?"

"Looking for you, no doubt." Bennington smiled. "Don't worry, Dora-ora. She forget soon enough."

Vicki usually did forget, but Pandora had a feeling not this time. There was something about that photo that had set her mother off. Otherwise, why would she get so angry with Pandora over a picture? Besides, anyone could have made those copies. There was no reason to think Pandora was the culprit. But Vicki *did* think Pandora had done it and this, for some reason, made her madder than a wet hen. But why such anger? It seemed overdone, even for Vicki.

Well, whatever the reason, Pandora wasn't sticking around to find out. "Thanks for the scoop, Benny. See ya." She left Bennington's office, the gears in her brain spinning furiously. Halfway across Vicki's office, she paused. This was a doozy of a predicament, but one that could reap big rewards if she played her cards right. Her mother had no proof that Pandora had anything to do with the copies so all she had to do was play dumb when Vicki confronted her about them. While she was busy making accusations, maybe she'd accidentally spill the beans about what was making her so mad. And the sooner Pandora found that out, the sooner she could figure out what was going on around here.

She turned back around and dropped one of the copies of her research report on her mother's desk. She sat down in a visitor's chair and ate her supper while she waited for her mother to return. The pie was excellent. Twenty minutes later, after Bennington had left to go home—she lived in Bedlam with her mother—Vicki breezed in looking flustered and out of breath. "There you are! I've been looking everywhere for you. Where have you been?"

Pandora smiled. For once she was going to look golden. "I was doing homework in my room. Then I headed to the cafeteria to get some supper. I thought I'd eat with you, so I came here. I also realized I forgot to give you the copy of that project I was telling you about. You know, the one I was making copies of while you were in here with Dr. Steele."

Oh, well-played, Pandora.

Her mother eyed her suspiciously as she walked around to the front of her desk. She picked up the stapled report and read the title. With each word she mouthed, her eyes widened and her skin turned white as the paper in front of her. "Pheromones and Attraction: Using Your Good Scents to Find a Mate," she repeated hoarsely. She cleared her throat. "Are you serious?" The wind chose that moment to slam against the building, making it creak like an old ship. Vicki didn't even flinch.

Pandora blinked at her mother. This was unexpected. She was always doing projects on unusual subjects. Vicki had never reacted this way before. "Perfectly. I've outlined my project and even created a questionnaire."

Vicki flipped through the pages. "What attracts you to another person?" she whispered. "Do you use all your senses when looking for a mate?" "If someone smells really good, do you like them more?" She shook her head slowly, as though stunned. The report, falling from her slack fingers, fell to the desk. She reached down and yanked open a drawer. "First this!" she cried, holding out a piece of paper. "And then, this!" She swooped up the report and shook it at Pandora.

"What's the first thing?" Pandora asked, staying calm. It was a defensive maneuver that drove Vicki crazy.

"Don't tell me you don't know. I found it in the copier."

"And you thought it was *mine*?"

"You were up to something earlier…"

"I was making a copy for you."

"No, no. It was something else. Something you weren't supposed to be doing. Where did you get this?" Vicki shook the piece of paper at Pandora.

Pandora shrugged. "Being as I don't know what you're talking about," a statement which could apply to just about everything her mother said, "I can't answer."

"Don't play dumb with me. *This!*" She shoved the piece of paper into Pandora's face. "Where did you get it?"

Pandora looked her mother in the eye, as all good heroes would do, then took the paper from her hand. She made a big show of looking it over, turning it this way and that. "I didn't get this anywhere." Ah, the truth. It was a slippery sucker.

Vicki's eyes narrowed. "Okay. Then where did you get the original?" Vicki was now demonstrating why she was the Director. She reached for the photocopy before Pandora could discreetly tuck it into her back pocket, forcing Pandora to hand it back to her.

"It's not mine," she replied, which, technically was true.

"Then whose is it?"

Pandora shrugged. "You know the college students use our copiers all the time. I suppose it's someone's boyfriend, or something."

More eye narrowing. Vicki's eyes could barely be seen now, just thin slits of annoyance. "And this topic?" She held up the report. "Does it have anything to do with Xavier?"

This time Pandora didn't have to act. She drew back, as though slapped. "Are you kidding me?"

Her mother started to look relieved. "So you don't, um, fancy him?"

"*Fancy* him?"

"Do you like him?" Her mother was now gripping the back of her chair, knuckles white as marshmallows.

Pandora was in a dilemma. It obviously bothered her mother to think her daughter might be falling for a hoodlum, which pleased Pandora immensely. On the other hand, telling the truth—that she found Xavier repulsive and vomit-inducing—might get her off the hook, and free her to do what she needed to do to save her posse.

"He's all right, I guess," she replied coquettishly, though she'd meant to say just the opposite. Apparently her need for attention outweighed her desire to save others.

Her response had the desired effect—her mother looked ready to explode, her eyes widened, her nostrils quivered. "What have I told you about him?"

"I can't help it. He's forbidden fruit."

"*No.* No, he's not that," her mother said in a voice that one would use with a wayward child who's about to do something foolish. "He's just like any other resident who lives at Nepenthe Manor. Right, Pandy?"

"Off-limits?"

"Exactly."

"What about when he gets out?"

Vicki froze. "Well, see...I...he's..." She was stuck. She couldn't tell Pandora anything about Xavier, or she'd be breaking her own strict rules of confidentiality. But she had to say something to stop her daughter from pursuing a delinquent.

"So that's okay?" Pandora jumped to her feet. "Rad!" Abandoning her tray, she hoofed it over to the office door. "Thanks, Vicki! I'm glad we talked. I feel so much better."

"What—? No! I mean—"

But Pandora had swung open the door and ducked outside, only to come face to face with Dr. Steele, who was heading toward the office with a stack of manila folders in hand. "Dr. Steele. Come on in!" She held the door for him.

Shoulder to shoulder, he stopped and gave her an assessing look. "Why is it," he asked in a low voice, "that whenever we meet I feel like I'm being used to further your subversive activities?"

She grinned. "Probably because you are..."

Midnight Meeting

16

THAT NIGHT PANDORA'S mother looked in on her, something she rarely did. It was odd how she trusted Pandora to be where she was supposed to be. *I'll never trust my kids,* Pandora promised herself. *Better yet, I'll never have any.* Luckily Vicki was making it an early night, coming up at a quarter to twelve instead of her usual after midnight bedtime, and luckily Pandora had heard the creaking of the floorboards outside her room and acted quickly, climbing up into her bunk as fast as a monkey. Lying flat, she yanked the covers over her head, then took deep, even breaths to feign sleep.

"Pandy?" her mother called softly as she stepped into the room. "Are you awake?" She waited a few measly seconds for a reply, then slowly closed the door again. After hearing the click of the latch, Pandora counted to one hundred, then pulled down the covers. Acting like she was changing positions, she turned to face the door and scanned the room for signs of anything human. She wouldn't put it past her mother to trick her daughter by staying inside the room and waiting for Pandora to give herself away. But as far as she could tell in the dim lamplight, no one was in the room.

Miffed at her mother's pathetic attempt at parenting, she slid out of bed and picked up a wool blanket lying in a heap on the floor. Moving quickly, she rolled up the blanket and stuffed it under her covers to look like a sleeping form. She pulled on her black sneakers, all the better for sneaking, and grabbed Frank's donut. She'd already delivered Cracker Jack's and Professor Robertson's pastries at around nine o'clock, leaving them, as she typically did, on a plate on their pillows while Jack was watching TV and the professor roamed the foyer searching for specimens. Like Frank, they didn't question the magical appearance of their pastries, but unlike Frank, they could use mental illness as their excuse.

After fetching her flashlight, she waited until the sound of the toilet flushing and then the closing of her mother's bedroom door told her it was time to make her move. She slipped into the secret passage and headed in the direction that would take her to the end of the third floor's hallway. The stairway to the attic was on the third floor—same as her room—but taking the hidden passage was more fun and made it less likely for her to get caught creeping about.

After looking both ways, she stepped out into the dark hallway. She had to move quickly now. Frank would be coming along soon to do his walk-through, which typically took him exactly ten minutes to do, as he tested each door to be sure it was locked, sweeping the hallway several times with his flashlight. Without the proper motivation to keep him hopping along, he would use the entire ten minutes to do a thorough search, which was unacceptable. While his unvarying routine made certain things easier to do, it also made it damn difficult to hold Midnight Meetings. Pandora wished they could meet later, but Charles would never last that long—he had a hard enough time as it was with his bad heart—and Sinclair would throw a holy fit if they changed things now. Besides, calling them 1:30 a.m. meetings didn't quite hold the same mystique.

She centered the donut on a little table at the far end of the hallway, flicked on a hall light to guarantee Frank would see it, then ducked back into the secret passageway. In two strides, she found the steps leading to the attic, pounded up them, and entered the large, high-ceilinged space that always reminded her of the inside of an airplane hangar.

First things first, she pulled off her shoes. After overhearing complaints about mice, or perhaps something larger, running about in the attic, she'd instituted the no-shoes rule. Birdy fought it for a while— she loved her heels—but relented when she heard the Hessian mention to another p.a. that she thought giant raccoons had taken up residence in the attic and had a mind to catch her some dinner if she heard any more from the tasty rascals.

Flitting through narrow corridors carved out amongst the towering stacks of boxes and furniture and broken-down junk, Pandora, sneakers in hand, hurried over to the main stairway and down the stairs to the attic door. She turned on the light, unlocked the door, then waited. Two minutes later, Frank's heavy steps announced his arrival. As usual, he was talking to himself.

"Don't you forget to check all the doors, Frankie boy," he muttered. "Be sure to remain vigilant at all—" He stopped. He'd spotted the light over the donut. The footsteps picked up pace.

After counting to five, Pandora opened the door and peeked out. Waiting at the cracked open door to the third floor were five faces. After checking to be sure Frank was enjoying his donut with his eyes closed, she waved them on. Light as chickens in their stocking feet, they hurried toward her. She pushed them past her up the stairs, closing the door just as Frank turned around. Dang! Sometimes it was like he had built-in radar. They hadn't made a noise, yet he had sensed their presence. Pandora quietly turned the lock and motioned to the others to get up the stairs to hide. "Frank's coming!"

When they reached the top, she flicked off the light and hurried up after them. As the door swung open below, she dove behind a musty, old trunk. The naked bulb in the stairwell popped on, emitting a dim, yellow glow.

Lucy was sitting three feet away from Pandora, back against a stack of cardboard boxes, sucking on her fingers. She seemed content. Charles was sitting next to her, on the alert, golden head swiveling back and forth, waiting to spring into action. Sinclair looked rather peaky. He was not made for stealth operations. Skippy and Birdy sat side by side, trying not to laugh. Pandora shot them a warning look. Their eyes widened and their lips pulled inward as they tried to keep the laughter in.

"If anyone is up there," Frank called in his deep voice, "Frank is going to be very angry." His voice echoed in the stairwell. "Frank will beat you on the head with his flashlight. Frank's got a gun, too, you no-good varmint!"

Birdy looked about ready to pass out from holding her breath.

"Are you the spirit?" he asked, his voice a little higher this time.

Birdy sputtered. Pandora had to do something before that foolish girl lost it. Luckily, Frank had just given her the perfect opening. Anyone who lived at Nepenthe Manor for any length of time—even the most skeptical—came to believe it was haunted. Pandora sort of believed it herself even though typically she was the source of the strange sights and sounds witnessed by the inmates and staff. She tried to walk quietly while moving about in the secret passageways, but once in a while she kind of forgot where she was, and subsequently, sometimes went bump in the night. Or she popped out of nowhere without looking first. So, of course, she had to go into acting mode, pretending she was a ghost. At the time, such discoveries had been a major inconvenience. But now Pandora realized that everything happened for a reason.

She inhaled, found her focus, and began her haunting. *"Begone!"* she cried out in a wavery voice. *"Begone, trespasser!"*

A sharp grunt, as though someone had punched Frank in the gut, traveled up the stairs. "Frank's sorry. So sorry!"

Just for giggles, Pandora was tempted to say, *You're going to be, you big dope,* but opted for a repeat of, *"Begone, trespasser!"*

"Frank's going. Right now!" The light went out, the door slammed shut, and footsteps thudded away. Five seconds passed, then the footsteps returned, the lock clicked, and away went Frank once more.

A moment later, Birdy burst out laughing, gasping and snorting like a dying pig. "Oh, man! That was totally too close. I almost died!"

"Shhh!" Pandora hissed. "He could come back, you know. Besides, the staff can hear you. Probably all of Nepenthe Manor, for that matter." She stood and turned her flashlight on. "Come on, let's go."

The posse followed after her through a maze of junk that seemed to grow more aged and decrepit with each step. The treasures that surrounded them—typically left behind by previous inmates who had since passed on to a better, or at least more interesting, life or death—always fascinated Pandora. Much loved dolls, favorite hats, well-used toys. Birdy used the place to update her wardrobe whenever she could. Skippy, too. Sinclair didn't touch anything—everything was too dirty for him. Charles didn't like being reminded that most of the people who'd once owned these objects were now dead. He never said so, but Pandora could tell he didn't like how all this stuff was hid away, neglected and left to rot. She did her best to convince him that using these things, looking at them and enjoying them, kept their owners alive, if only for just a bit.

"I don't want to be forgotten," he once confided in her. "I think that's the worst part about dying."

"Then don't die," she told him and he'd laughed, though he continued to be wary of the leavings in the attic, taking nothing for himself.

Lucy had no problem borrowing from the attic, but she had her own honor system. For each item she took, she replaced it with something of her own. Today she'd brought along a tattered, old teddy bear that had seen better days probably about half a century ago. She plunked it on top of a wooden box and went straight for a pretty doll lying on a nearby chair. The doll had curly, brown hair and blue eyes that blinked when you moved its head. It had been Pandora's, one of the few that had survived the Vlad the Impaler massacre. To her, dolls were useful for two things: sacrifice and experimentation. But for some reason, she had never touched this doll. And last week, no longer wanting its annoying perfection in her room, she'd brought it here for Lucy to find.

"She's so beautiful!" Lucy cooed. "I love her already." She crushed the doll to her chest and patted its back with hard smacks. "There, there, baby girl. Mommy's here." She didn't question where it had come from, which was good for Pandora. Imagine having to own up to possessing that hideously girly *thing*?

Way back in a dark, hidden corner of the attic, everyone sat down in a circular space they had cleared out several years ago for their meetings. Pandora had drilled a hole into the wall and hoisted up an extension cord so that even though there weren't outlets up here, they could have a lamp, which she flipped on. It was a Tiffany, borrowed from a corner of the attic, and its colored glass cast a soft rainbow glow over the posse. Each member had a cushion to sit on—Birdy's idea, being as how, according to her, her heinie was too delicate to sit on a wood floor. Pandora's cushion was purple velvet. Quite an appropriate choice, considering she most likely came from a long line of royal personages, on her father's side, of course. Mother's ancestor had most likely been the serving wench who'd gotten the Duke or Prince outcast from his family home because he'd foolishly fallen in love with her and was now doomed to roam the earth until one day his offspring could make their rightful claim to the throne, or extensive family estate. Pandora had no doubt that this offspring was her. If only she could find the necessary proof she'd be free to live her life in a style more befitting her majestic station.

"That was a close one with old Frankie," Birdy giggled. Pandora glared at her and Birdy sobered a little. "What? Are you still mad because I called you bossy?"

Stay calm, Pandora. Stay calm. "I'm mad because you called me bossy in front of our enemy."

"He's not *my* enemy. He's cute! Besides, you said he was your new friend."

"I was forced into saying that." She gave Skippy a fierce glance.

"Xavier's bad for us—" he loyally began.

"And that's what I like about him." Birdy grinned.

Pandora groaned. "Can we just start the meeting?"

Birdy shrugged. "I'm not stopping you." She spread herself out on her cushion, a red velvet piece the length of her body, and turned her attention to her fiery red fingernails.

Pandora took a deep breath. "Now begins our Midnight Meeting," she intoned, solemn as a druid about to perform a ritual sacrifice. Rain drummed on the roof overhead and the bulb flickered like a candle flame in a breeze. "Members of the Secret Six, please acknowledge your presence here tonight." Everyone did so, though Birdy's "here" was barely audible. She was staring dreamily off into space, slowly chewing her gum like a cow on its cud. Pandora felt her blood pressure rise. That tramp was always ruining things! "We have convened here tonight to discuss a very important *matter.*" She directed her haughty gaze at Birdy, who had the gall to be looking the other way.

"Mama." Pandora nearly jumped out of her skin before realizing it was the doll. She had no idea Betsy Wetsy or Whiny Wendy or whatever her name was did that. Lucy smiled and patted the doll on the head, the movement more akin to someone hammering a nail into a board.

"As I was saying…" Pandora continued, clearing her throat. "We have an important matter to discuss."

"It's about Xavier, isn't it?" Charles asked nervously.

"Yes, it is, Charles." She nodded solemnly. "I don't think he's very good for us. Neither does Skippy. Right, Skippy?"

"Righto," he proclaimed, his fingers tapping on a wood plank. "He's bad for us. Bad for the economy. Bad for mankind—"

"So I think," Pandora interrupted, "that it's in our best interest to stay away from him. Poor Sinclair shares a room with him, so it's going to be harder for him." Sinclair, in a manner atypical of him, nodded furiously. "But the rest of us don't need to have anything to do with him."

"I don't think it's in *my* best interest to stay away from him," Birdy asserted. She pushed herself upright, crossing her plump legs Indian-style. Her Kleenex-enhanced chest pushed outward like a regular Joan of Arc, ready for battle.

Pandora's fingers curled into fists. "Then maybe you should think about leaving the Secret Six, Birdy. You're always going on about how you want to."

"We cannot have a Secret Five," Sinclair burst out plaintively.

"Don't worry, Sinclair. We'll invite a new member to join our group. Someone who's not so much trouble." This seemed to soothe him, though he did glance over at Birdy a couple times as he made his repetitions. As much trouble as she was, she was familiar to him. Sinclair liked familiar, *and* he liked even numbers. In his mind, the answer to this dilemma would be to keep Birdy around. Pandora rushed to cut off that line of thinking. "Cause if Birdy stayed I bet she'd invite Xavier to be one of our Secret Six. That would make it the Secret Seven."

Sinclair's eyes widened and he began repeating Secret Six over and over, emphasizing the six part.

"So what if I did invite him?" Birdy defended herself. "It's not like you're our supreme leader, Pandora. Even though you act like you are."

I'll show you supreme leader, Pandora thought to herself. *Goes by the name of my fist*. "I only want to protect all of you," she said aloud. "Xavier is using you to help get himself out of here faster. He doesn't want to stay at Nepenthe Manor. In fact, he's threatened me so that I'll help him get released."

Birdy studied Pandora suspiciously. "Threatened you with what?"

Pandora didn't miss a beat. "He figured out that I sneak into town even though I'm not supposed to. I'm not sure how he learned that…" Pandora looked straight at Birdy.

"It wasn't me!" Her hand flew to her heart. "How dare you accuse me of such treachery? I've never been treated so terribly in all my life. Off with her head!" She pointed at Pandora imperiously. Pandora had to admire the gesture, if not the rationale behind it.

"Well, I certainly didn't tell anyone—" Pandora stopped. "Did you guys hear that?" About fifteen feet away from where they sat, something heavy had fallen to the floor, creating a loud thud. She put a finger to her lips and slowly pushed herself to her feet. "Someone's up here," she whispered.

"Oh, it's just a squirrel," Birdy snorted. "Now back to my idea…"

"I'm going to see what it is."

"I'll go with you," Charles volunteered.

"Me, too," Lucy lisped, clutching her doll under one arm.

"Me, three?" Skippy pleaded.

"All right, all right. But Charles, I want you to bring up the rear. You need to cover our backs." *And stay protected from whatever it is that's up here*, she added to herself.

He saluted vigorously. "Got it."

Pandora left her flashlight behind on the floor. She didn't want to let whatever, or whoever, it was know she was coming. Tiptoeing across the floor, with the posse in a line behind her, Pandora quickly reached the cleared pathway. She had gone only ten feet along it when a dark shadow darted in front of her, turned right, and headed toward the stairs. Startled, she lunged forward and tripped over her own feet. As she was going down she managed to reach out and catch hold of a bony part of the trespasser's anatomy. Turned out it was his ankle. She jerked hard and he went down with a loud crash.

"Hold him down!" she cried as the posse raced past her. She struggled to keep hold. "Show no mercy. Fart if you have to, Lucy! Lord, he's a slippery sucker."

The posse, with the exception of Sinclair, piled onto the slippery sucker with overzealous abandon. "Get my flashlight!" she yelled to

Sinclair. Ten seconds later he was back. He shined the beam into the intruder's face like it was a weapon. When Pandora saw who it was, she wanted to chew up that flashlight and spit out nails.

Xavier had found them.

17

Right Before She Died

"AGH!" XAVIER CRIED as though in terrible pain. "That horrible smell! Make it go away. Get off me!"

"Good one, Lucy!" Pandora shouted nasally, one hand pinching her nose. "Fire at will!"

"With pleasure," Lucy replied and promptly let loose another one. Pandora sometimes wondered what happened inside that girl to produce such odiferous gas. Even more magical and mysterious was how she was able to release it upon command. Her intestinal system was a thing of wonder.

"I said, get off!" Xavier started to buck like Shadow in a snit, and Sinclair followed every movement with the flashlight beam.

"Not until you're thoroughly punished," Pandora wheezed. "And not until you tell us how you found out about this place and who let you in."

"It wasn't me!" Birdy declared, holding down one of Xavier's arms with her chest.

"Sure, it wasn't," Pandora snorted. "So spill it, Newbie. Who narked?"

"Nobody," he gasped. "Not on purpose, anyway."

Pandora groaned. "Birdy!"

"It wasn't Birdy," he insisted, a tinge of amusement sneaking into his tone.

"Then who was it?"

"It was *you*."

"Me!" She let go of her nose. "I would never tell you anything!"

"Not on purpose, I'll give you that. But next time you want to keep something secret, don't talk about it in a stairwell with the door open. It's like a giant speaker."

"Ha!" Birdy roared. "Pandora narked on herself. That's the funniest thing I've heard in a long time."

"I did not." Pandora did not find this the least bit funny. "Skippy shouldn't have left the door open."

"How else was I supposed to talk to you?" he asked, sounding hurt.

"I don't know! More quietly?" Pandora grumbled.

"But he heard you, not me," he argued, growing annoyingly obstinate. Pandora wished he'd act like a man and just take the blame on himself.

"He's right," Xavier spoke up. "You said, and I quote, 'Let the others know about the midnight meeting in the attic. Oh, and remind them to keep quiet about it. We can't have Newbie finding out.' And I got into the attic by picking the lock."

"I knew it!" Skippy cried.

Pandora stewed. "How dare you eavesdrop on a private conversation? How dare you break the law in our home? I thought people had more principles these days."

"Can you call them off now, please? I think one of my ribs is cracking."

Pandora let go of his ankle and sat up. "Fine. You're free to go, trespasser. Escort him out, posse. I'll decide what to do with him later."

"You make me go," he threatened as he stood up and brushed himself off, "and I'll start yelling." He looked down. "You can let go now, Birdy."

She pouted and let go of his calf, where she'd slid to when he stood up. "I thought you came to see me."

"I came to see what was going on. I was bored."

"Nothing's going on," Pandora rushed to say. "We were bored, too."

"Oh, yeah. Didn't sound like it to me. Sounded more like you were plotting. I for one would like to hear more about you wanting to ostracize me."

Dang, he knew some big words. "Not ostracize completely, drama queen. We're simply going to protect ourselves from your unhealthy influence."

"By keeping me out of your club?"

"Why do you want to be in it?" Pandora demanded. Really, this boy had no boundaries! "You're leaving soon."

"Am I? I met with Dr. Steele again and he said I had to stay…indefinitely."

Birdy sighed wistfully. "How was Dr. Steele? I'm angling for an appointment with him myself. Word on the street is that he's god, I mean, good." She laughed wickedly.

"He's all right," Xavier replied with a shrug. "Thing is, he says my release has been delayed by your mother, Pandora." He stared hard at her.

"Don't look at me! I don't get it, either." She stepped forward. "Now why don't you just leave and let us get on with our meeting? I'm a busy woman."

"Are you saying you didn't do anything to influence her decision?" He sounded insultingly skeptical.

"Me, influence *her*?" Pandora couldn't believe what she was hearing. "I don't think so. Besides, I told you. I don't want you here. I want you gone. I would do everything in my power to get rid of you. But when Vicki makes up her mind about something, it's like drilling through a wall of steel to get her to change it back."

"*Dr.* Steele," Birdy giggled.

"Gross, Birdy! Would you give it a rest?"

Xavier frowned. "But why would she want to keep me here?"

Pandora shrugged. "Unlike everyone else in here, I'm sure it has nothing to do with your warped personality."

"Very funny."

"Or the fact that you tried to beat up Dougie Daft and then threatened to kill him in front of Officer Riley, who was holding you back. Dougie said you were raving like a lunatic."

"I wasn't raving like a lunatic! I was mad as hell, sure. But I wasn't acting crazy. That little jerk was about to kick a dog who was following him and I told him to back off. When he didn't, I let him know what it felt like to get kicked in the ass just like he was about to do to that poodle. When I hit him he started shrieking like a sissy and I only got in one more good punch before that cop ran to his rescue."

"But you tried to fight a cop, Xavier," Pandora tried again. Pursuing this line wasn't helping her case against him at all. In fact, he'd done exactly what she'd done to Dougie years ago. But she had to keep going. She couldn't just let him off the hook. Since coming to Nepenthe Manor, he'd refused to do things her way, tried to take her friends, and called her evil. He needed to pay for his arrogance, and for making her life more difficult. "That's just plain stupid," she went on, "some might even say *insane*."

"I wasn't thinking clearly, all right?" he growled. "I barely had anything to eat for two days and I got sloppy. That doesn't mean I should stay locked up in *here*. I'm *not* crazy." He rubbed his forehead as though it hurt to think. "It's like your mom has something against me, Belfry. Why else would she want to keep me here?"

A thought occurred to Pandora—a rather intriguing one. "You know, she did see that photo."

"What photo?" A threat edged his words and he took a menacing step toward her.

"The photo of that strange dude you've been showing around Bedlam. Who is he?"

His eyes narrowed angrily. "How did you get that?"

"Whoa, keep your voice down," she warned. "Someone's going to hear us."

"I don't care," he hissed. "Where is it?"

"I put it back. Well, Skippy did."

"Skippy?" He stared at Skippy in surprise and Skippy ducked his head.

"Yeah. I took it from the bathroom, made copies of it, and Skippy put it back. Unfortunately, I was almost caught in the act, and I accidentally left the copies behind. My mother found them amongst the pages of her daily report." She crossed her arms. "So who is the guy and why are you looking for him?"

Instead of answering, he said to Skippy, "I thought you were cool, man."

Skippy's brown eyes blinked in shock. "I am! But you were— I was only— Don't you see—" He stopped, his shoulders hunching forward, the pain sweeping over him like a tidal wave. The light in his eyes sputtered and died like a candle. "I'm sorry, Xavier." He held out his hands. "I didn't mean—" Xavier just snorted in disgust and looked away. Skippy sagged and gave up.

Pandora stared at her friend, then at Xavier. "How dare you say that to him! He was helping me. He's cooler than you'll ever be and certainly more of a *man*."

"You had no right touching that picture!" Xavier yelled back, his face growing redder by the second. "It's mine!" He pounded his heaving chest with his fist. "*Mine!*"

"How do we know *you* didn't steal it?" she taunted, feeling good and mad now.

"Because my mother gave it to me!" he howled, looking almost on the verge of tears. "Right before she died, you evil witch!"

"So who is he?" Pandora pursued relentlessly, refusing to be deterred. She had to know who that man was, was irrationally desperate to know. She had a feeling that if she could solve this one mystery, then everything would go back to the way it was—with her in charge and her friends looking up to her.

"I...Don't...Know, you idiot!" And to Pandora's horror, he burst into tears. "You all just stay away from me," he sobbed. When no one responded, he cried out again, "Do you hear me? Stay away!" With a stifled whimper, he wheeled away from the stunned group and ran down the passage. No one moved to follow him.

"Nice going, Pandora!" Birdy sniped when his footsteps died away. "Way to hit below the belt."

"What are you talking about?"

"He tells us his mom dies and you continue to interrogate him like some kind of criminal."

Pandora felt her face grow hot. "He is a criminal. Assault is a crime. Besides, I-I was just trying to help."

"Help what? Help him feel like crap?" Birdy accused. "Well done on that." She sighed. "Poor Xavier." She turned and headed back to the circle. "He didn't deserve that. You should be treating him like a hero, Pandora Belfry, especially since you hate Dougie Daft so much. I'd think you'd be happy Xavier tried to beat him up." The rest of the posse followed after Birdy, each taking their seat with an air of tragedy dogging their every move.

"Listen," Pandora started in as soon as everyone was seated, "just because his mom died doesn't mean he has a right to spy on us or treat us like scum."

"He never treated *me* like scum," Birdy insisted in her typically delusional way.

"Really? He told me you wanted to marry him, which he thought was crazy."

She tossed her head. "Liar."

"I'm not lying. I don't need to lie when the truth serves my purpose perfectly well."

"You're just jealous."

"Xavier's heart hurts," Lucy interrupted. "Cause he doesn't have a mommy."

No one had anything to say to this, and Pandora had the good sense to keep her mouth shut this time. She wasn't quiet on the inside, though. The Newbie had trumped her by playing the dead mother card, bully for him. But the fight wasn't over. She'd probably died ages ago, anyway. More likely she wasn't even dead.

She turned to Skippy. "Did you get into the records room?" His nod was slow, as though his head were encased in cement. "What did you find out?" He shrugged. "Anything on Xavier?"

"His mom *is* dead," he muttered around the hand covering his mouth, the palm of which he was using to prop up his head. "She died a month ago."

"Oh," Pandora breathed, feeling a little sick. "Well. That changes things, doesn't it?" she said brightly, trying to regain some ground. "Did the report say anything about a dad?"

Skippy shook his head, rolling his chin back and forth on his hand.

"Was there anything you found that we could use against him?"

"Give it a rest, Pandora!" Birdy snapped. "You're the only one who seems to have a problem with Xavier."

"That's because he threatened me. If he hadn't, I would've been perfectly fine with him being here."

"No, you wouldn't," Lucy said in a singsong voice.

Pandora stared at her. "What do you mean?"

"You think Xavier will take us away from you."

"I do not! I'm not *that* insecure."

"No, because then you might be like us," Birdy put in. "Lucy's right. Bravo, Lucy!" She clapped and Lucy gave her a half-smile in return.

"I like you both, Pandora," Lucy said. "Xavier should be part of our family. He can be the daddy and you can be the mommy."

Pandora and Birdy both groaned at the same time. "That's sick, Lucy!" Pandora cried.

Lucy's lower lip stuck out. "It's just pretend, Pandora."

"Okay, fine," she sighed. "But let's make Birdy the mommy. She's the one who wants him so bad."

"No way!" Skippy shouted, briefly coming to life. They all jumped. "He doesn't even like Birdy. He said so."

"Yes, he does, too!" Birdy's green eyes were fiery. "You two are just jealous because I have a boyfriend and you don't have anyone." She looked pointedly at Skippy, who turned red.

"That's because we're not willing to throw ourselves after the first skeeze that comes along!" Pandora cried.

"Please be quieter," Charles pleaded, looking worried. "Someone is going to hear us."

"I'll be quiet when you two admit Xavier likes me." Birdy looked at them both defiantly.

"It's going to be a long wait, Birdy," Pandora growled. "Cause he's just using you."

Birdy pushed to her feet, straightened her long gown, then drew herself up into a regal pose. "I know when I'm not wanted. I shall acquit these premises and never return!"

"It's about time!" Pandora found herself shouting. "We didn't want you here anyway, traitor."

"Please don't fight," Charles wailed. "*Please!*"

"You're making Charles hurt inside!" Lucy shouted, shaking her doll at them. Its eyes bobbed up and down. "His heart is going to explode!"

"That's not my fault, it's Herr Dictator's here." Birdy pointed at Pandora. "When she's out of the Secret Six, I'll come back. But only then!" She spun on her heel and flounced off in righteous indignation. The posse watched her go.

"Do you think she'll come back?" Skippy asked, his voice wounded and worn.

"She always comes back," Lucy answered.

They waited for half an hour, but Birdy didn't return. Every other time she left in a snit, she was back within ten minutes, unable to stay away. This time she'd actually meant what she'd said. She had left the posse for good.

18

AFTER FINALLY GIVING up on Birdy, Pandora helped the deflated posse get safely back to their rooms. The last thing she needed was for one of them to get caught by Nurse Hunter or her p.a., who was watching a dull-sounding training video in the office on the boy's side, or the lone p.a. covering the girl's section, and more likely working on homework than paperwork.

First Pandora dropped Lucy off, then returned to the attic to escort the boys, one by one, to their rooms. The p.a. typically did a quick walk-through every half-hour, so Pandora simply had to get her timing right and have the inmates crawl to their rooms to avoid being seen.

Everything went smoothly for once and Pandora returned to her room, relieved to have that nerve-wracking task done. But as she pulled the rolled-up blanket out from under her covers and climbed into bed, she found herself growing madder and madder. How dare Birdy quit the Secret Six? And then to threaten that she wouldn't come back as long as Pandora was still in it? Pandora had *created* the Secret Six! Without her, they would be nothing. They would still be sitting around, staring at the wall, their brains slowly turning to mush like a loaf of bread left out in the rain.

Pandora had saved Birdy from the maddening boredom of being an inmate at Nepenthe Manor, and what did she get in return? Betrayal, that's what she got! She was only trying to protect her posse, only trying to do what was best for them. If Birdy would just pry open her faux-colored eyes, she would see that Xavier was a threat to her mental health. She might also notice that Pandora was trying to eliminate that threat through whatever means were available to her. She'd done *nothing* wrong!

Well, leaving copies of the photo in the photocopier was a bit of a boneheaded move. But still, she hadn't done that on purpose. She'd made a mistake. An honest mistake. Granted, she made a *lot* of honest mistakes, but didn't some genius once declare that humans grow through failure? According to that line of thinking, and supported by any good Humanistic Psychologist, Pandora was merely trying to achieve her full potential. If she happened to mess up on occasion, that was all part of the process of becoming a fully actualized adult.

Furthermore, to blame her for interrogating Xavier about that photo was futile. She had only been doing what any good leader would do. Anyway, he didn't have to be such a wuss about it, getting bent out of shape over a picture of a man he didn't even know. Sure, his dead mother had given him the photo, but still...to freak out like that? Maybe his being here at Nepenthe Manor was warranted. His reaction to her justified demand to know the truth had been entirely irrational and downright unnecessary. She wasn't being pushy; he was being secretive. He was the problem, not her. Right?

Her conscience refused to answer, leaving her hanging.

Feeling restless and out of sorts, she punched her feather pillow several times, trying to get the lumps out. The shapeless thing was ancient and stained, but she never asked for another one. She never could quite figure out why, though. The pillow was so flat it barely resembled its namesake. Lack of funds was probably the main reason for her reluctance to ask Vicki to buy another one. Vicki was so stingy with the cash, Pandora didn't even get an allowance. Any money she pried from Vicki's cold, tight fists was hard-earned, for sure. Pandora could sympathize with those kids back in the old days who worked 18-hour days in noxious factories or out in the fields picking rocks for a pittance.

She closed her eyes and imagined herself as one of those poor children, her face pinched and drawn as a dried-up potato, with a streak of oil or dirt—depending on where she toiled—marring her cheek. Cold and shaky from hunger, she'd look so wretched it would break the devil's heart. Her whole demeanor would be so sad, so pitiful, so deprived-looking—

Her eyes flew open. She'd nearly forgotten that her Coke supply was getting dangerously low. Talk about deprived—she had only one bottle left. Just the thought of it made her feel a little shaky. *Tomorrow*, she promised herself. *I'll get some more of My Precious tomorrow.* Feeling somewhat reassured, she fell asleep to the sound of rain and wind against her windows, and thankfully dreamed of nothing.

She awoke the next morning refreshed and invigorated, though her watch said it was only half past eight. She'd gotten a mere seven and a half hours of sleep. It seemed she was growing stronger, less needy of physical comfort. Yes, she needed her Coke, but sleep? Sleep was for wusses.

Climbing out of bed, she headed for the window to peer through the rain-spotted glass. Though the rain itself had stopped, the day remained wild and windy, remnants from the nor'easter still stirring up havoc. It was not the best riding weather for Shadow, but it would be good to get away from Nepenthe Manor for a while until she could figure out what to do about the Birdy/Xavier situation.

Maybe while she was in town, she could also ask around about the photo. It would help immensely if she could get her hands on it again. Xavier had probably moved the original by now, but her mother had the copies, most likely stashed in her secret hidey-hole. The woman was naïve enough to believe she could hide things from her daughter, and *keep* them hidden. Ha!

Pandora quickly brushed her hair, re-did her braids, then donned faded and ripped black jeans that she safety-pinned at the bottom—a style that Birdy envied greatly, but couldn't wear because inmates weren't allowed to have sharps—and a ripped black sweatshirt over a black lace tank top. Black Doc Martens and black eyeliner completed her ensemble. She was dressed in her best and ready to go to town.

After scarfing down a couple strawberry pop-tarts for breakfast, Pandora filled up her backpack with empty glass Coke bottles wrapped in an old sweatshirt, and headed off to her mother's office, whistling. It was Wednesday, which was weekly staff meeting day. The meeting ran from eight to ten and was held in an empty room on the first floor in the North wing. Bennington would be attending to take minutes, so the office would be locked. Which presented no problem for Pandora and her handy-dandy key ring.

Outside the office, Pandora looked around, waited thirty seconds, then looked around again. When she was sure no one was coming, she whipped out her key ring and unlocked the door. Slipping inside, she pushed the door shut and locked it again. She didn't want any unexpected visitors popping in to say hello and finding her butt sticking up in the air as she snooped around.

Her mother's desk was a mess, as usual, but Pandora didn't touch anything on it. When she was seven, she'd made the mistake of moving some things around, thinking her mother wouldn't notice, but she had. She didn't know it had been Pandora, but her rants about it for well over a week were a good warning to be more careful.

As Pandora headed for the desk, it struck her as odd that Vicki had gotten so upset about finding a strange photo in her report. Finding strange things was par for the course at Nepenthe, and typically, Vicki would just toss whatever it was into another pile and go about her business. Besides that, the amount of paperwork that went through this office was astounding and could probably fill the back of a pick-up truck every week, so why would she take special notice of this one particular photo, and not a very good one at that?

Maybe she knew the man in the picture. Bedlam *had* been written on the back of the photo. Perhaps the man actually lived in town. *That's it!* Pandora's heart quickened with excitement. This guy had something to do with her mother, and what's more, still lived in Bedlam. That would explain her mother's strange reaction.

But who was he? A secret lover? Doubtful. A spy? Possible. A long-lost brother? Well, Vicki had always claimed to be an only child. Grandmother and Grandfather Belfry had produced her in their mid-forties. But maybe there'd been another child before her—a hidden one.

The plot thickens...

Pandora grinned as she rounded the desk and pulled off her back-pack. She set it on her mother's chair before lowering herself to her hands and knees and heading straight for the secret drawer. She quickly found and removed the necessary panel, then reached up inside the space. Once she found the hidden latch, she pressed hard—it always stuck—and slid the drawer out of the desk.

Drawer in hand, she scooted back out into the light. The copies of the photo were on top, simplifying Pandora's task immensely. She grabbed one, ran to the photocopy machine, made a copy, made sure to grab the copy *and* the original this time, and hurried back to the desk.

Seeing the time on the clock in Bennington's office, Pandora realized she'd better hurry or risk getting caught. The meeting would be over in ten minutes. And even though it often ran late, there were times when Vicki was able to wind things up early.

Pandora put the photo back on top of the stack of papers inside the drawer and was about to return the box to its secret place when something stopped her. Maybe she should check out those papers. Perhaps one of them contained information that would help her solve the mystery of the strange man. It was worth a shot, anyway.

She pulled out the thick stack and shuffled through it, scanning a sentence here and there. After a couple minutes she decided there was nothing of interest to her here. She put the papers back in order and was returning the stack to the box when a pale blue envelope fell to the floor. She replaced the papers and picked up the envelope. It was addressed to her mother in handwriting that looked more like chicken scratches than English. She opened the envelope. Inside was a letter. She pulled it out and unfolded it to read...

Dearest Vick,

If you're receiving this letter, then I'm dead. Sorry to spring it on you like this, but you know me, the ultimate procrastinator! I'm sure I was even late to my own funeral. The thing is, I have cancer. You know, of course, that I also have a son. It's strange that we both have kids, seeing as we swore never to have any. But things happen, as you know, even when we don't want them to. But this was a good mistake. The very best. Xavier is by far the most wonderful thing that ever happened to me.

Must have been a brain tumor that killed her, Pandora promptly decided. First, driving her to madness, then slowly choking the life out of her. Poor, delusional lady...

I was hoping that you could look after him when I'm gone. I know this is a lot to ask as we haven't seen each other for years, but I figure you're over our fight by now. What was it about anyway? All right, I remember—perfectly well, in fact, but notice I only admitted that once I was dead?!

Anyway, my mother is too sick to be of any use watching Xavier and I'd hate to have him end up at a foster home. He lives in the home where I grew up, right next door to you and your folks, so you'll know where to find him. Don't delay, though. He's not a big fan of my mother — you know what she can be like. Soon as I'm gone, I'm sure he'll be planning his escape. I know you didn't want even one kid, not to men-

tion two, but he's a keeper. Would I lie to you? Well, not now. Dying people tell no tales.

Until we meet again...
Judy, your BFF

Pandora re-read the letter twice. So that mystery was solved. Xavier's mother knew Pandora's and had asked her to look after her son. That was why Vicki was so adamant about keeping Xavier here. Unfortunately, the letter didn't explain about the man in the photo or why Xavier had come here searching for him.

Feeling as though she was missing something, Pandora scanned the letter a third time. Not finding anything, she was about to tuck it back into its envelope when her eyes settled on something odd. Judy had called Vicki *Vick* and to Pandora's ears, Vick sounded more like a man's name than a woman's. She thought about that. Maybe Xavier had read the letter and thought Vick was the man in the photo his mother had given him. It made sense. When Pandora had called her mother by her first name, Xavier's reaction might have been surprise, not disapproval. He'd come to Bedlam looking for a Vick and got a Vicki—totally not what he was expecting. Pandora almost felt sorry for him. *Almost.*

She slid the letter back into its envelope, then glanced down at her watch. 10:02. Agh! She shoved the letter in under the photos, stuck the box back into the desk, slid the panel home, and crawled out like a crab on hot tar. She stood up, folded the copy of the photo into a square, and slid it into her back pocket. Slinging her backpack over her shoulder, she ran to the door, unlocked it, and after checking to be sure the coast was clear, tiptoed out of the room. Turning around, she locked the door, her fingers swift and sure from years of experience sneaking around.

Footsteps tapped across the lobby and she promptly dropped her key ring on the floor. Years of experience, it appeared, had yet to tame her innate clumsiness. "Son of a biddy butt!" she cursed, ducking low to pick up the key ring. Running out of time, she dropped it down her shirt, where it sat in a lump.

She stood and spun around, ready to face whoever was coming... Dr. Steele, it seemed, and he was walking fast. Her breath whooshed out of her in one big rush. Funny how that happened whenever she saw him.

"Hello, Pandora," he called when he spotted her. "Up to no good?"

She nodded. "Yes... I mean, of course not, Dr. Steele!"

He laughed. "You seem to be growing an appendage out of your stomach."

She glanced down. "Oh, that. Just a fashion statement."

The twinkle in his eyes told her he wasn't buying it, but all he said was, "Interesting statement."

"So you've had your first staff meeting," she rushed to change the subject. "Scintillating, was it?"

"Terribly. We talked about a lot of things. But you know what was on my mind for most of it?" She shook her head, barely able to hope it might be her that had occupied his thoughts. He smiled broadly. "How cool it would be to be out riding in this wild weather."

"Oh, yes," she replied, vastly disappointed. "Riding. Cool. Messy, though." She bit her lip, needing the jolt of pain to rein in her traitorous emotions. "As a matter of fact, I'm going for a ride right now. It's nice to be free to do whatever I like." She pretended sympathy. "Poor you has to work inside all day."

He fixed her with a long stare. "I was also wondering how a girl of fourteen and living in an institute keeps herself occupied all day."

He *had* been thinking about her. She promptly stifled the goofy grin fighting its way to the surface. In circumstances such as these only mischievous grins were an acceptable response. "Oh, I do this and that. Lots of homework, of course. Riding. Long talks with my mother." She gave a bitter laugh. "Okay, not that last one."

"Your mother is a very busy woman, isn't she?" He looked concerned. He looked worried. He looked like an adult who was thinking about interfering in her life. As much as she liked his attention, this had to be nipped in the butt, *stat*.

"Don't worry about me, Dr. Steele. I'm fine. Absolutely." She gave him a thumbs-up.

"Well, if you ever want to talk—"

Ha. Like she'd ever do that. Once they talked, she'd be his patient. Then she'd never have a chance with him. "Thanks, but—"

"As a friend, I mean." He looked away from her and let his blue eyes slowly wander around the foyer, as though he had all the time in the world. "I imagine it's hard for you to live here, caught in between two worlds."

Pandora took a step away from him, feeling a spurt of rebellion fire up inside her. "As I told you, Dr. Steele, I'm cool. I have to go now. I'm sure you have *patients* waiting for you, ones who really need your services. See you around…" She flipped him an impudent salute, then pushed past him and toward the outside door, pulling the other strap of her backpack onto her shoulder. She fetched her keys from under her shirt and tucked them into her sporran.

"I'm here any time you want to talk, Pandora," he called after her, but she didn't respond. She didn't know how to respond. While she wanted to believe he meant what he said, she couldn't. The last time an adult on staff had expressed an interest in helping her, she found out her mother had put the woman up to it.

Never again. "*As a friend,*" he'd said. Yeah, well, friends like that, she didn't need. Anyone who was paid by her mother could not be trusted. Still…it was a tempting offer. Alone time with Dr. Steele, his undivided attention, those stunning blue eyes aimed solely at her—it made her feel all wiggly inside just thinking about it.

She sighed and straightened her shoulders. She had to stay strong and fight his gorgeous powers of seduction…much as she didn't want to.

19

Saved by a Giant

STAYING STRONG, HOWEVER, didn't mean Pandora couldn't take a few moments to ponder over might-have-beens. While saddling up a skittish Shadow and heading for Bedlam she dissected her conversation with Dr. Steele, tweaking it ever so slightly so that she came across sounding far more witty and sophisticated than she had in reality.

"As a friend, you say?" she imagined herself responding. "Why, I don't think any woman could be just friends with you, Dr. Steele." *Lean forward, touch him on the arm, have knowing look in eyes.*

Or...

"How do I keep myself occupied? Wouldn't you like to know!" *A coquettish, sideways glance at him under her lashes, a womanly laugh to let him know just how interesting those activities were.*

And the best...

"Sounds like you want to talk more than I do, Andrew. I imagine that being a therapist can be a lonely occupation. Why don't we ride together and we can talk then? Say, this afternoon?" *A glance at her wristwatch to convey disinterest in his response either way.*

Pandora wasn't sure why, but in her fantasies, she always spoke with a British accent.

Halfway to town, she gave up her mental ruminations. Shadow was giving her a hard time, fighting each turn, shying at squawking crows, ducking her head to chew on clumps of grass. By the time Pandora pulled up behind Simon's Supermarket, the small grocery store where she bought her Coke and an occasional chocolate bar, she was ready to kick Shadow to the moon. She wrestled the ornery mare up to the back entrance and was about to dismount when someone carrying a plump garbage bag banged through the screen door.

Shadow whinnied in fright and reared back. Pandora, concentrating on getting her foot out of the stirrup and not ready for the sudden move, flew off the horse. She had just enough time to yelp before she fell heavily onto her bottle-filled backpack. A loud crunching sound met her ears, then she hit the ground like a brick. Her breath flew out of her lungs and into the air like a blast from a steam train and her back bent absurdly the wrong way.

Footsteps thudded toward her along the cobblestone street and came to a stop right by her ringing ears. Pandora lay rigid on her back, staring up at the strip of gray sky between the store rooftops, stunned and unable to breathe. The figure kneeled down and rolled her onto her side. The broken glass in her bag tinkled merrily.

"Don't fight it," a low, calm voice told her, even though all she wanted to do was scream, "Stay back, you beast!"

Large, strong hands grabbed her wrists and lifted her arms above her head. Within moments, her abdomen relaxed and she was able to breathe once more. Back to normal, she looked around, feeling panic. Where was Shadow? But the horse had not bolted, and was in fact, nuzzling the stranger's neck. He reached up and patted her on the nose. Then he stood, letting Pandora recover for another moment before offering his hand to her. She stared at him suspiciously, then grabbed hold. It was a large hand. Huge, really. Once she was on her feet, she realized just how big her savior was. He had to be at least 6'5", and two hundred fifty pounds, and all muscle, judging by his biceps, which she could see under the gray t-shirt he wore. She'd been saved by a giant.

"Thanks," she muttered as she slipped her hand quickly out of his. She grabbed Shadow's reins and tied them to a post.

"Least I could do being as I was the one who startled your horse." The words came out slowly, almost haltingly, and Pandora looked him in the face. It was *him*, she suddenly realized. The guy with the haunting eyes, the one who'd come into the bakery the other day just as she was leaving it. The guy who pitied her.

"I suppose so," she muttered, feeling like a lobster in a pot of boiling water. She yanked off her backpack and unzipped it, not wanting to look at him anymore.

She soon discovered that not one bottle had survived the fall though she supposed she should be grateful the sharp pieces hadn't ended up in her spleen. The sweatshirt, though no longer wearable, at least not without something on underneath it, which could be cool, had saved her from getting sliced and diced. "All my bottles are broken," she moaned. "I use them for a deposit."

He picked up his garbage bag and threw it into the dumpster as easily as a guard tossing a basketball into the net. "Come inside," he ordered.

She nearly told him to stuff it, but as he was holding the door open for her, she shrugged and picked up her backpack. Might as well. No sense cutting off her nose to spite her face. She needed Coke, and Coke she would get. Some way. Somehow.

Once inside the store, she headed straight for the soda section, hoping against hopes there would be a sale on today. But when she arrived in aisle three, she found there was no sale, and without her deposit money, she didn't have enough to pay for a six-pack.

She sighed and turned away from the colorful display, slamming right into the boy, who stood hulking behind her. He grabbed her arms to steady her, then quickly let go as though she'd burned his hands.

She yanked off her backpack and shook it at him. It rattled glassily. "I get five cents for each bottle, but since they're all broken, I don't have enough to pay for my six-pack. How am I going to get my Coke? I need my Coke!" A small part of her mind noted that she was starting to sound like Al the Addict. Poor Al. He treated addiction as though it were a career. If the staff broke him of one bad habit, he'd promptly find another to replace it. Right now he was into eating pancakes, which although not nearly as destructive as some of the other addictions he'd taken on, was not very good for his waistline, or the food budget. In three months, he'd gained thirty pounds. Last month, Frank had found him in the kitchen at 1:30 a.m. making himself pancakes in the shape of teddy bears. The inmates, encouraged by Lucy, were starting to call him Al the Elephant.

"Did you say five cents?" the giant asked, looking down at her. She stared up at him. "Uh, yeah. *Five cents.*" She wanted to add, "Do you have a hearing problem? Should I talk louder?" but she clamped down on the words. She had to keep her cool and find a way to get her Coke. Insulting him, as fun as that could be, wasn't going to help.

His expression scrunched up, though she couldn't figure out if that was because he was mad at her or because he was thinking. "You should get ten cents."

"What are you talking about? Where's Joe?" She tried to look around the hulk, but he really was very big, nearly filling the narrow aisle. "He's my dealer. He knows I'm good for the money."

"Joe's gone. It's me now."

"You?"

He nodded. "I'll cover the difference."

"I don't want your *pity*!"

He jerked back as though she'd taken a swing at him. "But I broke your bottles."

"*I* broke my bottles by landing on them." She peered over at the Coke display. The brown drink looked so tantalizing, like liquid gold. She could really use a drink right now. She sighed. Apparently her dignity meant little when it came to satisfying her avaricious need for caffeine. "Fine. I'll pay you back next week. But what's this about ten cents?"

"You get ten cents a bottle for deposit."

"When did that start?"

He blinked slowly, like a cow. "It's been that way for ages."

Pandora's grip on her bag loosened and it hit the floor with a crash. "Are you saying Joe was cheating me? But we've known each other for years. I thought we were buds!" She couldn't believe he'd betrayed her. She had trusted him about as much as she could trust a person, which, admittedly, wasn't much. But it was *some*thing!

Taking a deep breath filled with resolve, Pandora decided she would learn from this experience. Joe's lie, along with Birdy's recent betrayal, would both serve as reminders of how treacherous the human race, and that included the captivating Dr. Steele, could be.

The giant reached down and picked up her bag. "You fetch your soda. I'll be back."

She could only watch helplessly as he ambled down the aisle, turned right, and disappeared. What was he going to do? Should she run after him, demand he return her bag? She could tackle him. *Yeah, right.* Maybe if she were riding a rhino at the time.

Having no other recourse, she grabbed a six-pack of Coke, which looked so delightfully jaunty in its red cardboard case, and headed for the cash register. She plopped the case on the wood counter, covered with scratches and doodles made by bored workers, and the bottles clinked lightly. Joe had made a few of those doodles while they were shooting the breeze, acting as though they were the best of friends. *That dirty, cheating liar!* Boy, if she ever saw him again, she'd be sure to scar his psyche for good. She counted mental torture as one of her most practiced—and enjoyed—skills, and was always looking for a good opportunity to put it to use.

Her attention wandered as she waited, and she found herself staring out the storefront window at Main Street. Cars passed slowly, an occasional person drifted by—a mother with a stroller that had a wobbly wheel, an old woman with a flowered scarf tied under her chin, the mailman, already wearing his gray shorts, delivering mail—nothing too exciting.

Then she spotted Dougie Daft. Just the sight of him made her skin crawl. She watched him slinking along the sidewalk on the other side of the street, all alone, hands in his pockets, eyes scanning the area like a psychotic robot. He looked his usual preppy self—clean-cut and perfectly attired. She felt an urge to run outside and push him into a mud puddle.

"Here's your bag."

Pandora turned her head, startled. For being so big, the giant certainly was a quiet one. He seemed to enjoy sneaking up on her. She took the bag from him, realizing it didn't jingle like it had before.

"You took out the glass."

He nodded. "Vacuumed up the inside, too."

She noticed one of his fingers was bleeding. She pointed. "You cut yourself."

He glanced down. "Hm." Then he looked back at her. "I saw you the other day. At the Chowder Shack."

"Did you? Can't say I remember you. Do you go there often?"

"When I can."

His mention of the Chowder Shack gave Pandora an idea. She reached into her back pocket and pulled out the photocopied photo of the strange man. She unfolded the paper and smoothed it on the counter. "Have you ever seen this person?"

He picked up the piece of paper with the hand that wasn't bleeding and studied it closely. "Can't say that I have. Your pa?" His dove gray eyes turned soft with pity, and Pandora felt her insides twist. That horrid, insipid emotion! She had a mind to take that pity of his and shove it down his throat.

Instead she took the high road; he *was* being somewhat nice to her. "My pa!" She laughed lightly to show how little such a preposterous question affected her. "What makes you say that?"

"Just figured, is all," he said, keeping his eyes on her the whole time. He was relentless with those eyes, but at least the pity in them was gone. The intensity of his gaze disturbed Pandora, but not in a Dougie Daft creepy sort of way, but in a "I can see into your soul" sort of way. She wasn't sure she wanted anyone seeing into her soul.

"Well, I'm not looking for *me*," she said, "I'm looking for a friend."

He gave the photo further study. "Then maybe he's your friend's pa."

"I don't think so—" She stopped suddenly. *Oh, duh.* Why hadn't she seen it before? Xavier thought the man in the photo was his father and had come looking for him. His mother had warned Vicki that he wouldn't stay long with his grandmother. But neither would he want to end up on the streets or a ward of the state. So what was his alternative, other than finding his dad? Pandora found it a little strange, though, that Judy, his mother, never told Xavier that the man in the photo was his father. Perhaps she'd meant to say something, but had put it off too long. Pandora snorted. Judy hadn't been kidding when she'd called herself the ultimate procrastinator.

Well, at least he still had a father. Pandora's own father was dead—killed in a car accident before she was born. If Vicki ever kicked the bucket, Pandora would be an orphan. She'd probably have to go live with the senior Belfrys, which would be worse than having to eat rotting goat cheese. A small part of Pandora envied Xavier his father.

What baffled her was why the boy didn't try to escape from the manor so he could continue his search. She'd found a way out, surely he could. Of course, she had had fourteen years to discover Nepenthe's secrets. But still…if he really wanted to get out, he'd find a way. Could it be that he didn't want to leave? She mentally shook her head. No way. That would be crazy. If she had the money, she'd leave Nepenthe Manor behind so fast she'd make everyone's heads spin. Which might be what was holding him back. No money. Too bad she wasn't rich. She'd give him the money for a bus ticket home and a few extra bucks for a decent haircut.

Out of the corner of her eye, she spotted Dougie crossing the street. He appeared to be heading for the store. "I've gotta get going," she said quickly, pulling her pocket inside out and dumping a crumpled bill and odd change on the counter. "This might be enough. If I owe you, keep track and I'll pay the rest next time."

"You don't owe me anything," he said, his gray eyes fixed firmly on hers.

"Oh, yes, well…thanks." She quickly shoved the six-pack and photo into her bag and zipped it shut. Dangit, she wished he'd stop looking at her. She had to regain the upper hand, get him to stop pitying her, staring at her, making her feel all weird inside. "One last thing…" She pointed a finger at him. "Next time you come banging out that door, just be sure there aren't any horses in the vicinity first. Got it?" He nodded, eyes never once wavering from her face. "Okay, good." She slapped the counter heartily. "Well, I'm outta here."

Pandora didn't wait for his reply, which was taking its time in coming. Dougie was nearly at the door. She had to escape before he saw her. She was pretty sure that the question he'd been about to ask her the other day was not one she wanted to hear. Or answer.

And anyway, she had to get away from the giant and his eyes. She had a feeling, though, that hard as she rode, they would follow her home as relentlessly as an angel searching for someone to save.

Make Some Mischief

20

ON THE RIDE home, Pandora's mind spun like an overheated engine—hot, sputtering, and heading nowhere fast. Apparently, Xavier had come to Bedlam looking for his father. But through a weird twist of fate, he'd ended up at Nepenthe Manor. Even stranger was the fact that he would have ended up at the old place anyway when Vicki took over his care.

Pandora had no doubt her mother would have followed through on her friend Judy's dying wish. Vicki had a nagging social conscience that would have made most people stick forks in their eyes. Whenever she had free time, she'd drive to the state hospital an hour away and scour the halls, searching for inmates to bring back to Nepenthe to live. She was always trying to save somebody. Pandora bet that after seeing that photo of Xavier's, Vicki must have figured out that he was looking for his dad so he could live with him and that's why she got mad at Pandora for interfering. Protecting the vulnerable was Vicki's own personal crusade; a regular Mother Teresa, she was. And to her, Xavier was at his most vulnerable. What she didn't seem to get was that Pandora was only trying to do the same thing—save others. Vicki never seemed to get it, though. Worse, nor did she ever seem to think that Pandora herself might need saving.

Pandora prodded at Shadow's flanks with her heels. The horse's reaching teeth were attempting to nibble at a shock of dead grass. "Knock it off, lazy bones! I want to at least make it home before the sun sets." Shadow, knowing quite well it wasn't even lunch yet, skittered to the left and back to the right, fighting the good fight to eat grass whenever and wherever she pleased.

Pandora jerked on the reins and spun the wicked horse about. She scolded and threatened. She whispered entreaties. She bellowed curses. At last Shadow settled into a reluctant trot that made the bottles in Pandora's backpack clink furiously. She could only hope the glass survived the rest of the ride without breaking and that the tops wouldn't pop off from being jostled about so much.

After a few more tussles along the way, they arrived at the stable, alive and with bottles intact. Pandora pulled off her backpack and hung it up on a nail to protect its precious, though volatile, contents. She then set about wiping down Shadow, and to thinking some more on what she'd learned about Newbie's dad, the elusive Mr. Carlisle.

If Xavier thought his father lived in Bedlam, then where was he now? Did he still live in town? If so, one would think the giant would have seen him about—he had enough height on him to scope out several miles, at least. Though, to give Giganticus credit, the photo wasn't a very good one. Its worn condition and bland color quality indicated that some time had passed since it had been taken, meaning the man was probably a fair bit older today than when the picture was snapped. He might not even look the same now. Old people had a way of losing identifying facial features, and hair, at an alarming rate.

Pandora snorted mirthfully as a thought occurred to her. Maybe Mrs. H.'s husband was Xavier's father. According to Mrs. H., who always seemed oblivious to what she was implying, the mister liked looking at a bit of fluff now and again. Perhaps, back in the day, he'd done a bit of touching the fluff, as well. Which, while an intriguing and somewhat repulsive subject, was best reserved for further contemplation another time.

Finished with grooming Shadow, who was now happily fed and covered with her red wool horse blanket, Pandora grabbed her backpack and emerged into the wild day, eyes on her Doc Martens as she crossed the damp lawn, pondering her next move. Overhead, gray clouds raced each other across the sky like hounds after a fox, but she didn't notice them, nor did she hear the wind whistling and charging around the buildings like a mad horse. She also didn't see the figure watching her from a window of the manor. She was aware of nothing but her inner turmoil.

After last night's debacle in the attic, Pandora felt she had to do something to get the posse's approval ratings of their leader back up, something drastic, if necessary. Not that what had happened was Pandora's fault, but Birdy's leaving was a big loss to the others. She had to do something to make up for that loss. It was also obvious they hadn't liked how Pandora had handled the whole Xavier and his dead mother revelation. She could have been more sensitive, she supposed, but how was she to know he was going to be such a crybaby? And why was Pandora always expected to be the adult around here? Her dad was dead and her mother a dictator, but did anyone see her crying? No way. Never. Not in a million and one years.

Her shoulders lifted in a sigh, then dropped low. Life at the top was lonely. Unfortunately, so few people reached the top that they could never truly empathize with what it was like.

That being the case, it looked as though Pandora once again would not gain the sympathy and understanding she deserved. But she'd make things right, anyway. She would find Xavier's dad, and she would bask in the glory of reuniting the two Carlisles. The posse would proclaim her a hero, her conscience would be assuaged, her mother would be forever grateful, and Dr. Steele would do...well, she'd have to think long and hard about what he would do. The possibilities seemed both deliciously endless and endlessly delicious. Really, Dr. Steele was just too beguiling for his own good.

Filled with purpose now, Pandora ran up to her room to deposit her Coke stash in her closet. She cleaned up from her horse ride, rebraiding her hair and changing into dry shoes. After touching up her make-up and checking her reflection in the mirror to be sure she looked suitably unearthly, she headed downstairs, two steps at a time, singing the little song she'd made up for whenever she was on a mission...

"Bugger off and cheerio. What, what, and tallyho! Here I come, and there you gooo... I'm off to make some mischief!"

"*There* you are."

Pandora froze on the bottom step, eyes darting back and forth, wondering if she could still escape her mother who was stalking toward her at an incredible rate.

"We need to talk."

That didn't sound good. "Now?"

Vicki gave her daughter her patented "don't be fresh" look. "No, next week." She motioned to Pandora. "Come on. We can talk in my office."

Escape was out. Pandora slowly trailed after her mother, noting that she was wearing the snazzy blue dress and matching high heels she ordinarily reserved for inspections and Visitor's Day, neither of which were happening today. After a few more steps, Pandora realized Vicki was wearing perfume, too—a light, floral scent that wafted in the air currents swirling in her wake. Pandora promptly decided she didn't like it.

"Are we having visitors?" she asked as she took a chair.

Vicki walked around the desk and sat down with a frown. The chair joints squeaked. "Why would you think that?"

"That fancy dress you're wearing. The heels. The perfume. Got a date?"

"A date?" Vicki pushed out a loud laugh that left her breathless. "Me?" She busied herself with the papers on her desk, shuffling them around like a deck of cards.

"Don't tell me you've changed your mind about Mayor Daft!" Startled, her mother glanced up and Pandora winked at her. She was purposely pushing a few buttons now.

"For heaven's sake, I'm just wearing a dress, Pandy!"

"But on a Wednesday? You never wear a dress like that on Staff Meeting Wednesday. Just seems odd, is all."

"Now don't you start analyzing me, Pandora Belfry," her mother wagged her finger at her. "Goodness, if this is what you're going to be like as a teenager, I shudder to think what's coming."

Pandora scowled. "I've been a teenager for over two years now."

Her mother shook her head and leaned forward on her elbows, two fingers massaging her temples. "I want to talk to you about Xavier."

That explained why she'd firmly closed the door behind them. There was a finality to the action that reminded Pandora of the last closing of a coffin lid. "So we can go out, then?"

"What? No! I mean…" She pulled in a deep breath, straight from the gut as Dr. Borger, the Behaviorist, had taught everyone during a lecture on *Controlling Your Anxiety Before it Controls You.* "Listen, Pandy. We have to talk about Xavier and the ways in which we must act around him."

"Okaaay…"

"Now I've asked you to stay away from him while he's here. But then you said you thought it would be okay to, um, hang out with him, once he's no longer an inmate. That's just not acceptable."

"What do you mean? Are you saying we can't be friends?"

Vicki gave an exasperated sigh. "Oh, come on, Pandy. I don't know why you have to be so stubborn about this. Just do as I say for once." She picked up her pen and tapped it twice on a pile of papers. "Oh, and about that photo I mentioned earlier… I figured out whose it is so you don't need to worry about it anymore."

Pandora straightened. "So you know who the guy in the photo is? What's his name?"

The pen slapped the paper like a whip. "So you *did* take it!"

Too late Pandora realized her mistake. "Uhhh…I saw the photo while I was making copies," she explained, while still telling the truth. "I didn't want to say anything about it…for confidentiality's sake."

"How good of you." Her mother's tone was dry as a desert.

"I do my best, Vicki. You see, I have a theory about that man in the photo."

Vicki fixed her with a dark stare. "Okay, I give. Let's hear it."

"I think he's Xavier's father."

To give Vicki credit, she didn't flinch too badly. "And why would you think that man had anything to do with Xavier?"

"Well, they sort of look alike, don't they?" Pandora was really reaching with that one, especially as it was impossible to tell from the bad photo, but she couldn't share the real reason how she'd figured out the connection. That wouldn't be prudent.

Vicki didn't say anything for several long seconds, just stared at Pandora like a hypnotist. Then, as though coming to a conclusion, she leaned forward on her elbows and gave Pandora her most serious look. "I need you to listen to me, Pandy." Her voice was deceptively soft and light. "We must do everything we can to help the people in our care here at Nepenthe Manor. They rely on us to look after their welfare and to do right by them. Xavier is vulnerable right now. The best thing you can do for him is to let sleeping dogs lie. I can't tell you any more than that. All I can ask is that you trust me."

Over the years Pandora had learned that whenever Vicki used this tone it was more important to listen to what she wasn't saying as opposed to what she was. The hidden message behind the words meant more than a bunch of blather, especially when her mother added, 'trust me' at the end of her little statements.

"So what should I do?"

"Just let me handle everything," Vicki said smoothly, the muscles in her face slowly relaxing. "Remember, this is for the best."

Pandora stood up. "Okay, sure. Whatever you say."

"I knew I could count on you, Pandy."

Pandora headed for the office door. "Say, *Vick*..." She turned in time to see the pleased smile that had been growing on her mother's face curdle like rancid milk.

"What did you just call me?"

"I called you Vick..." Pandora paused. "Hey, I thought you were okay with me calling you by your first name."

Her mother's mouth twisted. "I wouldn't say okay. I've adjusted. But...but why did you call me *Vick*?"

"It's just something I'm trying out, that's all. Shortening everyone's names. It's kind of the trend right now, you know."

"No, I didn't know," her mother said faintly, looking vaguely ill.

"So you don't mind?"

"Let's keep it Vicki, please. I'm too old to answer to anything else."

"Okay. No biggie."

Her mother's expression, while no longer pleased, cleared. She reached for the phone. "I have to make some calls now. Why don't you go do some homework, hm?" Already the conversation was fading from her mind as she dialed three numbers, the spinning wheel making its comforting whirring sound.

"Nurse Rackett, please..."

Pandora watched her mother's face for a few moments, then slowly closed the door behind her.

Homework, indeed. She had no intention of conjugating verbs when she had more important things to do. Her posse needed her and so did Xavier. Granted, he didn't want her help. But the one thing Pandora had never been good at doing was letting sleeping dogs lie. If you let them lie too long, they die. And what good would that do?

Absolutely none.

Right, *Vick*?

21

Perhaps a Purgative

PANDORA HADN'T MADE it far when she was waylaid by Charles, Lucy, and Sinclair. Lucy did the actual waylaying, racing across the foyer and wrapping her arms around Pandora's torso. "Skippy's dying!" she moaned, hanging on for dear life. Pandora, feeling as though a boa constrictor was crushing the life out of her, worked to loosen Lucy's grip.

"What's she talking about?" she asked Charles when she could breathe a little better.

Hands clasped together, wearing an expression similar to a prisoner heading to the chopping block, Charles told her, "Skippy won't get out of bed. He's been there all morning. He won't even talk or tell me what's the matter. They're gonna do a lobotomy on him if we don't help him, Pandora!"

Lucy let go of Pandora to pantomime sticking an ice pick up her nose. She pulled the invisible object back and forth like a warrior performing hari-kari. Her performance was eerily realistic, but then, she'd learned from the best.

"Well done, Lucy." The girl grinned happily, then proceeded to dance on her tiptoes. "But they don't do lobotomies here anymore," Pandora explained...not for the first time. The inmates lived in constant fear of being fried (getting electro-shock therapy) or sliced (lobotomy) and never quite believed Pandora when she told them that such procedures were no longer practiced at Nepenthe Manor, and that Vicki would rather get fried or sliced herself than subject one of her own to something so awful.

"They c-c-could always start doing them again," Charles said, stuttering slightly. "All the stuff is still there."

"True, but nothing works properly and the tools and machines are all rusty." Pandora was lying, of course, but she was doing it for the greater good. In this particular case, the truth would not set her friends free; it would only set them off. They had enough to worry about in the challenging life they'd been forced to live. They didn't need to add the threat of torture to the list. "So what's this about Skippy?"

"He says he wants to kill himself," Charles replied mournfully.

"His heart hurts cause he betrayed Xavier," Lucy added her two cents.

Sinclair shook his red head as though he didn't agree, whether with Lucy's assessment of the situation or Skippy's wasn't clear, but he didn't say anything one way or the other.

"Does Nurse Rackett know about any of this?"

"She's going to do her morning rounds soon. She'll find out then."

"Didn't anyone realize he didn't eat breakfast?"

"I told everyone he had a tummy ache," Charles answered. "I wasn't lying, Pandora. He looks like he has a tummy ache. He just lies on his bed and holds his stomach and groans."

"It annoys my ears," Lucy complained. Sinclair nodded, agreeing this time.

"I'll go talk to him. He should come round soon enough." At least that's what Pandora hoped. Skippy's moods typically came and went quickly. But sometimes he'd be stuck at one extreme for days. Last year he was in a manic phase that lasted three days. During that trying time, at least one member of the posse, and usually two, followed him around and made sure he didn't steal a car and drive to Mexico, call England and demand to speak to the Prime Minister about the whole Republic of Ireland situation, start work on inventing a time machine, which could also travel through space, or put into practice a myriad of other outlandish ideas. It had been an exhausting 72 hours.

The posse headed upstairs with Charles leading the way like a general. He and Sinclair walked down to Skippy's room and opened the door. When the coast was clear, Charles gave the girls the signal—a convoluted gesture made up by Skippy requiring several unnecessary moves when one would suffice. Lucy and Pandora were already halfway to Charles by the time he finished.

The room when they slipped inside was dark and smelled of dirty socks. Skippy was lying in bed, entirely covered by a dark gray, wool blanket. He looked like Jabba the Hut. Pandora went over and sat on the edge of his bed. "Skippy?" she whispered. "Are you awake?"

His only response was to groan and writhe about like Jabba in the sun.

"I'll take that as a yes. So I hear you're blaming yourself for Xavier's hissy fit." No response, but the writhing stopped. "Listen...you did nothing wrong. I asked you to do something, and as a good soldier, you carried out my orders."

"He's not responding," Charles noted.

"I see that. Skippy, we have a problem here. You did something, someone got mad at you, and now you feel bad. I'm sorry about that. But now Nurse Rackett is going to change your meds and you know what that does to you. Turns you into a brain-eating zombie."

"I deserve it," came the muffled reply.

Pandora felt heartened. "That's stupid, Skippy. If anyone deserves punishment, it's me."

"I was mad and wanted to get back at him. It's all my fault." His voice quivered.

"And I wasn't mad? What I did was worse, though. I went after him when he was down. That's not cool, is it?" She turned to the others and motioned for them to speak up.

"Not cool, Pandora!" Lucy scolded.

"You might have done things differently," Charles conceded.

"You acted like a bully," Sinclair added from his lookout post at the door. Pandora glared at him, but he didn't notice as he went back to watching while repeating his damning statement over and over in a whisper.

"Okay," she sighed, "maybe I did bully him a bit. But didn't Machiavelli say that the end justifies the means?"

"Machi Velli is mean!" Lucy shouted. "And that means his end isn't justified."

"Yes, well, nobody's perfect," Pandora replied sourly. "Not even you, Lucy. You *are* the one who started calling Al an elephant."

Lucy giggled. "That's not mean, that's funny stuff."

"Why don't I ask Al if he thinks it's funny?"

Lucy scowled. "I'm not trying to be mean, Pandora the Bore-ah."

"Well, neither was I and neither was Skippy."

"*I* was trying to be mean," Skippy mumbled unhappily. "I wanted to hurt Xavier, and I did."

"Okay, fine. So did I. He has a way of bringing out the worst in me. But now we can make up for our trespasses. We can come clean. We can regain our Karmic balance."

"What do you mean?"

Sinclair's arm started rising up and down in quick chopping motions. It took Pandora a few precious seconds to figure out what he was doing. Then it dawned on her. "Someone's coming! Quick. Under the beds!" Sinclair ignored Pandora's order and headed for the closet instead. Charles dove under Skippy's bed and Pandora grabbed Lucy and slid under Charles's bed. There were dust bunnies galore and one of

Lucy's pom-pom ponytails tickled Pandora's nose as she wiggled about. Pandora was going to sneeze.

The door opened and a pair of practical white nursing shoes and solid ankles encased in white nylons entered the room. "What's this I hear about a tummy ache, Mr. Stone?"

Pandora held her breath as she waited for Skippy's response. She also hoped to stave off the sneeze tingling in her nose. He didn't make a sound.

"Mr. Stone? Are you physically ill or is this one of your episodes? I really thought we had your dosage at the correct level."

Still, Skippy said nothing.

Pandora slowly lifted her hand and pressed upward on the bony part between her nostrils. "Come on, Skippy," she whispered softly. "Tell her what she needs to hear and make her go away." Lucy's hand suddenly darted out and grabbed something lying on the floor. Pandora couldn't see what it was before Lucy slipped it into her pocket. "Stay still," she whispered. Lucy froze.

"Mr. Stone?"

"What? Huh?" *Yes, he was responding!*

"Do you have a stomachache?"

"Um, I did. But it seems to be gone now."

Lucy wiggled with delight at the news that Skippy was feeling better. Pandora put her hand on Lucy's shoulder and she stopped, but now she wanted to sneeze again.

"Well, that's good news." Nurse Rackett sounded disappointed with his report. "I'll give you a laxative, though. That should move things along." Pandora, in addition to having to sneeze, now felt a wild urge to giggle. "Stay here. I'll need to request the proper medication from Nurse Devine, though don't worry, she should have plenty of laxatives on hand. I'll be right back."

"I'm not sure I need one of those, Nurse Rackett!" Skippy cried.

She left the room without responding. As soon as the door shut, Pandora sneezed twice, hard. Lucy howled, being that it was her hair catching the spit. The door swung open.

"Bless you, Mr. Stone. You must be coming down with a virus!" Rackett sounded downright cheery at the prospect.

He sniffed. "Just allergies, Nurse Rackett."

"Your voice sounded funny when you sneezed. Perhaps a purgative would be in order. A thorough cleansing should solve all your problems."

"No need for that!" Skippy's feet hit the floor like a ton of bricks. "In fact, I have to go to the bathroom right now. Thanks, anyway." His feet scurried out of the room like giant rats fleeing from a sinking ship.

"Humph!" Nurse Rackett snorted. "Well, then be sure you head down to lunch afterward and get a proper meal in you." She snorted again, then closed the door.

"Gross!" Lucy cried, though she waited a few seconds to do so. "Your snot is in my hair!"

"Sorry, Lucy," Pandora apologized. "But these are hard times. We must all make sacrifices."

"I need to wash my hair right *now*. You got your boogies in it."

"You can do that later. We're in a crisis at the moment."

"Now!" she insisted.

"Fine. But wait until Skippy gets back."

A few minutes later, Skippy returned and everyone emerged from their hiding places, wiping off dust bunnies and, in Lucy's case, snot. Sinclair, the smart one, returned to his post at the door, pristine as ever.

"Everything come out all right?" Pandora couldn't resist asking.

Skippy plopped down on the bed. "Very funny."

"So are you recovered from your mood?"

"I don't know. I don't feel like I am."

"You should feel better, you know. What you did—taking that photo—may end up helping Xavier."

He glanced up at her. "How?"

"Because now we can find his dad."

"His dad?" The posse all looked at her. "What are you talking about?"

"I figured it all out," she said matter-of-factly. "Xavier came to Bedlam to look for the man in the photo, who I'm guessing is his dad." She left out the part about his mother and her mother being friends. No need to impart too much information.

"So?" Skippy was determined to be difficult.

"So if we find his dad for him, he won't be mad at us anymore and all will be forgiven."

"How are we going to do that?" He still sounded unreasonably sulky. "We can't get into Bedlam."

"No, but some of the people who work here get around. We can show them the picture, see if they recognize the man."

He sighed. "I don't know."

"We'll be heroes." She paused, reluctant to add this next part. "Birdy *loves* heroes. I suppose she'll want to give you a hug, or something." That last bit was not easy to get out, but she did it. Talk about people making sacrifices. Pandora wasn't sure the remaining shreds of her dignity could take much more.

"I thought you and Birdy were fighting."

"We are. I didn't say she'd want to hug *me*."

"No, I suppose not."

"So are you with me?"

"I guess."

"Can you contain your enthusiasm, though? At this rate, you're going to bust a gut."

"Let's just do this." He pushed himself off the bed, looking more like an old man than a sixteen-year-old boy.

"Are you guys coming?" Pandora asked the others.

Lucy tilted her head to one side. "I suppose I can wait to wash my hair."

Pandora looked it over. "You can't even tell I used it as a Kleenex."

"I'll come," Charles volunteered. "You're going to need someone to watch your back. But I'd better put on my cape first. Just in case I need to fly. One never knows," he said, half to himself as he hustled over to his bed and picked up a red cape he'd left in a heap at the end of it.

"Sinclair?"

He looked back at her and blinked twice.

That meant yes.

Operation "Find Newbie's Father" was on.

Skinned Alive

22

BEFORE EMBARKING ON their mission, the posse agreed to eat lunch first. Proper sustenance, Pandora had learned from experience, was a necessary component to success. A hungry posse was a cranky posse. And cranky posses couldn't be relied on to do anything more than whine about hunger pains, dizzy spells, and the compulsion to resort to cannibalism.

While Birdy was the worst offender in these instances, Lucy could be trying, as well, sometimes making bomb threats and always kicking at shins. Charles would suffer in silence, though his trembling hands and inability to concentrate made him practically useless. Sinclair didn't need the food so much as he needed the consistent schedule. He typically resorted to tapping things in sixes, twelves, or twenty-fours when the time to eat was fast approaching and in danger of being passed. Skippy and Pandora managed better without food, but having to keep everyone in line while trying to carry out a mission just wasn't practical. It was simply better to eat first and only act once all bellies were suitably full, even though one had to exercise great restraint in doing so.

Sitting at their table, steaming lunch piles in front of them, Pandora leaned forward over her chicken potpie (which Lucy had promptly renamed chicken snot die, probably because it smelled more like chicken coop than chicken). The others copied her movement, looking terribly serious, except Lucy who was picking her nose.

"All right, guys," Pandora said in a low voice, "the key to our success is to maintain a low profile. We don't want to arouse suspicions, got it? You know how the staff like to gossip. We can't have Xavier finding out what we're up to until we're ready to present him with his fait accompli."

"I don't want to kill anyone!" Charles cried, growing purple.

"We're not killing anyone," she rushed to assure him. "It just means we're going to present him with his dad."

"Oh." He sat back and his skin de-purpled slightly.

"But what if we don't find him?" Skippy mourned. His right hand supported his chin while his left hand desultorily poked a spoon into the mottled piecrust.

"Then we figure out something else to do," Pandora soothed. "Don't worry. I've got it covered." She didn't have it covered. Not at the moment, anyway. But she would. She always managed something. That's why she was the leader of the Secret Six. That's why someday her name would be on the lips of millions, maybe she'd even end up in history books. Ah, yes...power could be so seductive.

"What if someone starts asking questions when we're showing them the picture?" Charles worried. "I don't like questions. And you know what happens to Lucy..."

Pandora nodded. If someone pushed Charles too hard, he started crying. Then he'd pass out because the crying made him dizzy and his heart just couldn't handle that kind of stress. Lucy always cracked under pressure. And it didn't take much of it. All someone had to ask was, "Why do you want to know?" and she'd spill everything in convulsive fits and spurts, like a cat coughing up a hairball.

"No biggie," Pandora replied breezily. "I'll ask the questions and you guys just sort of hang out in the vicinity and watch. If the person looks nervous or guilty, make a note of it. I might have to put the squeeze on them later." And by squeeze, she meant torture.

Sinclair looked relieved. He was good at watching. Those rust-colored eyes of his took in everything around him. Though perhaps that's why he was always so anxious—he noticed things most people never did...hidden anger, flashes of contempt, crushing disappointment. He saw below the nice mask most people wore in public and what he witnessed frightened him. Maybe if he missed more, lived like most people did, sightless and clueless as only humans can be, he wouldn't be such a mess inside.

"I can be your bodyguard!" Charles piped up. "I'll stay out of sight. Wouldn't want to scare anyone off. But I'll be ready to spring into action in case someone gets a bit rough with you, Pandora. You know how people can be, unpredictable, ruthless, dangerous..." He trailed off, his eyes growing dreamy as he imagined the scenario—the one where he flies to the rescue, beats up the bad guy, and saves the day; where he's strong and sure and best of all, immortal.

Pandora gave him a salute. "Good idea, soldier. Lucy will accompany you. Skippy, I want you to keep an eye on the perimeter. Alert me to anyone else coming along. I don't want to get caught with that photo by the wrong person. If Vicki finds out I have her precious Xavier's picture she'll skin me alive."

After agreeing on their various roles, they spent the rest of lunch pondering what someone would look like skinned alive. "A bit like those hairless dogs, I suppose," Skippy offered around a mouthful of chicken.

"I once saw a skinned squirrel," Pandora said in a low voice. "At the old Humphrey place." The old Humphrey place was a run-down mansion perched on a cliff overlooking the ocean. It sat just to the north of Nepenthe Manor, and was bordered by Bedlam on the other side. The man who lived there, a Mr. Choken, was rumored to be even crazier than most of the inmates at the manor. Last summer, bored and poking around, Pandora had come across the remains of six squirrels, sticks run through their bodies like hot dogs ready to be roasted over a fire, only with arms and legs. She was tempted to take one of the cadavers and study it, but she didn't quite dare. If she got caught and Vicki found out she'd gone outside the fence, she'd lose her freedom. The mental picture of those squirrels stayed with her, though—wet and red, gleaming, rounded muscles. Hands, feet, and entrails all missing. Head, too. Just meat and bones.

Charles, Sinclair, and Skippy didn't eat much after Pandora described what she'd seen. Lucy, on the other hand, was not in the least affected. Talking around a mouthful of crust, she said she hoped to draw a picture of the skinned squirrels for her art class this afternoon, and if there was time, color it with her new scented markers.

Only Pandora and Lucy's plates were empty as they went to dump their trays. After that, the posse left the cafeteria and headed for the foyer, talking excitedly. When they arrived, Pandora checked her watch. "We only have half an hour before your art class starts, which means we won't have much time to gather information. But we'll do the best we can." She scanned the area and spotted Frank, the security guard, loping down the hallway toward them. "Quick! Take your positions!" Positions ranged from Charles and Lucy ducking behind the heavy, red velvet curtains that hung from several of the main windows lining the foyer, to Sinclair leaning up against the wall near a giant, potted fern and standing perfectly still, to Skippy running up the spiral staircase to hide around its bend.

Pandora shook her head. The only one of any real help—Skippy— was now in the worst position possible. Sometimes that boy did not think things through. Ah, well, once again, she was on her own in a precarious situation. She felt a jolt of exhilaration shoot up from the depths of her stomach into her chest. Sometimes one had to take a walk on the wild side to enjoy life.

She stifled a giddy grin and hurried toward Frank. "Mr. Steen?"

His big, slick-haired head turned toward her and his eyes, hooded and dark, quickly found her. "Don't make Frank get behind on his schedule, Miss Belfry," he warned. "Frank don't like that."

"Wouldn't dream of it, Mr. Steen. I've got too much respect for your job to do something like that." He nodded in agreement. She whipped out the photo, running to keep up with him as he continued walking. She quickly unfolded the square of paper and stuck it in front of him. "Have you ever seen this man?"

Frank stopped suddenly. "He threatening you, Miss Belfry?"

"Well, no. But I thought maybe you might have seen him around. You see everything, Mr. Steen, don't you?"

He nodded again, his heavy brow furrowed. He took the photocopy from her and studied it, his thick thumb rubbing up and down on the smooth paper. "Nope." He handed it back. "Frank ain't never seen him."

"Not even in town?"

"Frank don't like the town. Too many folk gadding about. Too loud. Smelly, too." He rubbed his nose. "Frank's got to be going now."

"Okay, thanks, Mr. Steen," she called after him as he headed off down another hallway. She heard Skippy's sneakers thudding down the stairs to join her, but they suddenly stopped, then retreated just as quickly. "Hey, Skip—" she called, then stopped when she heard a loud, angry voice behind her.

"What did you just show that guy?"

Pandora froze. It was Xavier, and he sounded mad. She wondered if she could eat the entire piece of paper before he reached her, and decided probably not. Dang.

"It's that photo of yours, Xavier!" Birdy yelled excitedly.

Birdy? Damn her! Pandora swung around. "No, it's not!" *It's a copy of it*, she finished in her head.

"Well, it's a copy of it," Birdy said snidely. Arm in arm with Xavier, she stalked toward Pandora like a police officer intent on making an arrest.

"Give that to me!" Xavier yelled, pulling away from Birdy and rushing toward Pandora.

Pandora whipped the paper around her back. "It's not what you think."

"You have no right!" he shouted, his face red, spit flying. "I've been watching you. I knew you were up to something!"

Pandora stood her ground as best she could as she tried to keep the photo out of his reach. "I'm trying to help you!"

She spun away from him as he lunged for the photo. His shoulder slammed into hers like a linebacker, knocking her to the ground. "I don't need any help from you!" he bellowed and jumped on top of her. Before she could move, his hands fastened on her wrists and tightened painfully. "Where is it?"

The paper had dropped to the ground when Pandora had fallen and now she was lying on it. She scooted her butt this way and that to stay on top of it as he wrestled with her.

"It's underneath her!" Birdy shrieked, pointing.

"Ratfink!" Pandora yelled.

Birdy clapped her hand to her chest. "Did you hear that, Xavier? She called me a ratfink. Do something!"

"I want that picture," he growled, trying to flip Pandora over. She held her position, but she wouldn't last long. She might be wily and quick as a fox, but he was stronger. And those months of inactivity were starting to tell on her.

"If you'd just let me up," she panted. "I'd explain."

"Get off Pandora!" Lucy yelled from behind Xavier. Charles was next to her, hopping anxiously from foot to foot. She smacked Xavier on the head with the flat of her hand. "You're smushing her!"

"I am not," he shouted back. "Don't hit me." She hit him again and he let go of Pandora's wrist to defend himself. It was the moment she'd been waiting for—the moment to try out an awesome new move she'd seen in a wrestling match on TV. She slammed her knee into his back and he went flying forward. His hand, still swatting at Lucy, wasn't able to retreat in time to catch himself. Off-balance and falling fast, Pandora pushed him off her with her freed hands, rolled over like a ninja, and grabbed the photo. Seconds later, she was on her feet and standing in a karate stance that would have made Mr. Miyagi proud. Not that she could actually execute the move yet, but it certainly looked like she could. Creating an illusion was one of the many powerful weapons she kept stored in her arsenal.

Xavier jumped to his feet and began to circle her warily. "Just give me the photo, Belfry, and no one will get hurt."

"Are you threatening Pandora, Xavier?" Charles asked politely. "Because if you are, I will be forced to unleash my awesome powers upon you." He raised his hands and aimed them at Xavier.

Xavier glanced at Charles, then his eyes shifted back to Pandora. "Call him off."

"He's not a dog!"

"I didn't say he was, but this is not his battle."

"I can't take it anymore!" Birdy cried. "Just give it back, Pandora, before I have one of my spells!" She pressed the back of her hand against her forehead. "Oh, Lord. I can feel it starting already." She groaned and her eyes fluttered dramatically.

"Oh, stuff it, Birdy! Your spells are always nothing more than a bad case of gas."

"*Gas!* Why you little snot!" She rushed at Pandora, fists flailing.

"Birdy!" Xavier shouted, then did something entirely unexpected. He jumped between them, his back facing Birdy. Her forward momentum knocked him into Pandora's open arms, then Birdy bounced off him and onto her well padded behind.

As Pandora stumbled backward, she automatically reached out to grab hold of Xavier. The weight of their bodies and gravity did their work, pulling them to the floor, arms wrapped around each other with nothing to soften the blow. There was a sickening thud.

For the second time in a day, Pandora got the wind knocked out of her, and this time it hurt really bad. Xavier didn't look too good, either. In fact, judging by the odd contortions his face was making inches from her own, he was in a lot of pain. Together the two lay frozen on the floor, Xavier on top of Pandora, his hands stuck under her body. The sugary smell of lemon drops invaded her nostrils.

The silence that followed was soon filled with the sound of heels hurrying across the foyer. "*Pandy!*" a woman's voice cried out in horrified dismay. "*Xavier!* What are you two *doing?*"

Vicki couldn't have picked her timing any better, Pandora mused dazedly. She tried to talk and couldn't so she let her head fall back against the hard floor and hoped desperately to pass out.

23

All Wild-Eyed and Grunty

"ARE YOU TWO all right?"" another, deeper voice called out, the sound echoing in the high-ceilinged foyer, followed by the patter of running feet.

Pandora, of course, still couldn't answer. She could only close her eyes and wait on the cool marble floor for her breath to return. Xavier rolled off her, groaning and holding his left wrist. He ended up on his back, staring up at the foyer's domed ceiling and blinking back tears.

"What are you two doing?" Standing over them, Vicki sounded absolutely sick. "Are you...? Have you been...? Oh, dear Mary."

"Kids do fight sometimes, Director Belfry," Dr. Steele said calmly, coming to a stop beside her. "We'll get this sorted out."

Pandora opened her eyes in time to see him kneel down beside her. With the sunlight, which had momentarily broken through the dark clouds, shining all around him, he looked like an angel. She wanted desperately to say something, but all that came out was, "Uuunnhh..."

"Don't talk. You'll be all right in a moment." His hand found her shoulder and squeezed it; his strong fingers were warm and calming, and the smell of his primeval forest cologne filled her senses.

Pandora suddenly remembered what the Giant had done when she'd had the wind knocked out of her earlier and she lifted her arms above her head. Dr. Steele let go of her shoulder, which was a pity, but she thought it was preferable to having him seeing her like this, all wild-eyed and grunty.

Within a few seconds, she could breathe again. As quickly as she could manage, she sat up, though the movement hurt like the dickens. Vicki was kneeling beside Xavier, examining his wrist with a wrinkled brow. "It hurts in the bone?" He nodded with a grimace. "Then you might have broken it. We'll probably need to get it x-rayed."

Pandora peeked up at Dr. Steele, who was watching Vicki with an enigmatic expression. Feeling Pandora's eyes on him, he turned back to her, saying quietly, "I guess you won that round, huh?" He winked.

He was trying to make her feel better, but she didn't feel better. She felt horrible. A burning desire to run away from this mess surged through her body, making her skin itch and her lungs constrict. *Escape, escape, escape! She had to escape!*

But she couldn't. Dr. Steele was in the way, as was the posse. She was trapped like an animal in a zoo. They had him, and hence her, surrounded, all of them peeking at Pandora anxiously. Well, not Birdy…she was looking at Xavier. And not Skippy. He was looking at Birdy.

"I was only trying to help," she croaked. Her chest and stomach hurt like mad.

Vicki turned on Pandora. "What is going on here, missy? Were you two—" She paused, her mouth twisting. "Were you making out?"

Xavier started choking. "What?" he squawked, pretty much at the same time Birdy pretended to faint. Skippy caught her and laid her on the ground. His mouth straightened into two grim lines, but his eyes were dancing like a child's on Christmas morning. He looked oddly happy for someone tending to a friend in need.

Dr. Steele jumped up and hurried over to their side. Pandora now had another reason to hate Birdy. Her fake faint had stolen Dr. Steele away.

Through all this, Xavier glared at Pandora and she looked up at the ceiling to avoid meeting his eyes. "Why would she think that?" he demanded.

She shrugged. "I don't know. She seems determined to keep us apart."

"But why would she do that? What did you tell her about me?"

Pandora glowered at him. "I didn't tell her anything. Why don't you ask *her* what this is all about?"

"If you weren't actually…" Vicki put in, still focused on what she'd seen and not catching anything passing between them. "Well, what were you doing?"

"We were fighting," Pandora told her.

"Oh!" Her mother seemed strangely relieved. "About what?"

"This." Xavier reached for the photo. In a knee jerk reaction, Pandora whipped it away from him.

"What's that in your hand?" Vicki snatched up the copy of the photo that Pandora had stupidly placed in her reach. She studied it, her expression growing uglier by the second. "You snuck into my office and *stole* this?"

"I didn't sneak in there! I mean…" Ah, crud. The jig was up. She was so busted. She'd never see the light of day again.

"Then where did you get this?" When Pandora didn't answer, Vicki's eyes flared with reproach. "I'm trying to be fair here, Pandy. I'm trying to give you the benefit of the doubt, like I always do. But if I find out you broke into my private things…" Vicki stopped suddenly. Her head pulled back and she sniffed the air like a bloodhound. "What is that smell?"

"Fire!" Birdy screamed, sitting up and pointing at one of the red velvet curtains. Yellow and orange flames devoured the bottom of one, leaping upward like bounding deer.

"*Fire!*" Lucy repeated with relish. She grinned broadly and clapped her hands with glee. Or tried to. In one hand she clutched a pink plastic, tube-like object that was getting in the way. *Oh, no.* How could Lucy still have the lighter? Hadn't Nurse Rackett taken it from her? Apparently not, since Lucy still had it in her possession. Come to think of it, Nurse Rackett hadn't known about the lighter, only the p.a. and the nurse had seen it. And they'd forgotten about its existence. Or… Oh, crud. Pandora remembered lying under Charles's bed while Nurse Rackett interrogated Skippy, and Lucy had grabbed something and shoved it into her pocket. It had to have been the lighter. She must have tossed it under the bed before the staff grabbed her.

"*It was candy… Fooled you, fooled you!*" The memory echoed in Pandora's mind and she groaned. Not only had Lucy fooled the staff, she'd fooled Pandora, too.

Dr. Steele leaped to his feet and raced toward the curtain. "Get them out of here, Director Belfry!" he cried over his shoulder.

"Outside now!" Vicki shouted, suddenly snapping to her senses. She reached down and pulled Xavier to his feet. She tried to grab Pandora's arm, but Pandora jerked away. She had to get that lighter away from Lucy. If she was found with it, Pandora would be blamed and she'd be grounded until the day she died.

"Move!" Vicki screamed at her. Heavy black smoke was filling the large room, surrounding them like a fog at sea.

Pandora scrambled to her feet and immediately regretted the sudden move. Her ribs screamed in protest and her head pounded menacingly. In the thickening smoke, Vicki shooed the posse toward the doorway while Dr. Steele yanked on the burning curtain. It billowed and fought him like a living object. In seconds, the other curtain caught fire.

Pandora raced toward Lucy, who was lagging behind to watch, and grabbed her arm. Vicki had gone ahead to help Charles, who looked like he was about to pass out, and didn't notice them stop.

"Give it to me," she hissed at Lucy, swinging her around. "Give me back my lighter!"

Lucy shook her head, wriggling like a snake as she tried to get loose. "Finders, keepers, loser, weepers! So, go boo-hoo to somebody else, Pandora Poohead!"

"Give it to me now, Lucy, or you're out of the posse."

"No way!" Lucy stuck out her tongue. "You can't make me do nothing. It's a free country!"

Pandora glanced at the doorway. Her mother pushed Charles and Birdy outside and Skippy, Xavier, and Sinclair hurried after them. When they were safe, Vicki turned around. "Pandy!" she screamed into the smoke. "Where are you?"

"I've got Lucy," she cried back. "We're coming now. We're nearly out. Get the fire alarm!"

Vicki yanked off her shoe and used its heel to try and break the fire alarm's glass, while one arm waved at them to get moving. Pandora kept her eye on that arm. The open door was pulling at the smoke and surrounding Vicki like a magic trick. Soon she, and the door, would disappear.

They had to move fast. Pandora twisted Lucy's arm. "I'll never get you another donut again!"

"Donuts are stupid. They're *nuts!*" She giggled. "Get it?"

"Please, Lucy!" Pandora begged, then lunged for the lighter and missed as Lucy jerked backward. A sharp pain in Pandora's chest made her gasp and she inhaled a lungful of smoke. "Please, Lucy!" she sputtered, her lungs burning, her ribs protesting in pain.

The sound of shattering glass filled her ears like a scream, then the wail of the fire alarm filled the room. "Pandy?" Vicki shouted over the tremendous noise. "Are you still in here?"

Lucy wrenched her arm away. "You'll have to catch me, Pandora!" She started to run...away from the main door. Pandora raced after her, though her aching ribs made any kind of quick movement nearly impossible. Lucy gained on her, heading for the stairway. Pandora forced herself to run faster, forced herself to ignore the pain.

Luckily for them both, Lucy's short legs made her easy prey and Pandora caught her arm before she got too far. She spun Lucy around and shoved her toward the doorway, no longer caring about the lighter. "Get out, Lucy. Get out of the building!"

"But I want to see the fire!" Lucy shouted. In her excitement she sucked in a lungful of air. Her brown eyes grew big and she choked and wheezed, struggling for breath. "Can't breathe, Pandora!"

Pandora grabbed Lucy's arm and turned her around to face the door. "See that rectangle of light? It's the door. Go toward it. You'll be all right. But only if you go now!" Pandora pushed Lucy forward, again and again, like a mother horse urging her newborn to stand. "Keep going!"

Hacking and crying, Lucy stumbled toward the door. She was only about ten feet from it when she tripped and went down hard. Her hand hit the marble, knocking the lighter loose. It skidded across the floor, coming to a stop inches from Vicki's foot, which was about all they could see of her in the smoke. Pandora stared at the lighter in horror, her heart skipping a beat.

"Lucy!" Vicki cried, her shoe kicking the lighter back across the floor as she stepped forward. "What are you still doing in here? You must get out now!" A hand reached out, grabbed Lucy's arm, and dragged her away. Vicki didn't see Pandora in the smoke. She would think her daughter had gotten out.

A crash sounded off to Pandora's right. Dr. Steele had yanked the burning curtains to the floor. A billow of smoke from the raging pile engulfed her and she choked. She couldn't breathe. Dizzy and in pain, she turned around and around. She had to get out of the building. The smoke was too much for her.

But what about the other inmates? What about Dr. Steele? She couldn't just leave them in here. This fire was her fault. She had to save them. She had to get them out. The wail of a siren sounded in the distance, ominous as a banshee. Pandora would get Dr. Steele out of the smoke-filled foyer first, then she'd do what she could to help the other inmates.

Woozy from the pain in her ribs, she staggered toward the burning pile. The smoke was thicker and more acrid here, almost unbearable. Each step hurt worse than the last, but she was determined to make it to Dr. Steele. Her head swung drunkenly to the left and then to the right, searching for him. Where was he? He should be here, but she couldn't see him through the smoke. He must be on the floor, she decided, possibly hurt. She forced her feet to move faster. Quick, shallow breaths decreased the pain in her ribs, but made her feel dizzier and dizzier. She was nearly to the smoking pile when the inside of her head did a complete spin. Her body followed along and before she knew it, she was lying flat on the floor gasping for breath. Her ribs and her lungs and her eyes burned. She felt like she was on fire.

She was going to die. Everyone thought she was outside. Nobody would know she and Dr. Steele were still trapped in the smoke-filled foyer. Trying to push herself to her feet, her trembling hand landed on something plastic. The lighter. Pandora's fingers curled around the tiny item that had caused all this trouble.

"Save yourself, Dr. Steele!" she cried weakly, then passed out.

Ψ

The jarring sound of an insanely annoying trumpet filled Pandora's ears like a flood, and she came to, disoriented. Her itchy eyes darted about, trying to see in the smoke, but it was too thick. She started to cough, each bark like a cannonball hitting her chest. Her limbs felt heavy and her breath, coming in short pants, sounded like a dying vacuum cleaner.

"Where is she?" she heard her mother scream after the last trumpet sounded. She sounded far away. "I can't find her!"

"She must still be inside," Dr. Steele replied. "Stay here. I'll fetch her."

Still alive. Still in the manor. The sound of footsteps thudded toward her. "Pandora?" he shouted, unable to see her behind the pile of smoking curtains.

"I'm here," she gurgled.

"Pandora! Answer me!" He hadn't heard her.

"Here," she pushed through dry, swollen lips.

The footsteps faded. She closed her eyes. He was gone. She would be, too, soon enough.

And then, miraculously, he was back, and standing over her like a Celtic warrior. "What are you still doing in here, you daft girl?" he demanded, kneeling down. Her eyelids fluttered open, then drifted close once more. Her eyes stung from the smoke and she felt too tired to keep them open. He touched her cheek. "Never mind that. I'm just glad you're okay."

"The others..." Pandora whispered. "What...about...the others?"

"They'll be all right. The fire department just arrived. They'll take care of everything. Are you okay? Are you hurt?"

"And...the manor?" she asked, ignoring his worried questions. She opened her eyes and could see the concern on his handsome, soot-blackened face.

"Likely some smoke damage," he told her. "But easily mended."

"I'll...pay...for it." It hurt to speak each word.

"That won't be necessary—" His blue eyes sharpened. "Why? Do you know how the fire started, Pandora?"

"My fault," her lips barely moved as she spoke the words that would lead to her doom.

"I don't see how that could be. You weren't anywhere near those curtains. If I were to take a guess I would say it was that one girl—the one who likes to start fires." His expression urged her to agree.

She held up the lighter and her hand shook with the effort. "She got...this...from me. I didn't...realize she still...had it." The words were soft, but Pandora got them out. "*My* fault." He stared down at her, the look in his eyes somber as a hanging judge, then he took the lighter from her and slipped it into his pocket.

Pandora blinked back tears. "Sorry," she whispered, then another coughing fit seized her body and shook it like a giant, malevolent hand.

Dr. Steele didn't respond as he scooped her up into his arms and carried her toward the light, into fresh air. They passed a swarm of firefighters in black jackets and pants, racing up the steps, two of them dragging a flat hose like a reluctant dog on a leash. *They do look rather hot*, thought Pandora's addled mind. Lucy was sure to be thrilled.

Two ambulance crew members spotted Dr. Steele carrying Pandora out of the building and raced over to meet them. Dr. Steele laid her on the ground as gently as a child and then he stood and walked away. Through watery eyes she stared up at the sky as the EMTs tended to her, taking her pulse and blood pressure. Her ribs throbbed horribly and she felt an urge to throw up.

"Is she all right?" she heard her mother call in the distance.

"She'll live," Dr. Steele replied shortly.

A wave of dizziness passed through Pandora's head. Feeling full of shame and pain, she willed herself into oblivion, the sight of Dr. Steele's disappointed eyes following her down into the darkness.

For the Worst

24

THE SOUND OF talking invaded Pandora's dream and she tried desperately to tune it out. She and Dr. Steele were racing their horses down the beach, the wind wild and fierce on their faces. Pandora had never felt freer or more exhilarated in her life and she didn't want it to end, *ever*.

The talking grew louder and more insistent. Against her will her eyes flew open. "We're just in time everybody," a familiar voice screeched. "She's waking up!"

Pandora turned to her right and saw the inmates gathered around her bed, all staring down at her like she was some sort of circus freak. Light from outside silhouetted their five figures. She was lying in Nepenthe Manor's infirmary. She didn't remember much about how she'd gotten there. A blur of flashing lights from the ambulance, an endless series of x-rays and questions and proddings, and Dr. Steele looking down at her in disappointment—that's what came back to her. Little else.

But it was good to see that the place hadn't burned down. That her home, as much like a prison as it was, was still standing and things seemed back to normal. At least she had these two things to hold tight to even if she had lost her freedom and Dr. Steele's respect.

"It's about time," Birdy snorted around a wad of gum. "It's been nothing but Pandora this, Pandora that, for the last twenty-four hours!"

Pandora tried to sit up, but a pain shot through her ribs on her left side and she gave up the effort. She felt like she'd been run over by a Mack truck. "It's not my fault Xavier bruised my ribs when he landed on me," she grumbled through parched lips. She remembered that much about what Dr. Gara had said before she wrapped Pandora's ribs up tighter than a corset. Once she was finished mummifying her patient, breathing became a whole new adventure in pain for Pandora. Thank goodness for pain pills.

"Yeah, like that was *his* fault," Birdy snapped, pushing her way to the bed to loom over Pandora like a Marilyn Monroesque Grim Reaper. "You practically pulled him on top of you, you tramp!" Her baby blue fingernails clicked on the metal railing that surrounded the bed.

"Not on purpose!" Pandora wheezed. Just talking hurt. Dr. Gara had said something about smoke inhalation, too; that her lungs would be feeling quite raw for some time. "It was an automatic reaction," she added, less vehemently this time. "I was trying to keep myself from falling. I didn't realize he was such a lightweight. Thought he had more muscle to him."

"Yeah, well, if it makes you feel any better," Birdy sneered, "he broke his wrist because of you."

Pandora cocked her head. "Funny, it does make me feel better."

Birdy pursed her ruby lips in disapproval. "If I were you, Pandora, I'd be begging him for forgiveness."

"Well, lucky for us, I'm not you. The world doesn't need two Birdy Peacocks in it. Just imagine the drama."

Birdy blew an angry bubble, then sucked it back into her mouth. "You're just jealous Xavier likes me and not you."

"Did anyone else get hurt?" Pandora asked, deciding to ignore Birdy. "Did the foyer get gutted?"

"I got smoke in my chesties," Lucy replied, elbowing Birdy out of the way. "But not too much." She peered down at her "chesties," then at Pandora, her big, brown eyes squinting speculatively. Then she leaned over and said in a low voice that only Pandora could hear, "We gotta talk—"

"There's some smoke damage in there, but that's about it," Skippy interrupted, leaning against Lucy to get Pandora's attention. "Oh, and we need new curtains. Dr. Steele said he'd pay for the material if the home-ec class would make them. He said he's not very good at sewing straight lines."

"But what about the light—" Pandora asked, then stopped when she saw Lucy's eyes widen in warning. "I mean, did they figure out how the fire started?"

Skippy nodded, his fingers drumming on the railing. "The firefighters found Professor Robertson's magnifying glass by the window, which they figured started the fire. He must have dropped it there while looking for specimens. I swear he's lost about a hundred of those things. Maybe I should try to find them all. We wouldn't want another fire starting." The drumming intensified.

Pandora frowned. They couldn't really believe that a magnifying glass started the fire, could they? First, there was not nearly enough sun that day to produce the necessary heat. Second, there was the lighter Dr. Steele had taken from her. Third, there was Lucy, the miniature pyromaniac, who'd been on the scene.

"You see?" Lucy whispered in her ear. "It wasn't me. I might like fire lots, but I like Nepenthe Manor more." She pulled back and Pandora studied her earnest face. Was she lying? She seemed sincere, but then, she was good at that.

"And that's what the official report says?" Pandora asked.

"That's what the official report says," Skippy replied cheerfully.

"But what about what happened before the fire?" she wondered aloud. "With Xavier and the photo and Vicki?"

"I took all the blame for that," Skippy rushed to say. "It was the least I could do for not warning you about Xavier coming. I just thought it was another person to interrogate and I was getting back into position when I heard his voice, but by then it was too late to warn you." He gasped for air and continued, "But he wouldn't let me take the blame, even though I said we were just pretending to be spies, and now the Director is mad at all of us and we're being punished."

"*You're* being punished?" Pandora pushed herself into a sitting position, pain be damned. Why hadn't Dr. Steele explained what had happened? That it was all Pandora's fault?

"No *Scarecrow and Mrs. King* for a month," Charles explained sadly. "Director Belfry thinks it sets a bad example for us. But at least we still have *MacGyver*. She doesn't know about that show yet." He grinned, looking almost naughty.

"Xavier said I was cool about taking the fall." Skippy beamed. "He's so awesome."

Hmmm… It seemed that Skippy and Xavier were friends again. Pandora wasn't sure she liked that, though Skippy seemed a lot happier now. She did like that.

"It would've been cooler if no one *else* got into trouble," Birdy pouted.

"And the photo?" Pandora pushed, not even bothering to look at the sullen Birdy. She had to know all the details about what happened. She had to be sure.

Lucy grinned. "The evidence burned up in the fire and that means everything's a-okay." Still smiling, she took Pandora's face in her warm, little hands. "So when you getting out of bed, Pandora? We're bored."

"She'll get out of bed when she's ready to get out of bed, Lucy," Nurse Devine said, approaching the group with a small Dixie cup in one hand and a large cold pack in the other. "Coming here to ask me every half hour won't speed up her recovery any." She was a slender black woman with a lovely round Afro, whose vibrant black color

Pandora envied almost to the point of pain. Nurse Devine's tidy white uniform and shiny black skin made for a wonderful contrast, each emphasizing the vivacity of the other. She was competent, yet warm, and the inmates took every opportunity to get a little 'sugar' from their favorite nurse. She had a kind word and a sympathetic ear for everyone who came to see her, even for Mrs. Bodkin, the resident hypochondriac who faked every illness in the book. "Now you kids run along and get yourself some supper. Miss Belfry needs her rest."

"I could use one of those myself," Birdy hinted, nodding at the white pill lying on Nurse Devine's smooth palm.

"I already gave you one for your bruised fanny, sweetie, and it's too soon for another as you know full well," Nurse Devine scolded gently. "Now go on, all of you!" She shooed them away.

"Bye, Pandora!" Lucy yelled. "Sorry about your chesties!" She paused and turned back. "And sorry about that other thing, too..." She giggled merrily and skipped down the aisle between the rows of beds.

"Bye, guys," Pandora called. The boys waved, and Birdy rolled her eyes and flounced off, still angry. She had it in her mind that Pandora was trying to steal Xavier from her and Pandora was content to let her think that. That girl needed some payback.

"So when can I get up for real?" Pandora asked Nurse Devine when they were gone.

"Tomorrow, I think." She sat down on the bed next to Pandora and laid the pack on her patient's tender ribs. Her dark hand smoothed Pandora's wild, unruly hair out of her face. Someone had taken out her braids, but had done nothing to clean up the mess left behind. "Want me to take a brush to it?" the nurse asked, as though reading Pandora's mind. Her acuity made her such an excellent nurse. Times like these Pandora wished Nurse Devine was her mother.

"Not right now," Pandora said after swallowing the pill. It was big and tasted chalky. "Maybe when I wake up." She wanted to look terrible and pathetic. She wanted Vicki to see her like this and show mercy. Despite what the posse had said, Pandora was sure she was going to get into big trouble. Not even Vicki could let her off the hook for this escapade.

"That's fine. Get some sleep now, dear," Nurse Devine said softly as she stood up. "And no more fretting about your horse." She shook an admonishing finger. "Mr. Perkins stopped in yesterday to check up on you and overheard you mumbling in your sleep. He said to tell you he'd take her out most every day until you're able to do so yourself so you can stop worrying right now." Relieved to hear this, Pandora closed her eyes and soon fell into a hard sleep. Her dream of riding with Dr. Steele did not return.

When she awoke, the sunlight seemed unusually bright. A nurse, making up a nearby bed, heard her moan. "So you've decided to join the land of the living, hm?" She let loose a bubbly laugh. It was Joanna Burns, the gorgeous goddess.

"I've only been asleep an hour or so. It's still light outside," Pandora said, feeling muzzy and out of sorts.

"A few hours? More like fourteen, hon. It's Friday morning, don't ya know."

"I didn't know."

"Hungry?"

Pandora carefully pushed herself up into a sitting position and considered the question. "Famished," she replied.

"I'll get you some breakfast, hon."

When Nurse Burns returned with the food, Pandora was already feeling a little better. After eating the meal, which sort of resembled oatmeal and toast, followed by a passable glass of orange juice, she felt immensely better. Except for the ache in her mid-section and the fact that it hurt to breathe, Pandora thought she could get up. Besides, she really had to pee. She pushed the tray away, pulled back her covers, and swung her feet over the side of the bed.

"Whoa, there!" a voice called out, just as she was about to stand. "Slow down."

Pandora turned to see Dr. Steele approaching. He looked tired. "I have to go," she told him, her stomach twisting up in knots at the sight of him.

"What's the rush? Needed in surgery?"

"I have to use the bathroom. Really bad."

"Ah. Sorry, that *is* a rush." He came around to her side. "Come on, I'll walk you over."

Pandora regarded him suspiciously. Her pits were stinky, her hair was a rat's nest, and she more than likely had bad, bad breath. Besides all that he must hate her for what she'd done. "I'll be fine, thanks."

"Nonsense. Take my arm."

Reluctantly, she did. "Let's make this quick," she grumbled. She didn't like looking so awful, she didn't like feeling helpless, and she certainly didn't like that Dr. Steele was acting so nice to her. He should be yelling at her, telling her what an idiot she'd been. But he didn't do any of that and she felt herself grow more tense with each passing second.

He steered her over to the bathroom, which was nearly impossible to use without peeing on herself, being that her body didn't want to bend, then escorted her back to bed. The return trip was less painful, but climbing into bed sent a jolt of pain up into her chest. She gasped.

"You okay?" He pulled up a chair and sat down.

Her fingers wove together nervously. "Nothing a pain pill can't fix."

"Should I call the nurse?"

Pandora shook her head. "No, better not. I'd kind of like to stay awake today."

"Are you sure? Your mother wants to talk to you, you know…" He paused and looked out the window for a moment. It was a beautiful sunny day, the early May sky was blue and bright, like his eyes. "I'm going to be there, too, when she talks to you."

She glanced at him, but he was still looking out the window. Her heart gave a panicky flutter. "You are?"

"Of course."

Of course he had to tell Vicki the truth.

After a few more agonizing moments of weighted silence, he finally looked at her. His eyes were so intense, so penetrating, that they made Pandora feel weird inside. "Xavier is going to be there, too, you know."

"Urgh." *This just gets better and better.* She motioned to him to move back so that she could slide out of bed. "Fine. Let's get this over with." She would take her punishment for stealing the photo and for setting the fire all at once. Maybe then he'd stop looking at her with those mournful eyes, like she'd punched a little kid, or something.

"The meeting's not until this afternoon," he explained. Pandora fell back against her pillows. Apparently they wanted her to suffer a little longer. "Your mother has meetings all morning," he continued. "She can't make it before then."

She peeked at him out of the corner of her eye. "Is she really mad?" she asked, though she actually wanted to ask, "Are *you* really mad?"

"The way your mother has looked these last couple days," he answered, "I would say yes."

Pandora looked away from him. Her fingers started tapping on the bed sheet as she imagined typing up her last will and testament. *I, Pandora Belfry, being of sound mind and body—well, scratch the body part, and maybe the mind, too.* Start over. *I, Pandora Belfry, being not too nuts, hereby bequeath all my worldly possessions to my posse…*

Her imagination took off from there. Lucy would clamor for Pandora's animal skull collection. Skippy and Charles would share her

Dungeons and Dragons paraphernalia. Birdy would seize any jewelry she could get her hands on, including Pandora's skull ring. Sinclair most likely would commandeer her computer, after thoroughly disinfecting it, of course. Maybe her mother would want the photo of the two of them taken when Pandora was three. Her mother was tickling her tummy and both were laughing. It was hanging in Pandora's closet so Vicki would actually have to search pretty hard to find it. She probably wouldn't want it anyway. Not after she learned the truth about what Pandora had done.

"Pandora?" Dr. Steele waved his hand up and down in front of her face. "You still there?"

"What? Oh, yeah. Just daydreaming about my impending death."

"You're not facing the firing squad, Pandora. Just your mother."

She bit her lower lip, which was quivering traitorously. "Maybe I'll want to face it after all this."

"Do you really believe that?" he asked seriously, leaning forward.

Pandora had forgotten who she was talking to—a shrink. He didn't care about her; he only cared about doing his job. "*No*," she said hastily. "I don't want to *really* die. I'm of more use alive. But I wouldn't mind fast forwarding to a few weeks from now."

"Can't say I blame you." He checked his watch. "I have to go now. I'm meeting Nurse Rackett to discuss psychotropic medications." He didn't exactly look thrilled at the prospect. "I'll see you this afternoon. Your mother set up an appointment for all of us to meet in her office at one o'clock." He stood up.

"Dr. Steele?" she asked hesitantly.

"Yes, Pandora?"

"What do you think she's going to do?" *What are* you *going to do?*

Something strange flickered in his eyes. "I wish I knew. But whatever it is, I think you ought to prepare yourself."

She didn't like his expression. "Prepare myself for what?"

"For the worst," he said grimly, then left her without another word.

25

Flames From Her Mouth

TWO HOURS LATER, Nurse Devine gave Pandora the green light to leave the infirmary. She removed the wrapping around Pandora's torso, which instantly made her feel better—physically, anyway. "I don't know why those doctors keep wrapping injured ribs," the nurse mumbled, half to herself, "especially when you've got all that nasty smoke in your lungs. At this rate, you'll end up with pneumonia."

"Thanks, Nurse Devine." Pandora let loose a relieved sigh. "I can finally breathe normally again."

The nurse set the wrapping on the bed and dug a bottle out of her pocket. "Take these for the pain."

Pandora held up her hand. "I'd better not. Those things knock me out and there's something I have to face today." *Even though I'd rather stick pencils in my eyes.*

"These pills aren't as strong as the ones the hospital gave you, but you need to take them. I don't want you passing out again, you hear?"

Pandora took the bottle. She wasn't a martyr, after all. "I won't pass out again." She rubbed her aching temples. "I hope."

With a wave and a promise to "take it real easy" and check back later in the day, Pandora, still wearing her hospital gown, snuck up to their apartment to take a shower and change into real clothes. The hot water felt good on her skin, but it did nothing to soothe her burning lungs or jittery nerves. Seeing the state of the foyer hadn't helped her feel better, either. Black smoke stained the ceiling and marble floor, the curtains hung in tatters, and it reeked like burnt tires.

Not up to company, Pandora stayed in the apartment and ate a bowl of cereal and a banana for lunch. Time ticked by slowly as she fretted about Dr. Steele's warning to prepare herself for the worst. What did that mean? What did he know?

Eventually the clock showed five minutes to one. It was time to go. By the time Pandora made it down the stairs, though—she was used to moving at a much faster clip—it was already a little after one. She was late. It seemed a foreboding sign that the office, as she approached it, was as silent as a tomb. She pushed open the door, which creaked ominously, and popped her head in. Vicki was sitting behind her desk, the space between her eyes ridged with concentration as she did paperwork. Xavier was already there, looking out the window as though he hadn't a care in the world, though the stiff line of his spine told another story. He was worried. For some reason, this made Pandora feel a little better. Misery did love its company.

Vicki looked up. "Come in, Pandy." She sounded upset.

Pandora entered the room, feeling like an intruder. Where was Dr. Steele? Had he decided not to tell on her? Or had Vicki changed her mind and told him not to come so there wouldn't be any witnesses when she murdered her own child?

"Sit down." Vicki indicated a chair next to Xavier and Pandora lowered herself painfully into it. "How're the ribs?" she asked brusquely.

"Fine," Pandora replied in the same tone.

"I figured you'd bounce back. You've always been a tough kid." She looked at Xavier. "Pandy once fell off a horse and cracked her head open on a rock. She needed twenty stitches, and she didn't cry once."

He glanced over at Pandora. "Must be her thick skull."

Vicki laughed lightly. "Ah, yes. She does have one of those, doesn't she?"

Pandora scowled. She didn't like being ganged up on. "You don't like it when I cry so I didn't."

Vicki's laughter petered out. "Yes, well. I never did like seeing you in pain."

Yeah, right.

The room settled into silence. Pandora peeked at Xavier's arm encased in a white cast and propped up on the chair's black armrest. Over twenty signatures covered the surface, though Birdy's name, surrounded by a big red heart, stood out from the rest like a giant pimple. Xavier caught her looking at his arm and with a scowl, pulled it off the armrest and into his lap.

A light knock sounded on the door and Dr. Steele entered. "Sorry I'm late." He shut the door behind him, then sat down in the empty chair next to Pandora. She spotted the on-call beeper hooked to his brown leather belt. "I had an emergency to attend to." He looked at everyone. "Did I miss anything?"

"I haven't started yet," Vicki told him. She took a deep breath and looked first at Xavier, then at Pandora. "I imagine you have a lot of questions for me."

Pandora blinked. She hadn't expected this. Yelling, accusations, bolts of lightning coming out of her mother's head and flames from her mouth, but not this. "Questions?"

"You guessed, of course," Vicki went on.

Pandora stared at her mother. "Guessed what?"

Vicki looked at her, then turned to Xavier. "You must know, right? About that man? The one in the photo that Pandora had?"

Xavier shook his head, looking just as confused as Pandora felt. "I don't know anything about him. All I know is that my mom wanted me to have the photo—she didn't say why. I saw her addressing an envelope to someone named Vick. She covered it up before I could read the rest. I thought Vick was a guy, the same guy in the photo. But it was you." He stared at her defiantly.

Vicki was pale. "Do you... You think the man in the photo is your father, right?"

Xavier stared down at his cast. "I used to think that. I mean, why else would my mom give that picture to me? Now I don't know."

"Ahhh..." Vicki expelled the sound like a sigh. Her eyes returned to Pandora. "And what do you know about this man? You seem very interested in him."

Pandora shrugged, not wanting to commit to too much. "I don't know. I guessed he was Xavier's dad. Isn't he?"

Vicki looked like she wanted to be somewhere else. She glanced at her watch, fiddled with her papers, then her pen started tapping. "Well, yes, technically speaking."

"Is there any other way to speak of it?" Dr. Steele broke in. "What's going on, Director Belfry? Is the man in the photo Xavier's father, or not?" Xavier leaned forward, his eyes at the same time hopeful and anxious.

She ignored the question. "Pandy, you were just pulling my leg about wanting to date Xavier, weren't you?"

"What?" Xavier exclaimed, spinning toward Pandora. "Why would she want to do that? She despises me!"

Vicki's eyes narrowed into two dagger-shooting orbs. "Is that true?"

Pandora shrugged. "I wouldn't say *despise*, but he has been acting like a butthead ever since he arrived."

"Maybe because you tricked me and threatened me from the moment you saw me!"

"I was only trying to find out who you were and what you were doing here. You wouldn't tell me so I had to do some digging."

"Pandora Belfry!" Vicki cried. "You know the rules about confidentiality. You are to leave the residents alone. You have no right to any of their personal information."

"But I keep it confidential," Pandora defended herself. "I don't tell anyone anything!" The posse didn't count, and what she told Mrs. Hathaway was all made up, so she truly was in the clear.

"You're not staff. You cannot know these things."

"I'm not a snoop. I just wanted to know the truth!" Her hands gripped the steel arms of the chair.

"Well, you can't know. Do you hear me? You just can't." Vicki's cheeks flushed red. "You know, I'm beginning to think you stole that photo from my—"

"I wanted to help Xavier find his dad!" Pandora quickly interrupted. She hated that disappointed look on her mother's face.

"By stealing?" Vicki gasped. "From your mother?"

Pandora felt sick. She didn't know what to say. She didn't know how to fix this. Her head turned to see Xavier regarding her, one half of his mouth twisted upward. She looked away. She was so screwed.

"It was my copy, Director Belfry," Xavier said slowly. "I gave it to Pandora."

Vicki blinked a few times, but didn't take her eyes off her daughter. "Is that true, Pandy?"

"I just wanted to help," she repeated as she stared at the floor in shock. Had Xavier just rescued her?

"Even though I told you to stay away from him." Vicki wasn't going to let this go so easily.

Pandora looked up at her mother, adrenaline pumping through her veins. "You tell me to stay away from everybody."

Vicki stared at her. "Not everybody. Just the staff and the residents here at Nepenthe Manor."

"And the townspeople and our neighbors and anyone with a pulse," Pandora finished bitterly. "It's like you want me to live in this twilight world of neither here nor there. I'm not supposed to have any friends. I'm not allowed to do anything fun. Well, I'm sick of it. I'm sick of living in a place where I don't fit in!"

Vicki returned Pandora's grimaces with one of her own. "I can't help that, Pandy, and you know it. I have a job to do and if I don't do it, what will happen to the residents of Nepenthe Manor? There'll be no one to look after them and keep them safe."

"They'll have a new director to do that," Pandora said coldly.

"No, they won't! Not if Mayor Daft has his way." Vicki bit her lip, looking very much like she regretted admitting this.

"I suggest we all take a deep breath and calm down," Dr. Steele interrupted. "This is getting us nowhere." Vicki shot him a warning look to butt out, but he stared her down with a look of his own and she was the one to back off. "Good. Now let's get back to why you called this meeting in the first place, Director."

Vicki did not look pleased that Dr. Steele had steered the conversation back on track. In fact, she looked quite irate. Pandora smiled inside. At least something good was coming out of this, even if it was revealed that she was the one responsible for the fire.

"Yes, well," she started. "I was just trying to get at the truth. I needed to know if Pandy wanted to date Xavier. Her dating a resident goes against the institute's policy."

"Even after he leaves and is no longer an inmate?" Pandora pushed. Xavier shifted uneasily in his seat beside her.

"He won't be leaving."

"What?" Xavier squeaked, horrified. "Why not?"

"Because your mother, who was an old friend of mine, asked me to look after you when she died." She turned to Dr. Steele. "She had cancer." He nodded, his expression giving nothing away.

"I have to stay *here*?" Xavier yelped. "Please tell me you're kidding!"

"You'll no longer be a resident," Vicki went on. "You'll live here, though, and help Mr. Perkins with the groundskeeping while you finish your degree at Bedlam High."

"And what if I don't want to?" His lower lip jutted out.

Vicki shrugged. "Well, then I guess you can go live with your grandmother. Or there are foster homes that might take you in. You could also try to make it on your own, but there aren't many places that will allow a sixteen-year-old to take up residence. You'd need money for that anyway, and from what I remember of your mother, there probably isn't much of that. Here at Nepenthe Manor you'd get a wage—a small one, but a little something for after you graduate."

He looked sick. "I'll find my dad and stay with him."

"You don't know where he is."

His brown eyes studied her and then a spark fired up in them, as though he'd just figured something out. "No, I don't know where he is. But you do, don't you? You *know* him."

Vicki's cheeks darkened—only a little, but Pandora caught it. "I do," she admitted.

"Are you certain he's my father?"

"Yes."

"Where is he?" He slid forward, to the edge of his seat.

"I'm not at liberty to say."

Xavier's left ear reddened, starting at the tip and making its way down to his earlobe. "Why not?"

"Because I made a promise." Her pen started tapping again.

"To who?" Xavier insisted.

"To your father."

His eyebrow lifted in disbelief and he fell back against his chair, stunned. "He didn't want me to know who he was?"

"Not necessarily."

"What does that mean? Why can't you tell me?"

"Because if I told you who your father was, then I would be breaking my promise."

Xavier looked as confused as Pandora felt. "But you just said—"

"There's more, isn't there, Director?" Dr. Steele said softly. "Tell them everything."

She gave him a pained look. "I can't, Andrew. I just can't."

"If you don't, I will. I think I've got it figured out, but I don't want to get it wrong and make more of a mess of things."

Her shoulders sank low and after several long seconds, she said, "All right. I'll tell you what I can." She drew in a deep breath as she looked back and forth between Xavier and Pandora, then slowly released it. "I made a promise that I vowed to keep for as long as he was alive, so I can't break it. But I will tell you this." She paused and the pen tapped furiously. "That man in the photo is not only Xavier's father..." The pen fell from her hand and rolled off the desk to land on the floor. "He's Pandora's father, as well. You two are brother and sister."

"YOU'RE NOT MY mother?" Pandora cried, only grasping this small part of what Vicki had just said. "I knew it!"

"You don't need to sound so pleased, and besides, you've got it wrong. You two don't have the same mother, you share the same father."

Xavier regarded Pandora, his expression akin to someone inspecting road kill. He looked back at Vicki. "You can't be serious. You just can't be serious." He repeated this a few more times, softly to himself. He was starting to sound like Sinclair.

"But my father's dead," Pandora suddenly remembered. "So that means…" She glanced worriedly at Xavier, who appeared to deflate right before her eyes.

Vicki shook her head, looking pained. "He's not dead, Pandy. Your father is very much alive."

"What? You mean… He's still… But you told me…" Pandora stopped. At this point, she couldn't finish a sentence if her life depended on it.

"I had to tell you that." Vicki blinked rapidly several times. "He made me promise."

"So he's alive," Xavier summed up quickly, leaning forward, full of life again. "And you know where he is!"

"I can't tell you where he is," Vicki pushed out. "If *you* know his whereabouts, then Pandy will know, too. I can't tell either one of you where your father is." She drew herself up. "I broke one promise letting Pandy know her father is still alive, but I won't break another. I can't."

"Surely this is a promise that must be broken, Director!" Dr. Steele exclaimed with surprising passion. "They have a right to know who their father is."

"I have my reasons for keeping this promise," Vicki stated coolly.

Xavier pushed back his chair and stood up. "I can't stay here. Not with all these lies and crap. I got enough of that at home!"

Dr. Steele stood and went over to him, placing his hand on Xavier's stiff shoulder. "Please stay. At least for now. We'll try to work this out.

If you go, it will only make things worse, and then you might never know the truth about your father."

Xavier reluctantly sat back down and Dr. Steele returned to his seat. "Fine. But I don't like it." His jaw pulsed with repressed anger intermingled with spasms of fear. Staring at him, Pandora finally understood why he looked scared whenever they met. He wasn't afraid of her (even though he should have been), he was afraid of having nowhere to go, of being left to fend on his own. Now he had a dad, which helped a little, but even so he didn't know where his dad was.

Feeling strangely distant from everything, she hugged herself, making her ribs ache. She, too, had a dad. "My father is alive," she said softly. "All these years…" She felt like Alice in Wonderland. Big, then small. Lost, then found, then lost again. She didn't like it.

"I can't believe that of all the people I could have gotten as a sister," Xavier mumbled half to himself, "I get *her*."

"I'm sorry," Vicki said stiffly. "This isn't what I wanted. You would never have known, but you pushed and you—"

"I have to go now," Pandora blurted. Her head felt so light, like a dandelion fluff in the wind. "I have to go find my father." She shoved back her chair and hurried toward the door.

"Pandora!" Dr. Steele called after her. She heard his chair scraping on the wood floor and she took off like a frightened deer. She had to get away. She didn't want his pity. She didn't want to talk. She only wanted to be left alone. So she ran to her secret room to hide.

Some time ago, while searching for a better place to stash her dearest possessions, she'd discovered an old skeleton key in her closet, wedged up behind a piece of wood. She sensed at once that it belonged to the one door she'd been unable to open, a door that stood in the middle of the maze of secret passages.

And she was right. When she'd unlocked the door, she discovered a magical room furnished with Victorian furniture and built-in bookshelves lined with countless old books on fairies and magic and legends, all inscribed with the initials, *EN*.

After staring in stunned wonder for several moments, she explored every nook and cranny where she found numerous treasures, like the seashell and fossil collections, and an assortment of glass bottles filled with unidentifiable liquids. Later she ran and fetched a broom, a bag of rags, and a bottle of furniture polish and by the light of a lantern she'd found, gave the room a thorough cleaning. When she was done, she had only to hang a poster of Sid Vicious on the wall and drape an old red quilt over the back of a dark velvet divan to make the room her own. After saving up to buy another extension cord, she borrowed a dinged up lamp from the attic, which lit up the cozy room quite nicely.

She didn't visit her secret place as often as she'd like. She secretly hoarded a tiny worry that one day she would fall asleep on the divan, like in a fairy tale, and wake up to find she could never leave, nor would she want to. She'd happily die in that room, she liked it so much. But she would miss Shadow and the posse and they needed her anyway, so she knew she had to be careful not to let the power of the room tempt her away from her responsibilities.

After turning on a lamp, she sat down on the divan and pulled her knees up to her chest, clasping them tightly. "I have a father and a brother," she whispered to herself over and over as she rocked back and forth, relishing the pain in her ribs. The throbbing kept her from thinking too much. She didn't want to think too much.

But after half an hour of rocking and babbling to herself about betrayals and fathers and the pain, oh, the pain, she could no longer stop the thoughts from coming.

I have a dad somewhere out there in the world...and he doesn't want me to know him.

I have a brother who doesn't like me very much, and who's now going to live here at Nepenthe Manor.

I have a mother who lied to me and when offered the chance to make things better, decided not to.

I have bruised ribs that hurt every time I breathe and my mother could care less.

Pandora wanted to cry and rave and gnash her teeth about the injustice of it all, but she couldn't. The tears wouldn't come. Instead, like toxic worms, they burrowed themselves deep in her chest where they burned like hot coals. She wished she could cry, then maybe this wouldn't hurt so much.

Hurt.

Pandora sat up straight. A brilliant idea had come to her. As Nurse Rackett was so fond of saying, "There are Lessons to be Learned," but this time Pandora would be the one teaching them. Her students? Birdy, Xavier, and Vicki, of course. She would go after Birdy and Xavier first, then her mother. If she couldn't fix her life, she could at least fix those three.

Oh, yeah, she'd fix them good.

She glanced at her watch. Typically the posse would be gathered in the TV room at this hour, watching re-runs of *Bewitched*. Hopefully Xavier, who wouldn't know what else to do with himself while he waited to be discharged, would be there, too.

Pandora carefully locked the door to the secret room and headed to her bedroom to prepare. After some rooting around and several invigorating swigs from a newly opened Coke bottle, she found what she was looking for. She set to work, smiling to herself as she replayed the scene over and over until she had it clear in her mind exactly what she needed to do.

When she was fully prepared, Pandora headed downstairs to the foyer, her arms wrapped tightly around her torso. Keeping close to the wall to avoid being seen and to avoid seeing the damage from the fire, she was halfway across the broad expanse of floor when she spotted someone coming. It was Togs. His ever-present camera bounced against his concave chest as he hurried toward her.

"Miss Belfry!" he called. "I've got something for you." His thin fingers gripped a black and white square, which he waved at her with unexpected enthusiasm as he hurried toward her.

So much for remaining unseen, she grumbled to herself. She leaned against the wall for support as she waited for him to approach. All this plotting and running around was making her lightheaded.

"What is it?" she asked as he held out the square to her.

"It's a picture for you," he panted. His dry, sunken cheeks, which reminded Pandora of a peeled apple left out too long, lifted as he gave her a pained smile. "You look real nice in it so I figured you'd want to have it."

Pandora took the photo and studied it. *Oh, lovely.* It was the picture Togs had taken in the cafeteria, where Xavier had his arm draped possessively around her shoulders. Both were smiling at the camera, though Pandora's smile looked more like a barracuda about to attack. It was her bad luck that for once Togs's camera had actually had film.

She nodded. "Thanks, Togs. I'll treasure this photo," *for my dartboard.*

His head bobbed in a nod. "No problem, Miss Belfry. I was placed on this earth to help. And remember, if you have any special events you'd like to capture forever, let me know and I'll do everything in my power to accommodate you." He patted the pockets of his black slacks and gray wool blazer, which hung loosely on his scrawny torso, then frowned. "It appears as though I've misplaced my business cards." Blinking rapidly, he straightened his steel-rimmed spectacles, then ran a shaking hand over his spotted, balding skull. He scanned the foyer like a man who truly believed if he searched hard enough, what he desired would appear. It didn't. "Oh, wait," he realized at last, "you already know where I live."

"I certainly do. Thanks again, Togs." She waved the photo at him and he gave her another pained smile. "See you around."

Like a crab pursued by a relentless seagull, he scuttled off in his patent leather dress shoes, safe in the knowledge that he'd done at least one good deed for the day. Word on the street was that Togs had a bit of a martyr complex, driving him to wear a hair shirt and flog himself with a 'whip' (a bunch of shoelaces, cut in half and tied together into a knot on one end). At the end of the day his good deeds had to outweigh his bad ones (an infraction could be as small as leaving the toilet seat up) or he'd punish himself until the scales of justice were once again balanced. Vicki had once tried to take away his hair shirt and whip, but in the end, he was more miserable when he couldn't punish himself, so she reluctantly returned them.

Poor Togs. He had it all backwards. It was much better to punish others than to punish one's self. She looked at the photo one last time—he really was a very good photographer, she looked almost *otherworldly*—then tucked it into her back pocket. She crossed her arms once more and was turning to head toward the TV room when Dr. Steele called her name.

Boy, that man was *everywhere.*

"Can we talk?" he asked, his voice echoing slightly.

She slowly turned back around. He was walking down the hallway, which she had long ago christened Quack Central. It housed all the counselors' offices, and at the end of it was the most amazing library of all time. Unfortunately, the library was off-limits to inmates and Pandora, as it was being used, most unfairly, as the therapists' lounge.

When Dr. Steele reached her side, she asked cheekily, though really she felt anything but flippant at the moment, "Talk about what?"

He frowned. "Don't play coy with me, Pandora."

She sighed, considering for a moment whether or not she could outrun him. Probably not. He'd almost caught her when she'd fled her mother's office earlier. "I suppose you mean the lighter and how I let a pyro get a hold of one and nearly burn down Nepenthe Manor."

He frowned. "Not at all. I thought you heard."

"Yes," she pushed out. "I heard about the magnifying glass theory, but frankly, I'm not buying it. I can't imagine you are, either."

"They found about ten burn holes in the bit of material that managed to survive, Pandora. Apparently this isn't the first time that magnifying glass nearly started a fire. Thank goodness the fire snuffed out on its own all those other times."

"But there wasn't enough sun that day to start a fire!"

"It doesn't take long," he answered, looking at her strangely. "Especially if the magnifying glass is strong."

"But surely it takes more than a few *seconds*?"

His head tilted slightly. "I don't get you, Pandora. Do you want to get into trouble?"

She drew back. "No. No, I don't. It's just that… Well, it just doesn't make sense. Only a few seconds…"

"A few seconds can start a revolution. Why not a fire?"

"So you're not mad at me anymore?" she dared to ask, reaching up to tug on her braid.

"I was mad at you," he answered truthfully. "But then, after thinking about it, I decided you were pretty brave to take the blame when you could easily have placed it on your friend, Lucy."

"You know her name."

He regarded her steadily. "I've taken it upon myself to learn the names of everyone in your little group of friends."

Pandora didn't like the sound of that. "So if you didn't come to get me to confess to my mother, then why are you here? Why did you show up at the meeting?"

"I went to the meeting because your mother seemed overwrought and I thought I could be of help mediating between you two. I'm here now because I believe what happened this afternoon must have been pretty awful for you."

Pandora swallowed hard. "I don't want to talk about it."

He pressed one hand against the wall and ducked his head to look straight into her eyes. "When you're ready, then?"

Her shoulders lifted in a shrug. "Maybe."

"I wish this had gone differently for you, Pandora." His voice was soft, kind.

She bit her lip to stop the sob aching to escape her trembling lips. "Yeah, me too."

"Is there anything I can do for you now?"

She tried to look away from his gaze, but she couldn't. He was as mesmerizing as Rasputin, and possibly as dangerous. "Maybe get me a small fridge for my room and an endless supply of Coke?" She laughed jerkily. "Just kidding. No, really, you're a good guy, Dr. Steele. But I can handle this on my own, like I've been doing all my life."

"That's what I'm afraid of." He took a little of the sting out of his remark by smiling at her. "I don't want you to have to go it alone."

She felt unable to reply. She had a job to do and his kindness and sympathy were making it harder with every passing moment. "Well," she said lightly, "you know what Joseph Conrad said, 'We live as we dream – alone.'"

Dr. Steele shook his head, looking more than a little amused. "While I enjoy his work, I'm not sure Joseph Conrad is the best person to model your life after."

Pandora nodded in approval. The man knew his stuff. "Maybe not. But he's real, you have to give him that."

He grimaced. "Sometimes real is overrated, Pandora."

"This from a psychologist!"

"*This* from a psychologist." He looked at her meaningfully. "We'll talk again, all right? Maybe you can show me the stable? Help me saddle up Wily? Introduce me to Shadow?"

She gave a small smile, though on the inside she was singing. "Maybe." She paused, twirling her braid. "Say, now that you know the fire wasn't my fault, can I get my lighter back?"

He chuckled. "Not a chance." He pushed away from the wall and gave her a brief bow, an anachronistic, but oddly charming gesture. "We'll talk another time. Until then, try not to let your Shadow blot out your light," he added cryptically, then left her, with one last backward glance, to return to his office.

Feeling infinitely better about things between them, she squared her shoulders resolutely and headed to the lounge to take on Xavier and Birdy. But before she'd taken two steps she was waylaid again—this time, by one of her victims.

"Wait up, Belfry!" She stopped and turned around, hoping she looked suitably annoyed. Keeping her arms crossed should help. Xavier, wrist now supported by a blue sling, caught up to her.

"What good timing you have," she drawled.

Suspicion shadowed his face. "What do you mean?"

She reached into her back pocket and plucked out Togs's photo. She handed it to Xavier as though presenting him with an award. "Here's a little something to hang in your new room."

He peered down at it, brows furrowed. She figured he'd throw the photo into the next garbage can he came across, but to her surprise, he stuck it into his back pocket. "Thanks," he mumbled. "I'll hang it next to the picture of our dad."

She stared at him, feeling a little weird. What was he doing? Was he being *nice*? She supposed he did have it in him after he'd come to her rescue twice now. Once, while saving her from Birdy's attempt to tackle her. And the second time in Vicki's office when he told Vicki he'd given the photocopy to Pandora.

"So, um, what did you want from me, your unwanted *sister*?" she asked, the word tasting weird on her tongue.

He shrugged and looked around uncomfortably. She thought that if he could, he'd climb the walls to get away. But he stayed and he said what he wanted to say. "I just thought maybe…I don't know…maybe we should, um, talk."

"Talk? Everyone around here wants to talk." She crossed her arms again, irritation burning up the inside of her stomach. "Is this your idea, or Vicki's?"

He looked insulted, taking an exaggerated step back. "It's *mine*! I'm not exactly a fan of your mom right now, you know."

"Well, me, neither. I can't believe she won't tell us who our dad is."

"No kidding. She has no right to keep that sort of thing from us! How could she? She's so—" He stopped talking and his pale lips pressed together. His one good hand, which had been flailing about while he was speaking, curled into a fist and he pushed it into his pants pocket as though to keep from punching a wall. He looked like he desperately wanted to trash Vicki, but with obvious effort, he held back. Pandora felt a grudging admiration stir inside her chest.

"Say, listen," she said after a few moments passed. "I have an idea."

"We're not sharing a room," he stated flatly.

"Damn right, we're not. Where are you staying, by the way?"

"Above the stable with that Mr. Perkins your mom mentioned."

"You *lucky*!"

He stared at her. "I don't like horses."

"No way!" She laughed. "Well, I guess you're going to have to get over that. I think horse is the only language Carl speaks."

Xavier's top teeth clamped down on his lower lip, then he asked, "What's he like?"

"He's a bit of a curmudgeon so don't screw up. You'll pay for it."

Xavier looked worried, and Pandora reveled in his fear for a brief moment before relenting. "But he's fair. He won't overwork you and he keeps to himself."

Xavier relaxed a little. "So what were you going to say? You mentioned you had an idea."

She studied him for a moment, pausing at his earring before finally meeting his eyes. "I'm going to look for our father. And I'm going to find him, whether you help me or not." She hadn't meant to include that last bit—she'd planned on going it alone—but again, he *had* covered for her in Vicki's office. In Pandora's book that made up for a lot of his ornery behavior. If he hadn't come to her rescue, Vicki would have grounded Pandora forever, and probably make her push a boulder up a mountain, Sisyphus-style, to boot. And, he was being nice now when he didn't need to be after what she'd done, stealing his photo and harassing him. So, she guessed she kind of owed him something.

"I'll help you," he agreed, determination strengthening his jaw. For the first time Pandora looked at him as a human being and—weird as it felt—as a brother. After a few seconds of staring at him, while he grew increasingly fidgety, she decided he might not be too horrible.

"Good," she replied. "Now I'm going to go teach Birdy a little lesson and it'll be better if you're there. Are you coming?"

"Lead the way," he grinned.

Yes, she figured, feeling strangely buoyant, *he just might do.*

27

His Poisonous Claws

THE TELEVISION, WHEN they arrived at the TV room, was on, and Samantha, the witch, was wiggling her nose, intent on conjuring up a spell that would get her into worse trouble than she'd been in in the first place. During the commercials of each *Bewitched* show, Pandora and the posse religiously practiced their nose wiggling with varying degrees of success, though most of them had yet to conquer ultimate nose wiggling. Birdy, however, was quite good at it. No surprise there, Pandora thought snidely, since she was, after all, a grade A witch. She *should* be quite skilled at all things witchy.

Pandora came to a stop just behind the circle of chairs and slowly peeled off her jean jacket, grunting with pain. "Hello, everybody!" she called when she was finished. "How's it going?" Everyone turned around to greet her.

"Crikey, Pandora!" Skippy gaped. "What happened to your, um, *chest?*"

Pandora smiled coyly, then let her eyes slide over to Birdy, who was sitting draped across her chair, her own miniature mountains pointing at the ceiling. "Oh, just a little trick I picked up from Birdy."

Xavier's eyes fastened on Birdy's ample bosom, which had gained another couple inches since yesterday. "You stuff your bra?" he asked, right on cue.

Her cheeks flared red. "*No!*"

"Oh, yes you do, Birdy," Pandora rushed to say. "You even offered me some Kleenex to do the same."

Birdy's green eyes glowed angrily. "Liar! I wouldn't do something so childish." She crossed her plump arms over her massive chest, which promptly flattened like a leaky tire. "I don't have to put up with this, you know." She slid down in her chair, her lower lip protruding grandly. "You're awful, Pandora Belfry!"

"And you're a traitorous little b—" Charles's worried eyes widened and she reluctantly amended her choice of words, "—butthead." She lifted her chin in a *I'm being merciful* gesture. "But... I will let you back into our group, just to prove that I'm not bossy or disloyal or *always causing trouble.*"

Birdy scowled, but her eyes shifted over to Xavier to see how he was taking all this. "Don't look at me," he snorted, throwing up his good hand. "You'd better accept Pandora's offer and leave me out of it."

Birdy's mouth pulled down at the corners. "What if I don't wanna?"

Pandora was tempted to cry triumphantly, "Then good riddance!" Instead, she said calmly, "Then the posse wouldn't be the same without you." Technically Pandora was speaking the truth. It wouldn't be the same because there'd be one less person. She just hoped Birdy didn't pick up on that. Charles looked on the verge of tears.

"Humph," Birdy growled, not taking the bait, and her green eyes glared hatred at Pandora.

Fuming inside, Pandora decided to forget trying to patch things up. She and Birdy were not going to get along; were never going to get along again. If Birdy wanted to betray her and not be in the posse, well, that was fine by Pandora. She had other things to do. She clapped her hands to get everyone's attention. Lucy had returned to watching *Bewitched*—she especially loved little Tabitha, though Pandora preferred Serena herself—and only reluctantly turned around.

"I have an announcement to make," Pandora said, when everyone was looking at her. She glanced over at Xavier and he gave her the go-ahead nod. Seeing the exchange, Birdy's scowl deepened nearly to the point of being a destructive force. Pandora ignored her. "Xavier and I," she began, "have just found out that we're brother and sister. We have the same dad." She took in everyone's stunned expressions before adding, "He's going to be staying here now and living above the stable while he goes to school in Bedlam."

She waited for the posse's reaction, which was sure to be disbelief, possibly revolt. They knew Pandora didn't like Xavier and wanted him gone. So she somehow had to make it clear he was okay now, protecting him with her body if need be. She readied herself for the attack as everyone leaped out of their chairs and surrounded her and Xavier. To her surprise, they were laughing and clapping.

"Yes, yes, yes!" Lucy cheered, hugging both of them at once. "I knew you two were family!"

"That's awesome!" Charles shouted, patting Pandora on the back. Then he stuck out his hand to Xavier, puffing out his chest and looking as manly as he could with his child-like face and golden curls. "You couldn't have gotten a better sister."

Xavier gave Pandora a smug smile. "And she couldn't have gotten a better brother." Charles beamed in agreement. Pandora stuck out her tongue at Xavier. He just continued to smile. He seemed to like the attention.

Skippy clapped Xavier on the back. "That's so cool, man!" He bounced up and down on his toes, nearly falling over on his last bounce. "Now we can do stuff together. I had this idea for a machine I want to build. But if you don't want to do that, we could talk about computers, or something. We could do whatever you want. I mean, if you want to—"

"That'd be cool," Xavier told him, having already learned not to let the Skippy train get its head. Skippy's bouncing grew more frenetic and he looked about ready to burst with pleasure. Pandora rolled her eyes at Xavier and he just shrugged as though to say, "I can't help it I'm so awesome."

Sinclair faced Pandora and gave her a small, congratulatory smile that likely cost him a great deal of effort to produce. Then he turned to Xavier and asked in a polite voice, "When are you moving out?"

"Ha!" Pandora sputtered.

Xavier gave her a quelling look. "As soon as I can," he told Sinclair. Sinclair nodded as best he could through his mumbled repeatings of "When are you moving out?"

Birdy was the last to join the felicitations, watching the whole procedure with assessing green eyes. Finally, she rolled out of her chair and sauntered over to where the rest were gathered. "So you're brother and sister, huh?" Her tone wasn't exactly congratulatory. Lucy glanced back at her, then tightened her grip on Xavier and Pandora. Pandora's ribs protested and she wriggled a little to relieve the unrelenting pressure.

"Yep," she replied, wondering where Birdy was going with this.

Birdy looked at Pandora, then tossed her head at Xavier. "So that means you're stuck with this arrogant ass for the rest of your *life*?"

"Hey!" Xavier cried.

Pandora couldn't help laughing. "I suppose I am."

"I'm sorry to hear that." Birdy stared pointedly at Xavier and he looked away, out the window. "So how'd you guys find out about your dad?"

"Vicki told us," Pandora answered.

"So if you share a dad, then who is he?"

Pandora shrugged. "That's just it, we don't know."

Birdy gave her a disbelieving look. "*Vicki* knows who he is and you don't?"

"That's right and she won't tell us. Apparently she promised him she wouldn't." Pandora's anger reignited at the injustice of it all.

Birdy stared at Pandora for a few long moments. Everyone started to shift about uncomfortably, wondering what her response was going to be. One never knew with Birdy. "Well," she said at last, "that's just about the *stupidest* thing I've ever heard! Of course you have a right to know who your dad is. You poor, poor thing, Pandora!" Pandora noted that she didn't include Xavier in her sympathizing. In fact, she was making it a point not to look at him. "As your friend," she cooed, "I'd be happy to organize a search for your father." Before Pandora could assure Birdy that she and Xavier could handle that themselves, she went on, her smile gracious as a Southern belle. "Friends always stick together, right, Pandora? Through thick and thin? Right?" Birdy was attempting to exude a calm confidence, but the look in her eyes was pure scared.

"Through thick and thin," Pandora replied. "Definitely."

Birdy's hand flew to her forehead. "Oh, dear. All this excitement is making me feel lightheaded. Skippy, get over here! I need help to my chair." Skippy grinned and rushed to her side. She wrapped her arm around his waist while over her shoulder she gave Xavier a provocatively dismissive glare. He looked bored. Frowning, she turned her attention back to Pandora. "We'll hold a Midnight Meeting to discuss everything, all right, love? Members only, of course."

"Cool," Pandora replied and smiled, feeling like everything truly was cool. Birdy might be a pain in the butt, but she was Pandora's pain in the butt. The same went for the rest of the posse. They were a family of sorts, warts and all. And together they were something more than who they were alone.

Feeling pretty good about life, she looked at each member of the posse—down at Lucy, who was happily sucking her thumb, over at Charles and Sinclair, both who appeared to be quite relieved—Charles because the Secret Six would remain intact, and Sinclair for the same reason, but also because he was getting his room back to himself, and lastly, at Skippy and Birdy, who were laughing uproariously as they threw wadded up tissues from her bra at each other.

They were all good.

"Well, thanks for your support everyone," Pandora said, unlocking Lucy's arms from about her waist. "Now I have to go do something for Vicki. See you later, okay?"

"Later, Pandora." Skippy waved. Birdy giggled.

"Bye, Dor Dor!" Lucy shouted, then ran over to her chair and crawled up into it. Charles gave Pandora a salute, then followed after Lucy. Sinclair nodded stiffly to acknowledge her departure, his fingers working at the hem of his argyle vest. Xavier flicked her a wave over his shoulder then headed straight for Pandora's chair and lowered himself into it, which was annoying, but would have to be dealt with another time. Pandora had one last thing to do and she had to do it soon, before she lost her nerve.

Pivoting on one heel, she left the TV room and headed to the foyer. After checking to be sure her mother was working in her office and that its door was slightly open, Pandora ran up to their rooms and made the necessary phone call with shaking fingers. Then she pulled out the tissues in her strained bra before heading back down to the foyer to wait.

Twenty minutes later the giant gargoyle knocker banged loudly against the door, startling Pandora even though she'd been expecting it. With a quivery stomach, she marched over and pulled the door open. Dougie Daft was standing outside on the landing.

"You rang?" she joked nervously. He stared blankly at her. "Oh, just come in."

He stepped inside. "I came as you asked."

"Yes," she nodded. Her ears caught the squeak of the office door opening behind her. Good, her mother had heard the knock. "Ask your question," she hissed.

He looked around at the mess. "Now? Right here?"

She nodded vigorously. "Ask it...quickly!"

He gave her an assessing look with his pale eyes and she suppressed a shudder. "All right. Would you, Pandora Belfry, do me the honor—"

"Pandy!" Her mother briskly entered the foyer, her high-pitched voice betraying her panic. "I was wondering where you went!" She stopped a few feet away from them, her hands clasped firmly together in front of her. "Oh, hello, Douglas." She barely looked at him before turning to face Pandora. "Shouldn't you be in bed, young lady? You must still be in a lot of pain. I'll tuck you in, get you a heating pad for your ribs." She reached out to grab Pandora's shoulders to turn her about, but Pandora ducked away, moving to stand as close to Dougie as she could manage without gagging.

"I heard about your bruised ribs," Dougie said politely. "Do they still hurt?"

"Not in the least," she lied.

He looked disappointed.

"At least you should be resting," Vicki persisted. She was smiling, though it was forced. "Feet up, taking it easy? Maybe some TV?"

Pandora looked her mother straight in the eye. "You didn't care about my pain before this moment, Vicki. Why should you care now?"

Her mother drew back. "I do care, Pandy. I visited you several times in the infirmary, but you were sleeping each time I looked in on you. And I've been busy with our new resident's discharge papers and seeing about getting the foyer cleaned up and then there's that other mess. I—"

"Finish your sentence, Dougie," Pandora interrupted, hating her mother for calling what had happened this afternoon a *mess*, as though Pandora had made it, like a child getting into the pots and pans. "Ask me what you were going to ask me." She met his stare squarely.

He blinked at her a few times, conveying a look of innocence from every part of him, except his calculating eyes. "All right, Pandora. Would you do me the honor of attending the Spring Ball with me a week from this Saturday?"

Pandora spun around. She wanted to see the look on Vicki's face when she accepted. "Yes I would, Dougie." Pandora managed to catch seeing her mother's face wrinkle irritably before glancing back at Dougie. "Pick me up at six."

His resulting smile conjured up images of ghouls dining on flesh and Pandora's elation at getting revenge on her mother withered like a flower petal put to flame. Now she knew why Giganticus always looked at her with pity. Because he knew, simply by looking at her, just how pathetic and stupid she was. Yes, she had taught Birdy and her mother a Lesson. But in the end, Pandora was going to be the one who paid the price.

As Dougie turned to leave, his expression that of a gloating fiend, Pandora realized the price was going to be excruciatingly high.

But you can't back out now, she warned herself. She had made her bed; she would just have to lie in it.

But she could do that. She *would* do that. She was strong. She'd survived worse, after all. She would endure.

Or would she? What if the mayhem that was always a part of Nepenthe Manor claimed another victim? And what if, this time, that victim was Pandora?

The outside door banged with menacing vigor as it closed on Dougie Daft's triumphant figure. Pandora let loose a groan. Dougie had his poisonous claws embedded firmly in her flesh, and it was too late to undo the damage. Mayhem had won this round.

Pandora couldn't let it win the next.

About the Author

When author, Kristina Schram, was growing up she wanted to be a star. When that didn't turn out quite like she expected, she turned her mind to achieving other goals: Earning her Ph.D. in Counseling Psychology, working as an Artist-in-Residence at local schools, being a free-lance editor and reader, coaching parks & rec basketball, and publishing her first novel, a YA fantasy called The Chronicles of Anaedor: The Prophecies (Book One).

Knowing what it's like to struggle with self-doubt and lack of confidence, her biggest dream (in addition to owning a castle) is to stamp out low self-esteem for everyone, especially young people. "Feeling bad about yourself is the number one deterrent to achieving happiness," she says. "So for the sake of a better world, it's got to go." She lives in New Hampshire with her husband, three boys, her mother and various pets, and can also throw a tomahawk, if need be. For more information, visit her website: www.kristinaschram.com. She's also on Facebook and Twitter.

Other Books by Kristina Schram

The Chronicles of Anaedor: The Prophecies (Book One)

Strange things happen to fifteen-year-old Lavida Mors. Maybe that's why her father sends her to Portal Manor, a mysterious family estate she never knew existed. Lavida quickly discovers that not everything at Portal Manor is as it seems when she stumbles across a secret passage to a hidden world—Anaedor. Long ago, humans drove the Anaedorians, a civilization of magical and strange beings, into the dark world of huge caverns, frigid rivers, and bottomless pits deep within the earth. Malevolent forces, led by the evil Malvado, seek to control all of Anaedor, but an ancient prophecy tells of a hero who will save them from destruction. While trying to escape the dark realm, Lavida must battle overgrown leeches, survive a poisoned arrow, and outwit a giant, all while trying to convince the hopeful populace of Anaedor that she is not the savior they believe her to be.

The Chronicles of Anaedor: The Return to Anaedor (Book Two)

After escaping from Anaedor, fifteen-year-old Lavida Mors starts a training course with her guardian, Mrs. Keeper, in hopes of improving her magic skills before the dreaded Malvado returns. But while trying out a new spell, something awful happens, and she vows never to do magic again. When an unexpected discovery forces her to return to Anaedor, she is faced with her most terrifying challenges yet. Strife reigns in the hidden underground world as lootings and burnings break out, and numerous enemies conspire to capture Lavida, fight her, even kill her. Without magic, how can she possibly flee from dragons, escape the Goblins, outwit the ruthless Frio, and fight a duel with a young rebel intent on proving she's not the One? Time is running out. If Lavida doesn't learn to trust herself and her skills, a series of catastrophic events will ensure that she and her friends never make it out of Anaedor again.

The Chronicles of Anaedor: The Lost Ones (Book Three)

Sixteen-year-old Lavida Mors is in for a long, hot summer. With no way into Anaedor, the Lost Ones seeking refuge at Portal Manor are taking over the house, creating havoc and misery. Lavida is overwhelmed trying to keep up with her chores, learning magic, and fighting off the Pixies—tiny creatures who have made it their mission to harass Lavida at every turn. Meanwhile, unbeknownst to the residents of Portal Manor, the AAK is hard at work opening a Portal to the Upland. They are successful at last, and the twins, Loria and Darian, on the run from Malvado, and the AAK leader, Trey, manage to make it through the opening only to have it collapse behind them. With no way back into Anaedor, they are forced to take refuge at Portal Manor. As they try to settle into this strange new life, tensions between the humans and the Anaedorians grow, creating rifts between Lavida and her friends. To make matters worse, Frio, Amoral Hunter Leader, is hiding out in the Upland, and when he goes after Lavida, he starts in motion a series of events that could end up costing Lavida her life.

The Chronicles of Anaedor: The Uprising (Book Four)

In this final book of the Anaedor series, sixteen-year-old Lavida Mors is placed in grave danger when a group of young Anaedorians infiltrate the Upland. Their orders are to eliminate the evil one, whom they believe is Lavida, and then launch an Uprising to take over the Upland. Disguising themselves as humans, they befriend the unwitting Lavida and her friends, allowing them easy access to Portal Manor. Darian and Loria, Blendar twins and Lavida's friends, and Trey, ex-AAK rebel leader, have come to the Upland to warn Lavida about the intruders. But before they can, Darian learns something about Lavida's past that turns him against her. Surrounded by betrayal and danger, and faced with an astonishing revelation that makes her question everything about her existence, Lavida feels increasingly alone and afraid. If she cannot convince Darian and the others that she is not the evil being they think she is, she will lose everything to the Uprising.

The Wrath: A Paranormal Gothic Romance

When a cryptic letter arrives from Evalina Filmore's two aunts, she travels to England to find out what they want, figuring this will be the chance to experience the romantic adventure she has so often read about in her beloved gothic novels. When she arrives, she finds the eerie mansion, the strange atmosphere, and the adventure, as hoped. But there are troubles. On the train, she meets a man who, upon learning her name, walks away without a word of explanation. Not long after, she passes unharmed through a wood called the Wrath, even though, as she later learns, no one ever has. While in the Wrath, she meets a tantalizing and seductive stranger, one who just might be her gothic hero. But he has a secret. It seems everyone in the village does, including her aunts, and it's up to Evie to figure out what is going on before the Wrath lures her in and never lets her go.

The Battle to Become an Author:
When Great Expectations Go Awry

Are you looking to find an agent and/or get published? Are you a published author frustrated with the whole process? Or have you simply heard the horror stories and are looking for a ray of light before plunging into the fray? In this short booklet, author Kristina Schram discusses how one's unrealistic expectations about becoming an author can contribute to feelings of negativity and isolation. Dr. Schram offers a real-world discussion of this growing issue, humorously incorporating her own experiences throughout. She also offers insights and ways to cope with the increasingly difficult battle to become a published author. Come prepared to challenge your own expectations, to laugh and to cry, and to battle against the forces conspiring to keep you from reaching your writing potential!

www.ingramcontent.com/pod-product-compliance
Lightning Source LLC
Chambersburg PA
CBHW031416250626
47155CB00004B/1513